Antipater, Regent of the Em[pire]
of Alexa[nder]

=(1) Eurydice

=(2) Berenice, perhaps her niece

other children

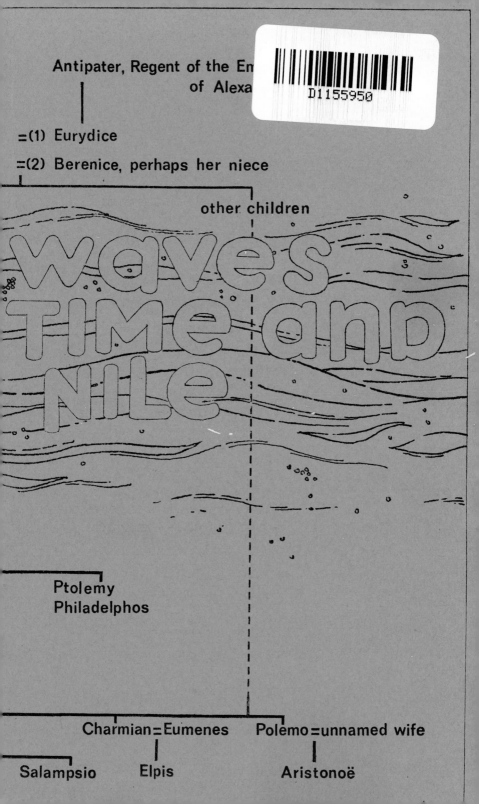

WAVES TIME AND NILE

Ptolemy
Philadelphos

Charmian=Eumenes   Polemo=unnamed wife

Salampsio   Elpis   Aristonoë

CLEOPATRA'S
PEOPLE

ALSO BY NAOMI MITCHISON

NOVELS AND SHORT STORIES

The Conquered
When the Bough Breaks
Cloud Cuckoo Land
Black Sparta
Barbarian Stories
The Corn King and the Spring
   Queen
The Delicate Fire
We Have Been Warned
Beyond this Limit

The Fourth Pig
The Blood of the Martyrs
The Bull Calves
Lobsters on the Agenda
Travel Light
To the Chapel Perilous
Behold your King
Five Men and a Swan
Memoirs of a Space Woman
When We Become Men

NON-FICTION

Anna Comnena
Comments on Birth Control
An Outline [of history] for Boys
   and Girls and their Parents
               (edited)
Vienna Diary
The Home
Socrates (with R. H. S. Crossman)
The Moral Basis of Politics

The Kingdom of Heaven
Men and Herring
        (with D. Macintosh)
The Swan's Road
Other People's Worlds
What the Human Race is Up To
              (edited)
Return to the Fairy Hill
African Heroes
The Africans

POETRY

The Laburnum Branch

PLAYS

The Price of Freedom
      (with L. E. Gielgud)
An End and a Beginning
As It was in the Beginning
      (with L. E. Gielgud)

FOR CHILDREN

Nix-Nought-Nothing
The Hostages
Boys and Girls and Gods
The Big House
Graeme and the Dragon
The Land the Ravens Found
Little Boxes
The Far Harbour
Judy and Lakshmi

The Rib of the Green Umbrella
The Young Alexander
Karensgaard
The Young Alfred the Great
Friends and Enemies
The Family at Ditlabeng
The Big Surprise
Don't Look Back

CLEOPATRA'S PEOPLE

Naomi Mitchison

HEINEMANN : LONDON

William Heinemann Ltd

15 Queen St, Mayfair, London W1X 8BE

LONDON   MELBOURNE   TORONTO
JOHANNESBURG   AUCKLAND

First published 1972
© Naomi Mitchison 1972
434 46801 0

Printed in Great Britain by
Northumberland Press Limited
Gateshead

CONTENTS

PART ONE

❦

Alexandria

PEOPLE IN PART I

Macedonians in Egypt

Queen Cleopatra VII
Her children:
Ptolemy Caesar (Caesarion)
Cleopatra Selene
Alexander Helios
Ptolemy Philadelphos (Philo)
Hipparchia, sister to Charmian
Polemo, brother to Charmian
Aristonoë, daughter of Polemo
Eumenes, husband of Charmian
Elpis, their daughter
Mikion, originally a Rhodian, husband of Hipparchia
Salampsio, their daughter
Kerkidas, their son
Phaedra, formerly sister-in-law to Charmian, Hipparchia
    and Polemo
Hellanike, her daughter
Kleanthes, one of the Queen's councillors

Her ladies:
Iras
Charmian

Egyptians in Egypt

Tahatre, and her sister Shepenese

Greeks in Alexandria

Pythokles, one of the Queen's councillors
Zenon, tutor to Aristonoë
Rhodon, tutor to Caesarion

Romans in Alexandria and elsewhere

Marc Antony
Octavian (Augustus Caesar)
Quintus Dellius
Lucius Mindius

In the Land of Punt

The Queen and her husbands

CHAPTER ONE : B.C. 26

'My sister Charmian told me to pass this on,' she said and looked across at the young girl, her niece Aristonoë. They were sitting on a wooden balcony with the vines growing up it and laced across to make a half shade, though one could see through the lattice of stalks and just bursting buds the port of Alexandria and the jostling of the boats, and hear from below the cries and quarrels of the fishermen. Sometimes the songs were not of a kind for ladies' ears, so they pretended not to notice and did not catch one another's eye, though a little trickle of a smile lifted the corners of Hipparchia's mouth. Some of the songs were in Egyptian, which neither of them understood well, only to give orders to the servants. But most, since this was, after all, Alexandria, were in coarse fishermen's Greek. They were above the fishermen's harbour at the Western end, not the Eastern harbour where the ships from Rome lay like black, gaping mouths to be filled with corn. That was a place which they did not much care for, either of them. 'You know,' Hipparchia went on, 'what is said about the Queen.'

The girl moved uneasily on the cushions. 'I know two things,' she said, 'two separate kinds of things.'

'Of which, one?'

'One is what is said by—by my cousin Hellanike, for example.' She looked away.

'And what marriage is proposed for your cousin Hellanike?'

'You know: that young Roman, Lucius Mindius—or something. I never can remember what they call themselves! But—he is certainly quite good-looking in his way. And not old. He will give her a good time. You know how it is.'

'I would have thought her mother was well enough off not to have to do this.'

3

'Oh it is not that!' said the girl. 'Not at all. But one needs a protector these days, and besides you know it is the thing to do. Visiting among the Prefect's staff. In her set at least.'

'And in yours?'

'Oh no. Besides I don't want to get married yet! And when I do—oh, I expect Father will know best.'

'Yes, you and Hellanike have been brought up differently. And you heard one story from her and the Romans. That is, I suppose, the story they put about that the Queen, having lost her youthful figure and so not being able to tempt the virtuous Octavian, killed herself in disgust?'

'My cousin at least said she did not even want to consider Octavian, but killed herself for love of Marc Antony, over his body.'

'That is not quite so evil a story, but still it is not true.' She watched the girl, who did not like being watched. 'You believe it?'

Aristonoë moved restlessly. 'I hardly know what I believe; surely, Aunt Hipparchia, it is beautiful that a great queen should love so madly?'

'It does not make sense of Actium—does it? When the Queen left the battle? Or do you believe she was just a coward?'

'No. I do not believe that: though my father does not speak of Actium, not to me. No.' The girl picked at a young vine leaf and tore it nervously away from the bud, bruising it between her fingers. It was a warm spring day, but they were on the north side of the house and there was a slight breeze off the ruffled blue, enough to flutter the edge of her dress where it dropped from the shoulder clasps, and cool her neck below the gold-brown curls.

'And the other story you know?'

'It is what my maid says. And Mother's dear old maid when she comes to see us. She always comes for Mother's anniversary: in strict mourning. They're Egyptians, very nice, respectable people from father's village. We don't really count them as slaves, nor do they think of themselves that way. My maid's brother is the head groom and Father says he's as honest as the day. One of those light-boned thin men. My little maid is the same. You know, I slapped her once; I was so ashamed: it was like slapping a flower. She—she went all inside herself and it took me weeks to get her back. Her name is Tahatre, that's quite a respectable name. It was after that when I'd said I was sorry, for really I was, that she began to tell me the other story. I was so moved, Aunt Hipparchia!

4

You see, I feel that what she meant was that this way she was making peace with me—through the Queen.'

'I expect so—if it was the other story.'

'The Isis story,' the girl said under her breath, 'the queen becoming a goddess. Not just poetically. But—visibly. So that all the people knew.'

'Yes,' said her aunt, 'but that isn't true either. Or only true in a certain way. Are you religious, my dear?' She leant forward, again watching the girl, whose mouth curled up a little at one corner. 'Naturally you go to the celebrations and so on. One must after all to some extent conform—'

'And see one's friends!' said the girl.

'And wear one's prettiest dress no doubt. But—I think your father engaged a tutor who had already published two or three philosophical treatises.'

'Oh, but Zenon's a darling! You've no idea. Sometimes he talks to me about Athens. He's any age, of course, and almost bald. But don't think he's against religion! Only against superstition. He took several of us to a performance of the *Oresteia*, for instance, and he was terribly interesting about the Furies and what they represented. You know it's a very modern play, one could almost place it in modern Alexandria, couldn't one? Altering the plot so that it could be some other kind of guilt and the Furies in our own minds—but naturally one can't believe in the gods as they're pictured, can one? I mean, not if one has any education. Oh, Aunt Hipparchia, I believe you're laughing at me!'

'Well, you know, I don't call all that nonsense about those old god-figures religion. After all it's nothing to do with the real search for God or the turning of our original guilt into expiation, with some kind of pattern that brings us together—'

'Yes, well...' How embarrassing one's relations could be!

'I'm sure you take no interest in the Mysteries, my dear, why should you at your age. But you see your Aunt Charmian, whom you should be proud of—'

'Of course! Whatever is true about the Queen, Aunt Charmian was wonderful. Father always says so.'

'Well, she said to me when it became clear what was likely to happen, that you were the one of all her relations that I was to tell. Specially.'

But why was that? Why was that? The girl knew she was

5

expected to ask and did not want to. It would lay an intolerable burden upon her. It wasn't fair! It would mean, yes she was certain, doing something, taking action, getting into the adult world of guilt and expiation, all that. It had been so enjoyable discussing moral problems with Zenon and what the choice of the good person would be in situations one had dreamed up, but that—well, that was philosophy and this looked uncomfortably like being life. She ran her fingers up into her hair from the nape of her neck; they came away smelling more of sweat than scent. One must stay cool. But Aunt Hipparchia was looking at her with those eyes that set up a kind of burning. Father was like that sometimes too, all the descendants of Queen Berenice had it. If you didn't answer—if you tried to get round it—well, it didn't do. Not that her father often spoke of his sister Charmian, the Queen's lady and friend who had gone with her to whatever unimagined place of brightness and certainty, whatever house of the gods—but no, she was thinking Egyptian!

'Why me?' she said at last, low and looking away.

'Because you have courage,' said Hipparchia, 'even as a child. You remember that time with the dog?'

'Only just. I wasn't really frightened so I can't have been really brave. Of course I was frightened afterwards when they all started talking, but by then it was over.'

'You see, you had the instinct for courage. That was what Charmian thought.'

Aristonoë tried to head it off. 'She had a daughter, if I remember right,' she said, 'a little older than me; I was rather scared of her. At least—not really, I suppose. Only she seemed to know so much. What happened?'

Her aunt's voice darkened. 'That's rather a tragedy. Luckily Charmian never knew the worst. Yes, the girl was taken to Rome with little Princess Selene, as her lady-in-waiting; she was just that much older. Then they were separated; Romans do such things. Rome is where she—your cousin—was last heard of. It's said she is quite a success. But I feel sick whenever I think of her.'

'Oh, the Romans are dreadful! They smell!' Aristonoë spoke quickly, to cover the break in her aunt's voice. But it didn't measure up. No.

Hipparchia recovered herself, spoke in an even voice: 'But you'd like to go there, all the same, to Rome? It could be interesting.'

6

Aristonoë turned and looked square at her aunt: 'This is part of what you want me to say—isn't it? Oh Aunt Hipparchia, don't keep hiding. I am beginning to guess. It is something to do with the Queen.' She thought back to her childhood and a lot of shining steps and a waving of fans and at the top a lady on a gold chair, a rather frightening, rather old lady, yes, she seemed old and far off. Had she a crown? Aristonoë simply couldn't remember. Her father had nudged her and she had gone right down on her knees and given the lady something—flowers it must have been. Country flowers. And then later the same day she'd heard her father say, 'Look at her talking to them—in their own hellish lingo!' And there was the same lady leaning forward and talking to two black men in feather hats and she seemed to be quite pleased and not frightening any more. That was the Queen. But Aunt Hipparchia went often to the palace, didn't she? To visit Charmian, and besides—oh what was it her aunt wanted to tell her about Queen Cleopatra?

After a time, Hipparchia said, 'Yes. I wanted to tell you about the Queen. There is so much you ought to know.'

'But why? Why?'

'I think you will understand. But I must go back to the early days.' She did not speak for a minute or two. Perhaps she was not going to. Then she did. 'Naturally, the Queen did not know at first what she wanted. She was proud and dreadfully touchy. When her young brother sometimes came strutting up saying, I am your husband, she would scream at him. If anyone spoke a word out of place about her parents or grandparents, and there were plenty who did, she always managed to get back at them. A savage, arrogant, handsome girl who didn't mind blood. People spoke of her back-back-grandfather, Philip, who found Macedon a tiny State that nobody noticed and in a few years made it the dead-centre of power. Yes, and of his wife Olympias who ran wild through the forests beyond Pella and bore Alexander to a God. Or so she said.'

'But—did the Queen herself think she was descended from that House?'

'From Philip of Macedon? It seems likely enough. Any of his friends and generals, Ptolemy's father Lagos among them, would have been proud to marry a wife who carried *that* in her. The Queen's back-grandmother, Berenice, who is also your own ancestor, the one who took Ptolemy Soter from Eurydice, she was a very strong woman, daughter of a god. Or so at least she is spoken

7

of. One way and another there were gods walking the woods of Macedon and the deserts of Asia. As it was told at Siwa.'

'That would have been—something to live up to.'

'Up or down. One does not escape from one's ancestors. Or one's children. The past and the future between which we slide like beads. Yes. But even as a girl the Queen was clever. It amused her to learn languages secretly. As she learnt Latin. She learnt Sanskrit openly; of course there were wise books in Sanskrit waiting to be read.'

'And in Latin. Or so my cousin Hellanike says.'

'Those dreadful clumping poets. Bad enough when they are obscene, but at least there is a certain wit present. But when they pretend to go back into their own history, Aeneas and that stupid Romulus... ! Well, perhaps they write what is expected of them. After Queen Cleopatra was fluent in Latin and allowed it to be known, her tutor began to put on tedious airs about these poets, and much else. She arranged a boating accident for him. Naturally, she was well read in Greek.'

'My maid says that she spoke with priests and people in—well, in their own language. In Egyptian. To be sure, we all know a few words. But—could that be true?'

'Certainly it is true. Isis would speak in her own tongue—and with force. I take it that this is what your maid told you?' Aristonoë nodded, but uncomfortably. It did not seem right. Her aunt went on: 'She could speak with people from the South, far down into Africa. When it came to buying iron ingots from Meroë, it was she who got down to business. The first time this happened it was quite startling for the Treasury officials who had been handling the deal up till then. After she had looked through the figures—and she was quick here too—she had one of them flogged. A Macedonian of quite good family, a University man, I believe: flogged by the men of Meroë. She looked on. She had hard eyes.'

'But not—not always?'

'Not to Charmian. I think never to Charmian, her mate. But for trade, yes, always.'

'Trade?'

'Trade, not tribute.' Both of them thought about the Roman corn ships. How expensive everything had become now that so much went to Rome! Not only corn but all the treasure which had once backed their credit. Of course the Romans could buy up any-

8

thing and if, for example, you had early manuscripts or any absolutely guaranteed work of art, you could be assured of a very
handsome price. Greek antiquities, of course. Egyptian or Indian
only if they were gold or precious stones. Which would probably be reset. However good!

'You don't mean, Aunt Hipparchia,' said the girl, 'that the Queen
actually went up, herself, to Meroë?'

'Yes, and away beyond to the land of Punt. You have heard of
it?

'Far, far South. Where Queen Hatshepsut sent her captains in the
old, old days. But she never went herself.'

'The Queen did. She was young then. Charmian went with her.
She was betrothed to her future husband, who was, as you know,
in command of the Queen's guard. One of the handsomest young
men I have ever seen. Though always rather quiet, except in action.
You would never believe, seeing him now, how handsome Eumenes
was as a young man. My dear, dear Charmian. She wrote back to
our mother, long letters. I have them still. But she never told the
Queen's secrets. Only I seem to know entirely what it was like,
being the Queen's mate.'

'How was it, then?' Aristonoë asked, half whispering.

And her aunt looked away, away, as though her thoughts were
still with her dead sister, far up the great river.

CHAPTER TWO: B.C. 44/45

The banks went by slowly; on a dropping Nile, the farmers climbed like ants down the damp ground, making their little terrace gardens and planting quickly in the damp earth, so that all was dotted with green. In the broad-beamed boat with its golden, beast-headed prow and stern, the rowers tugged upstream against the current. Three other barges, less beautiful but as well built and well crewed, followed them, heavily laden with the stuff of trade. Earth and water were brown, but the crop edge which caught the light between bank and sky was a shining ribbon. Often the long poles jutted out over the water and the buckets rose and fell; sometimes the bank would drop so that one saw inland to a village, a crowd of roofs and people and fruit trees, and perhaps a small temple, standing back from the furthest place to which a high Nile might come.

From time to time a string of barges passed them, on their way downstream, laden as deep as safety allowed with bags of corn or other produce, sometimes green fodder and sometimes livestock, small cows or oxen, sheep or goats, tied to the gunwale, staring out, their silly heads reflected in the water. Captain and steersmen bowed to the deck when they saw what boat it was they were passing. Sometimes the Queen demanded to know the cargo and there was shouting across from one barge to the other.

Almost all of this was the Queen's land, though sometimes a little had been left to a temple. Her peasants grew what crops the land could best support. They took their orders from government officials, in turn under the direction of the Treasury who kept a careful eye on prices and demand, both at home and abroad. Wheat always came into the rotation and usually a green crop which fed the cattle. But the cattle too were royal property. In a two-year rotation there might also be an oil-seed crop, perhaps sesame, which was the most valuable, or safflower or a fodder crop. There might be beans or lupins, both good for the soil, or flax, with linseed oil to be pressed from the seeds. All oil seeds went to the Queen's barn somewhere in the centre of the district and when this was full the sacks were carried to the river bank, loaded and floated down the Nile to the oil factories, where the pressing was efficiently carried out and the oil was stored in bulk in huge earthenware jars. Equally the wheat went to the Queen's barns here and there and so on to the great granaries in Alexandria where brick and plaster kept out the rats. It would either be milled and eaten in the city, or exported whenever a Mediterranean scarcity put the price up sufficiently.

The peasants had enough left over to keep themselves and their families, but not to sell. There could be no free market. Indeed it had been so long since there had been one that country people had almost forgotten about private trading. The duty of the officials was to see that the peasants had enough to keep themselves healthy and able to work and sufficiently contented not to grumble too much. When the Queen saw that the peasants looked hungry or did not greet her enthusiastically or were dirty in a way that showed they were despairing, she would send for the official concerned and tell him he must do better. Or else.

All the time, as they moved slowly Southward through Egypt, the long valley strip, the age-old green snake, the Queen kept her eye on all this. Wheat was the prosperity of Egypt, but if not wheat, and now they were getting too far South for wheat, there were other corn crops. These were almost as valuable as food for peasants or for export, not necessarily to the Mediterranean, but elsewhere in the hungry world which was touched by Egypt's thousand hands. The date plantations seemed good and here too was money.

Charmian was less interested in the crops; she could not immediately tell what variety of millet or beans the peasants were growing. Nor did she care for their food, though she had to eat it and pretend to enjoy it, as her dear mistress, in a strange way and because she had somehow tuned in, perhaps *did* enjoy it. For wherever they tied up at sundown and the locals came down from the villages in great boring, staring droves, comically dressed up but one mustn't laugh at them, Queen Cleopatra the Seventh of

Egypt asked only for the food of the place. But she asked them courteously and in the Egyptian language, which was something altogether unheard of. They were used to interpreters, twisting what was said unless you paid them. Now they looked at one another and whispered and oh, thought Charmian, how pleased they are! They know that they too are considered as persons.

These by now were darker people, burnt by the hotter, quickening sun, with thicker lips and curlier hair, smelling different. Some of them had scars on their foreheads or cheeks, given to them in the name of their gods. But which gods? Not, surely, those which were worshipped by well-off Egyptians in Alexandria or Thebes or even Philae which they had passed, it seemed now many days ago. But there were always upper-class Egyptians, properly shaved and pumiced, among the administrators and priests, especially near the important temples with the widest lands. Yet there it was: they were only Egyptians, when all was said and done. Eumenes, commanding the Queen's guard, was so splendid, tall and thick-chested, with blue eyes and hair that waved up as soon as he took off his helmet: a Macedonian of the old vintage, unmixed with lesser wines. Oh lucky Charmian, what pleasures she would have! Sometimes the Queen teased her, saying things that made her blush and cry. But it was important, in bed as in the market or in government and diplomacy, to know as much as one's opponent. More. Caesar had known much more than Cleopatra: once. But the Queen was a quick learner. She had learnt a great deal from him, especially about Rome. The price was Ptolemy Caesar: Caesarion. But what of it? People had sniggered once, but a few lopped heads or hands had demonstrated that this was unwise. Caesarion was her son, her own; he would only lay claim to his father should this become politic. Beyond that, he was an intelligent child. He would have the best education in the world. He would be able to deal with the Mediterranean end of things. One day she would take him to see it all. She and Caesarion, perhaps in disguise, an ordinary mother and child? Next year perhaps. To Rome? Oh, it would be thrilling. She dreamed sometimes of this, as the banks went by and the storks flew overhead and the ducks rose or did not even rise but rocked in the small wave of the boat, so little they cared for traffic.

Before Caesar's tutoring, the Queen had been a proud and violent girl, but without technique and without the patience to consider or understand trade or the ordinary people whom, as a child, she had despised, not thinking they were in the same world as herself. Now she had technique and the patience that is needed to sift out the grain of reality from the welter of talk or to notice what her councillors omitted to tell her or even concealed. Not that one did not also need a certain patience, a certain ability to delay and probe and watch for omissions in matters of the bed. This too she had learnt, partly from Caesar who was expert. Control was not only in the muscles but in the practising mind. Though muscles too needed practice.

Control for ruling. As Cleopatra of Macedon she would lie sprawled on cushions while the water made a faint rippling and the waving fans patterned shadows over her skin or fluttered the loose folds of embroidered muslin; Charmian would comb out the long tresses of her hair, away from her face, gently, gently. From there she could note the bodies of her guards without actively desiring them, but with the knowledge that she could have them if she chose, which meant that she did not choose. As Cleopatra of Egypt she walked in stiff and hieratic almost-nakedness, her hair hidden, but knowing that no man could look on her with desire for the shown flesh. Should it fall to her, masked and in duty, to consort with a masked high priest, the point of desire would be cut from the heart and head; eyes and lips would be unaware.

As Cleopatra of Egypt she was led down strange ways, to an infinitely complex music of gods and animals. She saw many things painted and apparently moving as the torchlight moved and flickered. They were from far back, when her ancestors of Macedon wore wolf skins and clubbed one another with sticks and stones. But, as Egypt, these gods and half-gods also were her ancestors. In these moving pictures was the journey of the dead, the guardians and the judgment. The gods were hidden behind their masks in which the beast nature was made plain: the devouring lion, the trampling hippopotamus, the dog-toothed marauding baboon, the narrow and brainless ibis. The snake that kept the gates between life and death: the tiny, powerful asp. Or else the goddess stretched from dusk to dawn and again from dawn to dusk, her eyes becoming stars. Yet where did all this notch with her knowledge of living Egypt?

Something else more nearly did. At a certain point a priest had come out in a small skiff, his robe white against the brown river, his shaved head shining in the direct light. He asked her to moor her boat at a place he would show them. She thought for a while, looking at him curiously, analysing and delaying, then gave orders. She went ashore with him attended only by Charmian, with Eumenes and a few guards discreetly following. As she had supposed almost at once, he was a heretic, a follower of the light, Aton. And she herself was, if anything, Isis. But by no means entirely. There had been times in the long story of Egypt when it was death to be a discovered heretic, though now it appeared unimportant, since the officially acknowledged priesthood, although pretending to be all-powerful, were only half believed in. And had not been able to resist when their land and much of their riches had been taken by the Ptolemies. There were other ways of evading complete death beyond those controlled by the official priesthood of Egypt. And also there were now other people who owned the green strips of ever fertile land. Macedonians. Greeks. The Queen herself and the Queen's carefully balanced and chosen friends.

She went with the priest, down steps carved out of the enormous rock, the body of the world, and through a narrow door. Charmian shivered a little, unable to share this intense curiosity, but, once they were inside, there was a lamp burning and then another and another, as the priest went round lighting them. And gradually the walls sprang to life. Yes, it was life this time, not the masked, two-dimensional gods stalking their rounds, but people and animals, not cruel animals but those who lived happily with mankind, flowers and fishes, the colours scarcely faded. And there were the rays of Aton, coming down to earth as helping hands. The Queen looked carefully at the pictures, these very Egyptian faces, but the King wearing the same crown that she herself had worn and would wear again. The priest kept whispering the name, but she already knew it: Akhnaton. And there, naked and head cropped and pretty, were the Princesses, his children. How much she herself would like a girl baby, a successor! Someone must make her one.

There was a great fresco on one wall. King Akhnaton preached to the multitude and the sun's blessing followed his words. There were people of all nations, carefully distinguished; she looked at them with interest, knowing more about them than the priest knew. There were Greeks and barbarians—yet perhaps to the Egyptians Greeks were barbarian. She laughed to herself: a strange

14

idea. Among them were barbarians from the South, yes, the shape of the head, the tilt of the body, men and women from the land of gold and ivory and the perpetual dripping of the incense trees, Africa, the blessed land. Where she was going now.

And this king wearing her crown and stretching out to the people was something to do with her. The priest knew and yet did not know; his knowledge broke down into a desire for money which came between his tongue and the words he could have used. He was poor. He had only that little skiff, a fish net and a small patch of garden. They left the tomb, blinking out into the strike of the sun: Aton. She turned to Charmian who turned to the purse-bearer where he stood, an old tired man, among the young, upright guards. It was too late now for the priest, his hands full of money, bobbing over it like a bird drinking, to tell her that this also was a way out of death and he could show it. Death. But surely one would stand and welcome it when it came, like a greater wave out of the sea? But not yet. Certainly not yet.

Walking back to the moored boat and casting an eye on the trade barges to see that orders were obeyed, she was silent. Those faces of all lands. In her mind now came another king, but not a king crowned with the signs of Upper and Lower Egypt: Alexander the founder who had made his generals, among them Ptolemy the First, out of the common clay of soldiery. Alexander, her half-brother in the long running of time. He also had seen all the nations of the world and blessed them, but he had a sword instead of little helping hands from the sun. Yet perhaps the sword might also be part of this bringing together. Only wasteful, uncertain, untidy. Standing on the prow of her ship that day she had looked with pleasure at the well-weeded cornfields and rows of beans and sesame plants, the trained vines, the well-spaced palm trees and the straight, narrow irrigation ditches between the vegetable plots. Her peasants were serving her well; she hoped their gods would serve them equally.

South and on into hotter nights and larger stars, an increasingly different, an African look to the people. When the river became suddenly fast and fierce, ox-carts were filled with pillows, the fanners walked beside them. Whole villages came running and kneeling, as was right. The Queen broke barley bread with the village headman, then passed on a gift. He brought beasts for slaughter, sheep and goats and goddess-eyed small cattle.

When the river became very sluggish and wide, small boats went on ahead, chopping reeds and rushes, pulling out mats of slimy green. The Queen's barge moved after them slowly, then the others. Behind, the weeds closed again. At long last they came to the slag heaps of Meroë, some cold and ancient, others still hot and smoking with a smell of death. Once, long ago, the Egyptian people had been conquered because they had not been interested in the new thing, iron, and when men came from Meroë with iron swords and spear points, bronze was useless. Cleopatra of Egypt asked many questions, since she already knew the language of Meroë, so that the interpreters who had been instructed beforehand on what to say, now found themselves dumb. She was not always answered or shown, but it was clear that the stuff out of which iron was made came from hilly and lumpy ground, reddish. Egypt had been born out of the Nile, centuries and centuries of dark mud spread like a blanket over a sleeping child by a good mother. Iron was elsewhere.

But she was not the only buyer and there was hard bargaining. Her people had samples of wheat, olive oil, wine, dried figs, chestnuts, linen and woollen cloth. There were also men from India, long-robed, bringers of spice and jewels, trade rivals. Some were princes; she spoke with them courteously, quickly learning their language of greeting. They were happy that this queen knew the great books of Sanskrit, the learned tongue. But the princes also made sport for her, shooting and javelin-throwing with marvellous skill and beauty as she watched them. One, she fancied; he, her. But Charmian, whose help was called for, Indian-fashion, looked away, not wishing to see her Queen thus pleasured. Later, in a deep sweat, the Queen scolded her a little. She could have learned and copied. This was not ordinary enjoyment, but something for every fibre, which melted the body and forged it anew into cutting strength. Would Eumenes do as well?

'I would not wish it! 'said Charmian, stammering a little. 'We shall marry and have children, it will not be for this!'

The Queen laughed, demanding that stupid Charmian, who would not go to school, should now help her to do what would stop a child she did not choose to have. In Caesar's time she had not known this. Charmian devotedly brought the sponges; when she put her cool fingers on to the Queen's flesh, it leapt again, still able to speak the language of no words. Both of them laughed and laughed and the Queen caught hold of the smooth, unsweaty virgin Charmian and rolled with her, marvellous, darling Macedonian mate, mouth to mouth. Now Charmian too was covered with the Queen's new-smelling sweat and heat; her breasts too prickled as the Indian scent came at her. But was it right? No, it was not right. It was not proper. Queens and noblewomen needing pleasure should use eunuchs who had been made safe for just this purpose, but could still do their duty and could be liquidated if need be or have their tongues cut. Though some grew old in the service of merciful queens, such as her own lady.

It gave the Queen an ally in her game with Meroë, insisting that none of their iron should go to Rome. The prince suggested through his counsellors and by letter, marriage. The letter smelt of delights. For a little Queen Cleopatra hesitated, seeing a joint empire spreading far to the East. The prince, too, had spoken about the monsoons, the strong winds which brought ships to India and were then, by divine intervention, turned about to take them back. This was something she had heard of, but she did not know the secret. If this was to be her wedding gift...? Could she resist such a double temptation? She temporised, tasted him once more. She even had inquiries made, but regretfully felt that his kingdom was too small and much surrounded by enemies, against whom he would doubtless hope for Egyptian armies. No, no, she had other matters to consider, among them the now proved dishonesty of some of her own officials. Which must be dealt with publicly.

One barge went back, North, heavily laden with iron in many shapes. The other two came on with the Queen, far and beyond Meroë, days and weeks going by, the old groupings of stars slowly dipping while new ones rose ahead. The way which the rare trading expeditions had used before was by sea, leaving the Nile valley at one of several points and taking the caravan route East to the coast and then again by ship South over the curve of the world to one port after another. But the Queen did not care for long camel journeys. No doubt her fleet could meet her, but this would mean leaving a temptation open to certain inquisitive or greedy neighbours. And again, unless there was a Northerly wind, of which one could not be certain, there would be uncomfortable waiting in foreign harbours which were not even under Egyptian rule. No, better to go with Mother Nile, on, on. There was no way of knowing what was happening, away North in Alexandria by the sparkling blue sea. But Cleopatra had chosen her Council carefully and trusted some of them, at least, and there was another Roman garrison who would, up to a point, be useful and even loyal.

Yet this for the moment was more important, this stretching of knowledge and boundaries; she would come back a lion refreshed. She had teams of local rowers and steersmen, taking her from village to village, even at night, when the moon was full. On such nights she and Charmian would lie in the bows, watching the wet, shining heads and tails of strange beasts or the wake of sudden fish scudding through the water. And so, quietly and peacefully, but, as they knew, much heralded, on into the blessed land of Punt, land of no desert, but of hanging trees full of marvellous birds whose feathers she immediately desired, and rivers rolling with gold; land of fruits and sweet gums, roast meat and wild honey. The palace of the Queen of Punt had carved pillars of wood and a roof of thatch, even and thick, skilfully patterned and fastened, coming down into eaves of deep shade. Inside, one's eyes must get used to darkness, partitions of silk or cotton from India, of stamped bark cloth and also, as Queen Cleopatra was glad to notice, of embroidered linen from her own country, probably coming in through Meroë, where a hefty percentage would be put on to it.

Here again she knew the greeting phrases, having learnt them carefully from the guides. Delighted, the Queen of Punt rolled off her throne. Layers of fat made her infinitely desirable to her subjects; her great bottom was a cushion of fashion. She spoke in the tongue of Meroë and there was also an interpreter. It was too soon yet to talk trade, so the Queen of Punt pulled the Queen of Egypt down beside her, on the leopard skins of her golden throne. Her husbands stood around her, lean and tall and aloof, carrying spears and hide shields, splendidly plumed and girdled. The Queen of Punt offered her guest a choice of them. Their skins were brown and unblemished like beautiful fruit, their eyes were agates; they were somewhat afraid.

Charmian, standing against a slung leopard skin, hoped that her mad mistress would say no; she watched her digging a fingernail into the throne, doubtless exploring to see if it was solid gold. The Queen of Punt beckoned one of her husbands and whispered to Cleopatra, who put up her hand and stroked the young man's thigh, intimately. 'What does he say?' she asked.

'He wants to know,' said the other, rocking with amusement

from buttock to buttock, 'how a Queen can be so thin. Is she sick?'

'Tell him no,' said Cleopatra giggling. 'It is because we are so active. We are like hunting lions!'

So she is on her mettle again, thought Charmian, she means to show him. I am sure she will uphold the honour of Egypt in the struggle. But at least, and she glanced at the young man quickly, I do not think they will want me to help.

'I have learned many new words, Charmian,' said the Queen later. 'Listen, what do you think this means?' She whispered and giggled.

'I think,' said Charmian, 'that this is a word which the Queen's majesty knows in several languages.' The Queen reached over and smacked her.

'Beginning with Latin,' said Charmian, looking reprovingly down her nose, 'a word taught to me by the Queen's majesty in person, who had learnt it from a certain interesting old man—it was—'

But the Queen pushed her over and kissed her. How far, how gloriously far this was from Latin or from Rome, the adversary. Or the Latin word which indeed she had learned from the old man, Julius Caesar, a wise and clever soldier. Sometimes even a good man in his way, not cruel or careless. But far, far from the warm forest, the singing and drumming, the trumpeting and squealing of elephants at night and the young man whose necklace and belt had pressed so hard into her that she could feel them still. And more. What had he said about her to his mates when he left her at the end of night, wrung out by this foreign lioness?

It was almost morning and a little cooler. Charmian, preparing her mistress for the day, found a tiny red feather where no feather should be and held it out to her lady with the hint of a grimace. 'Ah,' said the Queen, taking it, 'now I shall be able to make magic. He's mine!' Charmian frowned; it was nothing to joke about. The Queen had decided to dress Greek-fashion here, in a long robe of finest bleached linen. Egyptian-fashion might have seemed just wrong.

Trading agreements went well. It would be possible to build a rest house for merchants from Egypt under royal patronage. Cleopatra discovered from the other queen that nobody here knew of Rome nor indeed of any of the Mediterranean ports. India was at the edge of their minds and there was a trade route out to the East. When the Queen of Punt had many enemy prisoners she sent them off that way, but there was no regular raiding for slaves. There would be a slight market for them in Egypt, certainly, but rather as curios. On the other hand, if there was a possibility of finding dwarfs or acrobats...? Girls, the Queen of Punt suggested, milk-fed, round-rumped girls? But Cleopatra thought this would not be a very successful trade.

For a moment she thought of asking for the young husband with the scarlet-feathered loins. No, it would be tactless. And besides, after a while, what would she do with him? One could not simply sell the innocent husband of a fellow queen. No, no, back to essentials. Gold dust and nuggets. For that throne was pure, soft gold, though possibly on a framework of hard wood: gold would scarcely stand up to its lady's weight. Ivory. Well-cured skins. Incense and spices. Timber such as made the palace pillars, if it could be floated North on a full Nile. And where, could they tell her, would one find oneself if one went on further and further South into Africa?

The other queen explained, speaking of yet darker forests, yet stranger animals, of serpent-necked deer with eyes like beautiful women, of butterflies a handspan across the wings, of roarers and hummers and death-dealers. She spoke of man-eating men and she would tell Cleopatra the part which they preferred to eat: roast. Yes, the Egyptian Queen certainly knew its name in their tongue—'He told you!' and she pointed to the husband. She had heard that there were yet other nations where the people had three heads apiece, but she had not seen them. Some had poisoned arrows, others threw their enemies into a deep sleep, some spoke the languages of beasts and birds.

Thus there was pleasant converse and an increase of knowledge. Among a crowd of bead-wearing, busily playing little fat girls, the Queen of Punt pointed out two of her own. Their beads were soft gold and one toddled to her for a small suck at mother's great loving teats. But the young virgins who had outgrown their mothers' milk were almost as slim and almost as naked as the husbands. Night was as warm as day. The silver cup of the newly crescent moon held over it the faintly luminous full ball, as though it might at any moment float away. Stars surrounded it, growing in vigour the further they scattered. The two queens snuffed the air, heavy with new scents of plants and earth. Cleopatra's tent was of fine linen; an incense provided by the other kept away the many night insects. 'We must certainly take back some of this,' she said to Charmian and turned to the secretary who was taking notes of the day's proceedings and would write them up later: a competent man, if rather ugly. She would free him after they got back. He deserved it.

Charmian was sewing the edge of a dress which had caught in a thorn. 'Caesar said to me once,' said Cleopatra, one hand at her cheek, thinking back, 'that one day Rome would rule the world. I did not say what was in my mind, even then. That he and his legions could try to rule the world, but I, Egypt, I would have the power even without more soldiers than I need to keep order and frighten my stupid neighbours. The ones that do not understand trade.'

'Or interrupt it, like our neighbours in Arabia.'

'Yes. One day I shall get control of the Arabian coast: somehow. Too many kings try to do it the Roman way: by rule, not by money.'

'But money can be an unkind master too? Surely.'

'Yes, yes. Money is not everything. It is only the bridle on the horse. The beautiful horse: all the peoples of the world, caught gently between my thighs; liking it my way. Alexander of Macedon would have understood. My half-brother. When he went to see the oracle at Siwa, what do you think they told him?'

Charmian knew what the Queen wanted. 'Perhaps they foretold you, my beautiful Majesty. But,' she added, for one must not give Cleopatra all she wanted, it would be bad for her, 'if so, they were cleverer than most oracles. I have never heard you say you believed in oracles, Ma'am!'

Cleopatra laughed. 'We will go to Siwa—some day, when I have time. When I am not busy. For there is no trade at Siwa. Only gods.'

CHAPTER THREE : B.C. 26

Polemo was going through the farm accounts with the bailiff. On one side of the table were the outgoings: wage lists, seeds, new picks or hoes, saw blades, rope; on the other the sales of wheat, fruit, beans and other vegetables, wine and beer. There was a third column for the taxes and levies in kind and these surprise visits from the army of occupation. But that must be thought of with a separate part of the mind. The flax was fairly good, but, apart from the linseed, the oil sales were bad, even given that there had been a sudden extra levy on sesame seeds. His sesame had always been a success, but he had never hit on the right olives for his soil. And it took so long to show if they were a success! Cuttings seldom succeeded. He had tried grafting Licinian olives on to the local stocks, but they never bore well. The olive, anyway, was not native to Egypt. Olives need low hills and a wind to ripple their leaves and perhaps a cooler winter than they ever got in the delta.

'At least I hope there is enough for my own household?' Polemo asked. The bailiff answered nervously that he hoped so, but—'Bad enough in the old days buying Greek oil, but now it is ruinous. What else?'

They went on to discuss the smaller of the two vineyards, which would have to be renewed. Some of the older vines might be brought back into bearing with a heavy pruning and a good basket of pigeon dung round the roots, but at least one in three must be thrown out. 'Do you think the layers have taken?' Polemo asked.

'Yes, sir,' said the bailiff, 'but I think we should do an exchange. I've got my eye on some Bumast grapes for the early market.'

'Is it worth it?'

'Harder for them to spot. When we make wine—'

'Yes, they've got their noses into the butts before the pressing's through. Very well, get a few Bumasts; we'll see how it goes.'

After that the bailiff pointed out a few things on the stock side. There were transfers of draught oxen. Several donkeys had foaled. A bull had died for no known reason, though the bailiff hinted at witchcraft. Polemo frowned at this; he did not like to suppose that this was believed, however much he knew it was. However, the animal husbandry was less important than the crops; most of the sheep and goats were consumed on the estate and their hides made into shoes or cloaks. But there was likely to be a levy on the stock; he had it from someone close to the present Prefect of Egypt. Going into the stomachs of the legions, of course. Some had better be kept for this. 'You will know which,' he said, looking at the bailiff. This was understood. The bailiff would loyally protest to the Roman officials that they were the best. It had happened before.

It was a pleasant room, one side open but curtained against sun and dust. A breeze caught one of the curtains, which billowed in. Two or three of the papyrus sheets blew off the table; the bailiff dashed after them. Polemo counted a pile of gold coins and weighed them in his hand; it felt like bad measure. Clipped probably; anything went, in Alexandria, at any rate now. In the Queen's time you did not expect these things to happen. Those who clipped coins were liable to be caught and punished publicly and to the end.

The old tutor, Zenon, came in and said that the lady Aristonoë wished to see her father when he was free. Polemo nodded; the tutor went out. Then he turned back to the table: 'I think that's all, Dromon. But take care what money you accept. I don't care for this.'

'A drachma's a drachma, even from a Roman,' said the bailiff.

'Maybe. But look at this.' He held up a coin; clearly something had been shaved off the edge.

'I'll look through them, sir. I'm sorry. I think I could get off a few into the tax collection.'

'Yes, but be careful. If we get into trouble with the tax farmers it won't do.' Polemo had been lucky to keep his estate. At one time he had held another, further along the canal. That had gone to one of the conquerors, a client of Agrippa, not an agreeable man; one or two of the Egyptians who had worked there had

23

run away and were now with Polemo. Risky, of course, but what wasn't? Some people had lost their entire estates; an excuse could always be concocted. But Aristonoë was at the door; he wouldn't think of such things for a little. The bailiff tied the papyrus slips together, making two bundles for filing, and made his way out, after polite greetings. He could remember Aristonoë as a skinny little girl chasing the hens—yes, and once getting bitten by the big gander, not that she seemed to care.

'And what can I do for you, my rabbit?' said Polemo, a good-looking man still, with his tunic of fine, home-woven, sun-bleached linen, and handsome scarlet cloak dating back to his soldiering days laid over a chair. But, best of all, someone one could talk to. Aristonoë was wearing the brooches he had given her, pinning the shoulders of her dress, so that the overlap floated prettily, half covering her small, high breasts.

'Father,' she said, 'I don't know what to think.'

'Your old thoughts have been disturbed, rabbit? Not by Zenon, I believe.'

'Oh no! Philosophy never disturbs me. It is too far off. This—this was near.'

He thought he knew now. 'You have been talking with my sister, your aunt Hipparchia?' She nodded. 'Yes, she can be disturbing. And she was talking about—what?'

'You know, Father. I think you must know!'

'The Queen, I suppose. It was time, perhaps. And yet I could wish ... What did she ask of you?'

'To go to Rome. To see the children and to find out—what I could. And also to see my cousin, Aunt Charmian's daughter.'

'Elpis. I am afraid— And you were to go with whom?'

'With her father.'

'So Hipparchia has it all arranged. Macedonian fashion, the women only telling one when nothing can be altered! Well, well.' Polemo got up and half drew a curtain, to stare out into the sun and the garden, neat-rowed, the peach trees in flower, the budding figs and the imported apricot seedlings, each with its little embankment for the daily watering. The lettuce and radish were coming on nicely. The bees were busy. Not that any of it mattered. He went on: 'Your uncle Eumenes. You must have made some kind of judgment about him, my rabbit.'

'He seems so quiet. That I can understand. To lose them both,

24

his wife and his daughter. And all when he was so badly wounded. I think, too, he hates to have this crippled hand.'

'That was a sword cut. He was lucky not to lose it.'

'I see. But could he make an effort? If it was needed? Suppose I couldn't do it all myself?'

'He was a good soldier once, from an old Macedonian family, if that matters. Perhaps not any longer.'

'Hipparchia thought—if we could somehow get the children away, and most likely Elpis would come. My uncle would make the practical arrangements. But—would it be possible?'

'For one of them, no. I only heard—what—a few months ago. The Romans are a savage people. Yet perhaps kings are always the same and Octavian has made himself almost a king. Some say more than a king. Kill, kill. Any head standing higher than the grass must be lopped. That went for Caesarion, of course, betrayed by his Greek tutor within days of his mother's death. And then Alexander Helios, our little sun-child, who had been given Armenia, Media and Parthia, he was growing up in Rome. He was beginning to be almost a man. He may have been asking what was the truth about his life. He could have been looking beyond Rome and Octavia's house. Yes, I believe Octavia tried to shelter him; he had been her child for four years, as well as being her husband's child. But it was no use. Alexander Helios is dead. After all, there were plenty in Rome during the proscriptions who offered brothers, uncles, sisters' husbands, sons even, anything to get out from under Octavian's axe. I am sorry, rabbit, I could not bear to tell Hipparchia and it was known only to a few here. No place, no date even. The poor little lad, all alone.'

Aristonoë, stricken, murmured: 'Octavia? I cannot see why ... why she comes in.'

'She was Marc Antony's wife. Under Roman law. There is no getting over it. She was used by her brother Octavian, for politics, yet she must be a good woman. She and Marc Antony had two daughters, but she took and brought up all the children: his by his wife Fulvia and his by the Queen. Also she had children by her first husband, before she was taken away from him by her brother to be given to Antony after he had divorced Fulvia; yes, she had them all to bring up. It is hard for a woman to be that kind of pledge.'

Before sorrow for the Queen's son, Aristonoë felt pride that her father should have told her. Her and not Hipparchia, though now Hipparchia must be told. This golden boy, Alexander the little sun: yes, she remembered a curly-headed boy in a golden tunic, perhaps only threaded with gold, but it had seemed to her all golden. She had been a young girl then, taken to the Queen's palace to see her aunt Charmian and her cousin Elpis, who had scared her rather, because she seemed to have such grand friends. But this boy had been friendly, had run up to her and greeted her nicely; they had played ball. And now he was dead. But then, so many people were dead. She stood firm, watching her father.

'As far as we know,' said Polemo, 'the other two are still safe, in the care of Octavia. She is, however, as I told you, Octavian's sister: which immediately puts them into danger. It is possible that they may be arranging a marriage for Selene; she must be nearly of age and perhaps docile. If you remember...' But he looked away from his daughter, he could not bear to say it straight at her, '...she and her brother were made to walk in Octavian's Triumph behind a car with a gross image of their mother, in wax, made with all the indecency of which Rome is capable. That must have been shattering, though perhaps, being the Queen's daughter, she could draw on a stock of pride and courage. Perhaps, too, she was trying to shelter her brother Ptolemy Philadelphos. The little one would have been carried, but no doubt with a label round his neck so that such of the mob as enjoy throwing rotten fruit and filth at a three-year-old, could do so.'

'Don't, Father!' Aristonoë had suddenly felt less firm.

'You have to know what to expect of Rome. If you cross the will of the rulers it will not be at all what Hellanike and her set think. Anyone dealing with Roman affairs must be prepared to realise that anyone can be a spy and an informer, that there is no true loyalty anywhere near the top, and that they use words which once had meaning simply as political weapons. Do you follow me? *Pietas, auctoritas, libertas.*' He spoke the Latin words with distaste, as though he were spitting them out. 'Whichever party gets to the top uses them, most probably when murdering its opponents. It appears to take in some of the middle classes even, but perhaps less than it did. They want something more substantial than words. The mob gets money and food and amusements. The businessmen get what they want. But those who believed in the decencies have little left to them.'

26

'If Rome is like that, will it be safe for my uncle Eumenes? Surely they know who he was?'

'Eumenes was never anything but a good soldier. They understand that. Perhaps it is the only decent thing they do understand. After it all happened he was like a man struck on the head. He said so little. He is only now beginning to recover. You will not find him good company, my rabbit. You must at least take a maid whom you can talk with easily and who is loyal.'

'I shall take Tahatre.'

'Perhaps we could find you a Greek, a girl with some education. In fact, I think I know—'

'No, it must be Tahatre. For reasons. Besides—I think I want to learn Egyptian properly, as the Queen did.'

'You are growing up, rabbit. But listen. Forget Aunt Hipparchia. I do not think you should be involved at all. I had hoped she would not speak to you. It is dangerous. Yes, I know you like the sound of that, but danger is very unpleasant when it comes too close. Not beautiful at all. Not something in a philosophy lesson or a piece of poetry. We can all of us, I hope, die well, but to be tortured and laughed at and to know one has endangered others, that isn't so good. It might happen. Even to you in the world Rome has made. I would not think any the worse of you if you said no. Nor would your mother if she were living. My own mother would be glad. We had begun to think of a marriage for you. How do you feel about that?'

Aristonoë went over and stood by him: 'You had my horoscope taken, Father. What did it say?'

'I am not sure whether I believe in such things. It was the women: your mother mostly. They wanted it done. But why should the stars be interested in us? They may be further than one thought.'

'What did they say?'

'It appeared that there would be—a long voyage.'

'Would I come back?'

'I tell you, rabbit, I think most of this is nonsense. The voyage normally means going out and returning. It was done by a reputable man, old Philammon to be exact. He was not alarmed by it. Of course, if you do go, you might not have much chance of seeing the children, or, if you did, of influencing them. You would not be expected to do anything which—which a girl of good family should not do. Then you would come back, having at least done all you could, and we would go ahead with preparations for your marriage.'

'Had you anyone in mind, Father?' Her heartbeat had quickened a little and her stomach tightened. She had laughed about this with her mates, knowing it was still a certain way ahead.

'Naturally we would tell you at a definite stage. We would not force you. Your happiness is ours.'

'And if I said that my happiness lay in danger—'

'I would say you were a true Macedonian woman, throwing back to that far grandmother of ours who was also a grandmother of the line of Ptolemies. Queen Berenice was a lover of danger. As also our own Queen. But Cleopatra made very certain that the danger was worth it before she walked in. She herself went to Rome, you know, with the little boy; there was a possibility that Caesar, whose only daughter, Julia, was dead and who otherwise had little but uncertain bastards, might have felt a useful father-hood towards Caesarion. As it happened, he did not do so. He was too much involved with his fate, knowing that he had done everything, had been a conqueror and a ruler, had the utter loyalty of his soldiers, and yet it had all come to nothing. He had done something irreparable to Rome which was the only idea he cared about. He knew at that time that men whom he admired were wanting to get rid of him for reasons he understood, and he could do nothing about it. He did not even want to see the Queen of Egypt, let alone his son. That visit was a failure and she admitted it. Except, of course, that she got to know something of Roman politics.'

'And she met Marc Antony.'

'He was a young general then, very attractive, she said, but as far as she was concerned he was part of Roman politics. And nothing else. They met and she laid herself out to get answers to certain questions. She wanted to understand the civil wars, but he was bad at explaining. He could really only talk about himself and his own family.'

'I suppose you heard about it from Aunt Charmian, Father?'

'Yes, yes, the Queen always took her about, and Iras. They were the Queen's mates, the ones she talked to and the ones who could speak back to her. She could be close to them as she never could be with a man. I wonder if you understand. You see, she once got

28

very close to one of her own councillors, but when the others realised this, it stopped the Council being any use. You look worried, rabbit?'

'I don't see, Father. Did she ... did she ... ?'

'He was a very pleasing man. An Egyptian, as a matter of fact. Quite fearless, always laughing, with a passion for astronomy. It was that which interested the Queen first. They used to go out on to the roof together to look at the stars and he explained his theories, getting excited, laughing. And she with him; it was a relief from thinking about trade and war and alliances. High on the roof, under the stars. Charmian knew of course, but it was a long time before it filtered through to the rest of the Council and upset them so much. He is dead now. No, it was an illness, nothing to do with anyone. Charmian told me, long afterwards.'

'I think I understand, Father. Did Aunt Charmian write back to you, from Rome?'

'She had to be very careful. One never knows what happens to letters, what with spies and pirates. You must remember that. Apart from Alexandria, which is never quiet and wouldn't like to be, we have had a very peaceful time in Egypt compared with some other countries. That is why we have so much corn and such old and full-bearing trees. Apart from those wretched olives of mine! A letter would get from here to Upper Egypt without interference and without being secretly opened, as fast as a man could carry it. It was very different writing from Rome.'

'But how did things go for Aunt Charmian, about her marriage?'

'Oh well, it was always being put off. But she was married before the Queen went to Cilicia to meet Antony. She and her husband both went, of course, for it was very much a State visit. Yes, Elpis was born and left with our mother; she was rather a sickly baby, but Mother fattened her up. Poor Charmian had a difficult time at the birth. Perhaps she had been leading the wrong kind of life. I don't know. At any rate there were no more children. But certainly the Queen needed her in Cilicia. Needed her more than ever before.'

'Cilicia. I never understood quite why she went there, Father.'

'Perhaps I can explain. It was like this.'

CHAPTER FOUR : B.C. 41

Council meetings always took a long time. Naturally the Queen had consulted with everyone worth while, all heads of departments and, especially on this, the army, even if it had to call itself the faithful auxiliary army of the Egyptian alliance and had a certain number of Roman officers, as well, of course, as the legions of the Roman garrison, who were quartered separately. It was no doubt annoying to know that, if it were ever to come to war, the Roman legions could walk over Egypt, boots and swords and all. But it was not going to work out that way. Let them call her a subject ally. They were fond of big words. It was her father's weak-minded doing, hoping for powerful protection. And Rome was an accident. So nearly overthrown, time and again, by the Italian cities: older cities than Rome, some of them, more civilised, more beautiful, nearer to Hellas. Or to Macedon. A pity it had not happened. Rome had clung on obstinately in the body of Italy, growing and ugly, like an unwanted child in the womb that cannot be shifted, and always with this will to conquer and thirst for money to pay the legions, throwing the ancient cities with their temples and gardens and tombs like bones to dogs for the soldiers to loot and the veterans to settle on.

Force was necessary sometimes, but it was always ugly. It had been ugly to kill the great Pompey, and, as it turned out, politically stupid. Her brother had been ill advised on that, as on many other things. He had not had the will to think for himself. If he had not turned her out of Alexandria it would not have happened. Pompey and his dreadful, white, mummified head, which had made Caesar cry. Dead men went on in the minds of others. Dead women. The Queen, sitting not on her ceremonial throne, but on a raised seat cushioned with imported African skins, tawny and gold and black,

30

frowned a little, thinking about her sister. It had been stupid; other people again, advising Arsinoë wrong, till she ended walking chained in Caesar's Triumph along with dirty, long-haired barbarians. And now she was back, probably ill-advised again, plotting, dodging in and out of sanctuary like a rat, trying to get the mob on to her side. Which would not happen; but still, it might be necessary to get rid of her.

If one lived a private life, then such things need not happen. One could go untouched by guilt and grief through a quiet passage between birth and death. Guilt and grief and joy, these were not for private persons, but for the gods, forever guilty of the dooms which they alone laid on mortals, forever grieving at the folly of these same mortals who can see no way out, but joying at themselves being other, not doomed.

She listened to her treasurer, glanced round to see that the secretaries were taking notes. At the back of her mind moved the figures of the gods, not only the gods of Olympus with Tyche—with Fate herself forever taking their free will—but the gods of Egypt and above all Isis, who suffered because of the guilt of others and most of all her husband and brother Osiris. The priests of Isis seemed to have breathed a knowledge into the Queen, an intimacy, so that now she knew Isis, knew her grief and joy, could rest in her.

Parts of a Council meeting were always boring. She reached over and stroked one of her cats; it sprang on to her knee and kneaded at her with its claws, but she pushed it off, whether or not it was sacred. The old men of the Council always laid one thing against another, but in their equations they left out the human spirit, the will to win the game. She looked past them out of the wide, pillared windows and there was the tall tower of the as yet unlighted Pharos, square and strong at the base, but lightening as it went up and at the top the great bronze statue of Poseidon: guardian of Alexandria's trade, as the dead Alexander from his tomb guarded her honour.

The business before the Council was this. The Roman General in the East, Marc Antony, was going to send for the Queen; there was some story that she had befriended Cassius, one of Caesar's killers, a good general too. While they debated this, her mind went back to Cassius in Rome; she had met him briefly; Pollio had warned her against him. She had been stupid not to have made more

31

of a friend of Pollio. But she had been put off by his tough manners. Although he was a real friend of Caesar's, yes, she thought,
probably one of the truest, he was a strong Republican, really believing in some of those Roman values which seemed to her such
nonsense, and, because of this, against foreigners, especially
foreign women.

Why did Caius Asinius Pollio care for Rome and all it stood
for, she wondered. He did not come from one of the great noble
houses. His grandfather had died fighting for the Italian cities
against Roman tyranny. What was it then, that made him think
Rome was worth while, even Rome with Julius Caesar, whose
policies he so often criticised? Order, authority, loyalty and faith.
What did they mean?

Cassius had come to Alexandria at a tricky time when nobody
was sure whether Rome would go to the Liberators or to Antony
and Octavian. Brutus had even visited the city, shortly, a sad and
anxious man, grieving for his wife Porcia, left in Rome. He had
spoken of her to Queen Cleopatra. It was only a few words, but
she, quick at such things, had remembered their devotion and
offered him not a dancing girl, but womanly sympathy. Cassius
had been married to a daughter of Servilia. Well, one can always
be reasonably sure of one's mother, but in Servilia's case the father
was less certain. It had been an entirely political marriage and
Cassius was not averse to being provided with an Alexandrian
substitute. Yes, the Queen had found some money for them,
enough to keep the occupying legions quiet. It was unlikely that
this would cause trouble with Antony.

Cassius and Brutus both dead, dead by their own hands, honourably. And Porcia had died too, not accepting to live after Brutus.
Could she ever feel that way about a man? She frowned, doubting
it. In any case it would not be fitting for a queen. Ah, now here
was the envoy, Antony's man. She sat up straight while Iras, behind her, adjusted the diadem. Cleopatra was not wearing the
crown of Egypt, nor, for that matter, the dress of an Egyptian
queen. Her blue robe of the softest wool, so fine it would pass
through a ring, was worn in strictly classical fashion; the shoulder
pins were ancestral, from Queen Berenice. Her diadem recalled that
of an Olympic winner. Only her snaky bracelets, gold and lapis,
were of Egypt.

Quintus Dellius behaved with great propriety, giving respectful greetings and making no immediate demands. He seemed more civilised than most Romans. Yes, truly he had brought a letter from his master, Marc Antony, who was hoping to have the honour of meeting Rome's noblest and most beautiful ally. But he must not trouble the Queen. With a gracious gesture she sent one of the secretaries to take the letter.

A more auspicious meeting must be arranged. Did Quintus Dellius care for classical music? Or for acrobats? For dancing? Or just a little gambling? And of course all his expenses would be seen to. A hunting party would be immediately organised. Or perhaps he would prefer hawking in the marshes? Meanwhile she would busy herself with reading the letter. When the interview was ended, the Roman envoy was escorted out of the palace, slowly, so that he would appreciate the pictures and statues, the malachite vases and dishes of lapis or onyx, set in gold, the tame hunting leopards with their golden collars and chains and the beautiful weaving in and out among the pillars of the lesser cats.

Meanwhile Queen Cleopatra was reading the letter; at the end she handed it back to the waiting secretary. It was correct, unimaginative, a soldier's letter. She found herself somewhat unable to remember Antony. She had not noticed him much when she was in Rome. There was always someone gossiping about him and his wife Fulvia, but she found Roman gossip obvious and unamusing, depending too much on crude indecencies. She murmured to Iras: 'What was he like?'

'Blond, handsome, drunken, something of an athlete when sober,' said Iras in her ear; 'always showing off. That supper party when Caesar didn't come—'

'I remember,' said Cleopatra quickly, then, turning to the eldest of her councillors, Pythokles, a man sufficiently well-off to be uninterested in bribery and at the same time not an intolerably tedious talker: 'You have read the letter?'

'It was only to be expected, Ma'am,' he said. 'No doubt those who are less certain of themselves will be hurrying there. The lesser kings.'

'Egypt will not hurry.'

'The Queen has spoken wisely. We shall, however, have to send something—considerable—if we are to hope for an adequate return. Which he no doubt has it in his power to give.'

'There are the spice lands in Arabia. But one cannot be certain.

It seems from the earlier discussion that there are Treasury funds available. Meanwhile, the Roman garrison here—has it been tested recently?'

'On his side,' said Pythokles, and tapped on the shoulder of the man sitting in front of him, on the lower step: 'Would you not agree, Pathrophis?'

'Certainly,' said this councillor, whose face and name showed him to be more Egyptian than Macedonian or Greek: 'I had the officers over at my place for a hunt. Even when they were drunk —still more when they were drunk, I would say—there was no question. The legion has some of Caesar's veterans; there had been an exchange earlier on. The middle ranks are much the same. One of the ablest centurions, a Gaul, a brother, I think, of Fango, devoted to Caesar's memory, has a small shrine in one corner of the camp, very properly laid out. He is from one of these Gallic chiefly families up near the Alps.'

'A place I should like to see,' the Queen said, half to herself. Caesar had told her once of the guardian mountain range and the tough trousered Gauls from the foothills and lakes, who enlisted in his armies and enjoyed a good fight.

Pathrophis went on: 'I understand that earlier on one company had declared themselves for the Liberators. They were flogged of course, and there has been no repetition of the incident.'

'Would you say,' said the Queen, leaning forward, 'that they were more interested in Marc Antony or in Octavian, who, after all, declares himself the legal heir?'

'I would say, Ma'am,' said Pathrophis, 'that they have drawn no clear distinction—yet.' He paused. 'Marc Antony they know and have seen. Some have fought under him. The other is only a name.'

'And no very pleasant name—if you have relatives in Rome,' said the Queen; and then, 'I shall draft a letter which this Quintus Dellius can take back. But not until he has been well loosened up. As we can do in Alexandria. Or, at least, I pride myself that this is so.'

She looked round, catching the eyes of two or three councillors, who laughed discreetly. One of them said: 'When do we consider the draft, Ma'am?'

'Will later tonight suit, gentlemen? This will of course be a preliminary. After which I think—yes, I think a slight leakage to the envoy would be in order. On the matter of what might be expected from the Treasury. Only a slight leakage.'

'Not too much, or off go our heads,' said another councillor.

'Just that, Kleanthes! By the way, there is a merchantman in from Italy, with wine, I think, and probably a load of slaves from the north. We should find out before this evening what the news is. Yes, let me know immediately. Meanwhile, gentlemen, I shall make my draft and arrange a party for the envoy.' She rose in one balanced movement and all the Council stood with their heads bowed as she passed. In her grandfather's time they would have been expected to kneel. Such things were unimportant.

The draft, somewhat lengthened, was approved. In the evening the room was different but equally pleasant. The lamps ringed it from the night. One at each side of the Queen's chair balanced on a slender bronze stand, shoulder high. The oil was scented, so that a pleasing feeling wafted across the room. On the ledge outside the fanners, slaves from elsewhere, who did not understand Greek, saw that no flies or beetles came blundering in out of the night. One saw their moving shapes, the arms and the long fans, faintly against the pale glare of the lighted Pharos, another moon.

The party for the envoy was held in a different part of the palace, somewhat more Egyptian in general décor, which the Queen herself matched. After a good warming up—and how these Romans ate and drank!—she had the envoy come and sit by her couch. She noted how he averted his eyes from the transparencies which covered her vital parts, and took occasion to take deep breaths or curl an arm above her head. Questioned, he mentioned that Antony indeed had lavish tastes. He also mentioned Glaphyra, Queen Mother of Cappadocia, a beautiful woman. 'But you, Your Majesty, if you come, Glaphyra would go home.'

'Really?' said Queen Cleopatra. 'So you mean that this General expects his allies not only at his feet but in his bed. How interesting.'

'Oh not at all, Your Majesty, not all of them!'

'I would not suppose, for instance, that Herod the Idumaean— but perhaps your General has peculiar tastes?' She opened wide eyes at Quintus Dellius.

'Oh not in the least, Your Majesty! He does not care for boys. But there, I see—the Queen is teasing me! I am only a poor ignorant soldier. But I would only make one suggestion, just the faintest and entirely in your interest, Your Majesty, that if you should care to come in your own person, the amount that would be expected in actual money might be considerably less.'

'And the accusation about Cassius?'

'Thin air, Ma'am, thin air! Nobody with any feeling could suspect Your Majesty of incorrect conduct.'

'How you relieve my mind, my dear envoy!' She stretched one leg, slowly, her thigh and calf muscles giving infinite promise. At the join of the lovely legs, a jewel of great elegance held together the folds of the gauze, so that not all was visible, even if one dared to look. She folded the stretched leg over the other, the toes relaxing and curling; her eyelashes fluttered, her eyes observed. She felt with some satisfaction that the envoy would soon need a dancing girl.

Once the envoy had taken the ship back to Asia Minor with the Queen's letter, there was much work to be done. Nor could the Queen neglect foreign policy in other directions. One day, yes, one day she would sail South again, up the Nile and deep into Africa and to the golden lands. Was the fat Queen still ruling the land of Punt or had she, in the fulness of time, been taken to her ancestors, willingly or not, and been succeeded by a glossy and milk-fed daughter? There was considerable trade with the East. Once or twice she thought of the prince she had met at Meroë. Might there not be equally agreeable princes with larger and more stable kingdoms? It would be pleasant to take a long rest from politics on the back of a gilded elephant in the arms of a delightful prince. A husband? But would one's interest survive? No, better to reign alone.

Perhaps, she thought, her ultimate policy might lie in a withdrawal from the Mediterranean world, which was becoming more and more involved in Roman politics. One should not be in any way dependent on these barbarians, for that, after all, was what they were. They were unintelligible from any rational standpoint, but clearly they were getting worse and worse, everything tending to increased violence. This terrible, yelling Roman mob that could be driven mad by words. The dynastic murders and marriages among the noble families. Rome. If only she could get rid of the legions! Drown them like rats.

The calm of the summer seemed pleasantest for the voyage to Cilicia. Let the rest of the so-called allies hurry to kiss Antony's feet. Egypt would take her own time. Antony apparently had been making a show of himself in all the Greek cities as Apollo or

36

Dionysos. Very well. She, Cleopatra, rising from the sea, passing to Tarsus from Cyprus itself, birthplace of the goddess, would be Aphrodite. It would appeal to Roman tastes. And if her loyalty to Rome was doubted, it might be sensible to come in such a way that Marc Antony was disarmed. Whatever follies he committed, he had the armies of the East and he was a thoroughly competent general. But he was unlikely to set his armies on Aphrodite. The costumes, or lack of them, were duly put in hand.

They met in a burst of play-acting, all on a much more elegant level than anything Antony had devised or been entertained by in any of the Greek cities. Even Athens seemed provincial—and indeed was, these days. He responded, and gradually, from laughing at his clumsiness and lack of wit, the Queen began to be a little sorry for him, the big blond bear of a Roman. 'He is trying so hard to be civilised,' she said to Charmian.

'And can't quite make it!'

'Yet he is escaping a little from being entirely Roman.'

'Perhaps we should take him to Alexandria,' Charmian said, 'and see what that does for him. It might do a lot.'

'This winter,' said the Queen slowly, 'without Fulvia. And without Glaphyra.'

'Neither of whom would be missed,' said Charmian, 'if the Queen's majesty would condescend—or has she already? Almost, almost. But tongues will wag, my dear love, and tongues can hurt.'

'They were wagging a great deal in Rome when I was there. For nothing on my part, as you know. But it seems that Antony attracts this—waggishness. It is a pity, because he is a good soldier. And honourable in a way. He is a very loyal man—as Romans go. It is a pity that he is loyal to Octavian. That could perhaps be altered. And then—yes, I could get fond of him.'

Charmian hesitated. They were walking in the evening along the bank of the river, their barge a cluster of lights below them, the guards ahead and following at a discreet distance. 'My husband was telling me,' she said, 'that there is talk in Rome. About this very Octavian. It is said that he will not allow Antony to share the power. Even if he becomes Consul.'

'Octavian is Caesar's heir,' said the Queen. 'Legally. Whatever that comes to in Rome.'

'It is said,' Charmian went on, and the Queen was aware that she was passing on a message, 'that when he took a certain Italian city, Perusia, which had held out on the side of the Republic, he put the captives to death and the town to flames. This was not thought well of.'

'No,' said Cleopatra. 'No. Even Romans feel suddenly that things can go too far. Perusia. I think I have heard the name. One of the noble cities. You said it was on the side of the Republic. They call it that, do they, after the death of Brutus and Cassius and the rest?' Charmian nodded. 'The Republic. An honourable name. Against, I suppose, tyranny. Would Marc Antony make a good tyrant?'

'He is too careless. Perhaps too generous. You should know better than I do, love. But this young Octavian for whom things fall out strangely well—my husband thinks: yes. A tyrant.'

'Ah,' said Cleopatra. 'Hold the lamp low, Charmian.' She stooped and picked up a small stone from the path and threw it into the river. She listened for the faint plop as the stone vanished for ever, and appeared to come to some decision inside herself. 'We shall bring Antony to Alexandria,' she said.

CHAPTER FIVE : B.C. 26

They were down at the farm, with the flat delta country stretching round them, every inch cultivated. The corn was ripening and there were certain things which Polemo must see to himself. Hipparchia was there with Mikion, her husband, a Rhodian by birth, but now entirely Alexandrian. His land marched with Polemo's and they made use of irrigation water from the same canal, but his farmhouse was less comfortable, in fact little more than a reed-thatched shelter. The only one of his family who enjoyed going there was young Kerkidas, who was good at killing snakes, but he had just started going to lectures as a grown-up student in a proper student's tunic. It was a pleasure for Hipparchia and Mikion to see their son growing up. But the girl Salampsio, who was just twelve years old, liked best to be around with her cousin Aristonoë.

When they were at the farm, the two girls went out in the early morning and helped to hoe the bean rows. They wore their old school tunics and had their hair tied up in coloured kerchiefs, out of the way. The women laughed and taught them songs in Egyptian and asked them all the old riddles. When they didn't guess, everyone went off into fits of laughter. The men were getting up the water from the canal, which was now fairly low, or whacking the donkeys that brought in baskets of earth to lay down in the stables, after which, well dunged, it would be taken out for field manure, or else preparing seed beds for the summer vegetables. At noon they broke off; the women settled down under the palm trees to eat their bowls of cold porridge or barley bread and onions, and suckle their babies in peace. Aristonoë and Salampsio went back to the house. Two men had just brought in some pigeons. The pretty things lay there, in the yard, not yet cold, their necks wrung and drooping. I shall enjoy eating them, thought Aristonoë, but it is altogether too easy—to kill.

Their baths were ready; their maids sponged them down, telling them they shouldn't work so hard, they were young ladies, not serfs! Then they sat drying off, while their hair was combed. Salampsio was fairer, but the ends of Aristonoë's long brown tresses had just the same kind of gold glint. Salampsio's maid was really her old nurse, but this she pretended not to know. Aristonoë's Tahatre was a far better hair-dresser and she picked up languages easily. She could do a mimic of Roman guests at table that sent them into fits; it would be no big step to learn Latin. I must tell her soon, Aristonoë said to herself. But meanwhile the pigeons were roasting, what a gorgeous smell! If only he gets the stuffing right this time. And I could eat a mountain of salad. But all the same, why do we have pigeons now instead of at supper? I thought it would be just cheese, like Father has always.

Tahatre answered that their Aunt Phaedra—she was really their step-aunt—was coming with Cousin Hellanike—and her Roman.

'Oh, really!'

'Not to make a naughty face!' Tahatre said, and half patted, half smacked Aristonoë.

Salampsio said, 'I suppose he might be useful.'

'How?' said Aristonoë quickly, for she had also thought this.

'Oh well, he could get us things. They always have so much money. He has these horrible friends among the businessmen. At least he never brings them here. But they can get hold of—anything.'

'We must certainly never ask for anything, Salampsio. Or even hint it. Not even to Aunt Phaedra. But I hope they arrive in time or the pigeons will get hard.'

'And they haven't worked all morning,' said Salampsio virtuously. 'I'm hungry!' However, just then one of the girls brought in a bowl of delicious sour milk and, what was more, a little jar of honey to go with it. So if the Roman was late at least they wouldn't be thinking of eating one another!

He was, however, almost exactly on time, not a bad-looking young man and courteous to his host and the ladies. He spoke pedantic Greek, but said that his betrothed was already quite a good scholar in Latin; she was reading Virgil and indeed had already read many of the older poets such as Naevius and Ennius. But

40

naturally there was much—too much unhappily—which no young lady should so much as look at. He quoted a line or two to Polemo and Mikion.

Hellanike was an only child, her father dead. She was something of an heiress. Would this Roman sell her farm and go back to Rome? One didn't know. However she seemed cheerful enough, showing off her Indian silk dress and her new bracelets and ear-bobs. Dinner was served, pleasantly, under a tent. The pots of flowers from the front of the house made a splash of cool colour at the four corners. There were couches for the adults, but the three girls sat upright, their hair partly veiled. They drank the light beer of the countryside, leaving the wine for the rest of the family.

As dinner went on, Lucius Mindius, an officer of course and quite high up, but more interested perhaps in the diplomatic side, since he was on the staff of the Prefect of Egypt, kept on talking. His elders listened. He talked a lot about Octavian, whom he now called Augustus or the *Princeps*, using the Latin word—nobody quite knew what it meant. From time to time, Aristonoë, listening, caught her father's eye: here, or here, was something which had to be noted and remembered. Apparently they were making a great thing in Rome of the peace of Augustus, having various ceremonies, building a great altar and so on. Peace? But what did that mean? Peace for the Romans who no doubt needed it after all that blood-letting. But the peace of a conquering empire only rests on the back of the conquered. And possibly on those who for some other reason have to be put in their place in case they become a threat to the peace of Augustus. Lucius Mindius took on himself to speak disparagingly of the late Prefect of Egypt, Caius Cornelius Gallus, who appeared to have been one of these threats. He had duly cut the arteries in his wrists and expired, not too uncomfortably. Mikion, who had known him and got on with him reasonably well, remarked that it was an honourable death.

Lucius Mindius seemed to take this badly. 'Ah well,' he said, 'you Egyptians have a speciality in suicide. Asps in aspic!' He picked another pigeon out of the dish and crunched it, rather like a lizard crunching a moth.

Aristonoë tried to catch her father's eye, but he had turned away. Nobody made any comment except that Hellanike's mother murmured 'Quite'.

'Caught a real nest of little traitors that time,' said the chief guest, determined to show these provincials where they got off; 'that guy Pathrophis—knew him, did you?' For Polemo had winced a little. 'He squealed all right—once we'd tickled him up. He wasn't let off so easy as the Prefect. Not likely. Nor the others. Anyway, that old Gallus didn't die for love! He was a one, I can tell you: kids everywhere. Not that you didn't have a bit of that in high places yourselves! Not that it pays,' he added, realising that nobody had laughed, so at least he might make them grimace. These foreigners! 'We know,' he said, 'we know what went on—in that so-called palace!'

Polemo leant over and said, rebukingly: 'The young girls!'

'Young girls!' said Lucius Mindius. 'Mine knows what I think. And she thinks it too. As she should.' He was beginning to look angry and Polemo shook his head at Hipparchia, shifting the conversation, saying that the desert lions were getting too bold and that something must be done. What did their guest think? A hunt, yes, certainly. Oh, he would organise it! Soon afterwards the ladies withdrew.

When they were out of earshot, Aristonoë stood very straight in front of her cousin, with her eyes narrowed: 'Cousin Hellanike,' she said, 'do you believe these Roman stories about the Queen?'

'I don't know what you mean!'

'Yes, you do.' Aristonoë took a step nearer. 'About the Queen and this wretch Octavian—'

'Well, it's likely enough, isn't it? Anyway I don't care! He's going to be my husband, isn't he? I'm not going to be tied down by what people think here! And if you are nasty to me now, Aristonoë, I'll take it out of you when I'm one of the Prefect's staff wives, you see if I don't!'

Her mother began to cry. Hipparchia said: 'Anger gets us through no gates. Perhaps Hellanike will be able to see our side of the truth some day. Meanwhile, Aristonoë and Salampsio, you had better do a turn on your looms before you rest. I shall come and set the clock for you.'

They curtsied and left. 'In front of the servants, too!' said Salampsio. 'And he was going to get ever so much worse. Oh why have we got to have Romans!'

'That was before the Queen's day,' said Aristonoë going over slowly to her loom. 'It was her father's fault, Ptolemy the Flute

Blower who forgot how to stand up to anyone. He made his children wards of Rome. He ought to have known. Stupid men are often frightened. Because he was a coward this happened to us.'

Hipparchia came in and half filled the bronze top of the water clock. 'They will be gone by the time this is through. At least I intend so. But you must not speak so to Hellanike.'

'Why not, Mother?' said Salampsio. 'She deserves it.'

'Possibly. But she may repeat it. I do not wish to have any suspicions of this house. For reasons.' She looked hard at Aristonoë. 'I disapprove of this marriage. But it is not in my hands. I think, however, that she has sufficient family decency not to repeat anything.'

Salampsio said suddenly and violently: 'Mother, if the Queen had lived would we have had to have Roman soldiers?'

'I suppose,' Hipparchia said. one hand on the loom post, 'one might say that if the Queen had lived and been able to carry out her full plan, it might have been possible not to have them. If she had even been able to carry out half her plan they might have been a different kind of Roman soldier. Not Octavian's.'

CHAPTER SIX : B.C. 37

The Queen told her Council of the plans which were beginning to come clear in her mind, putting forward her reasons, or most of them. The Roman Empire was now split. At one time the division had been almost stable, with Octavian holding the West, Antony the East, clearly defined, and Lepidus holding Sicily and North Africa. But Lepidus had misjudged Octavian, blundering badly. He had been eliminated, in the name of peace and order, and now Octavian held both his provinces as well as Rome and the West.

Either of two things could happen now. The Queen leant forward, speaking slowly, looking at one face after another. Genuine friendship between the rulers of East and West : or else war. There had been attempts at friendship. After Fulvia's death, Antony had married Octavia, Octavian's sister. They had seemed for a time to be happy. But there had been no son, in spite of Virgil's Golden Age. And Octavian had never sent Antony the legions which he had promised earlier. Antony had defeated the Parthians, yes, after terrible losses. Better, he had won and consolidated Armenia. But Parthia and Armenia were a long way from Rome. Octavian and his Consuls had easier Triumphs. Octavian's men were in all the key places; Marc Antony had trusted him too much. It was possible that loyalty would be Antony's downfall.

'So the Queen tells us it will be war,' said Pythokles.

'On the contrary, I am asking for your advice—all of you.'

'I too think war,' Pythokles said, 'though like others of my age, I am sick of war. As they must be in Rome.'

'Only the young want war and this will be a large and dreadful war, a whirlpool into which all will be dragged,' said another councillor; 'but is there a way out for Egypt? Has the Queen thought?'

44

'I have indeed thought,' said the Queen, 'that there might be a way out. The middle sea, the Mediterranean, out there, leads to Rome. But it is not far from that sea to the other, the sea that leads one way to India and the other way down the African coast to the land of Punt. In India there are emeralds, rubies, silks, dyes and spices; in Africa ebony and ivory, hides, slaves, incense, above all gold. Supposing none of this was allowed to go through to Rome or only at a great price. What then?'

'They might cut off things we need just as badly,' said Kleanthes, 'tin, for example.'

'I have seen Indian swords, Kleanthes,' the Queen said, 'and it seems to me that there are other sources of tin besides the tin islands of Britain. Perhaps as far beyond India as Britain is beyond Rome. And now let us think further. It would be possible to build another Egypt looking to East and South. It would be possible to move ships from one sea to another. It is level ground. At one time there was a canal, but it was allowed to silt up; you may have seen traces of it. When I saw them myself I asked until I found out. Yes, Kleanthes, it is worth asking questions.'

'But—Your Majesty—another Egypt? That cannot be your plan —to go from here!'

'That is what I propose.' She looked at them, together and separately. 'That is my way out.'

'Leaving Alexandria!' said Pythokles. 'Surely the Queen cannot mean that? Taking the ships—the ships from the best harbour in the world!'

And now others began to see the enormity of the thing proposed. 'Leaving Alexandria, the Pharos, the docks—no!' 'Leaving the temples, the library—' 'Your own palace!' 'Leaving the bones of the founder!' The voices here and there barked with displeasure. Others looked round, silent so far, shocked.

The Queen said: 'Alexander, my kinsman, founded Alexandria where there was nothing but a mud village. Other cities can be founded. High up the sacred river, beyond Thebes, out of their reach. This is one way out of the destruction that we all see.'

'And if the councillors begged yet further thought from their Queen?'

'The other way is to take some action which will make this war between Romans of the East and of the West, this war which we foresee, end in the destruction of—both.' She dropped her head in her hands. She was no longer the slim, exciting girl, packed with energy, able to live to the full hour after hour, day and night; she was a woman, heavy-hipped, solid-breasted. She could become tired. She moved well still; she had good bone structure; she had balance. But her councillors thought of her less as a female creature than as a politician, as a dealer in statecraft who could see not just round one corner, but round three. She had their entire respect. They listened carefully to what more she had to say.

When she put forward some part of what was in her mind, there was long discussion, including some assessment of what would be needed from the treasure of Egypt. Once or twice the other idea came up, the possibility of basing themselves on trade between Africa and India. But could they risk all their Northern markets? Worse, it was a retreat: did the Queen not feel that this was unworthy?

'Alexander retreated from India,' the Queen said. 'It is the sign of great generalship to be able to retreat.'

But was she an Alexander? She was not afraid of danger; she was not even afraid of being thought a coward. She was simply very tired. She had not wanted to take this action. It was exhausting, trying to come to a decision of this importance, most of all when her Council could not see as far as she did. Unless she was completely backed and encouraged, she would not be able to carry out the decision to move: perhaps not, even if she was, even if she could lead out all the people of Egypt, a thing which could only be done by one considered as God. It would be bound to leave her for a time somewhat helpless, like a snake shedding her skin, and the Romans would see. Only a complete diplomatic double-front would make it possible. And the Council did not look like giving her that.

No, it would have to be the other way. Inducing the Western Romans and Eastern Romans to destroy one another, and to hope that, when Rome's power was at a low ebb, the Latin cities would turn on her and complete what was necessary. Clearly, it must mean, as a start, strengthening Antony. And could she be sure, could she be utterly sure, that she did this out of policy and thought for Egypt and not because he was the father of her children, the god twins, the little sun and moon, Alexander Helios and Cleopatra Selene? Octavian would probably decide to fight; he was a murderous type, like many other physically delicate people who feel they must show the world that they are as strong as the next. If he did not fight, then Antony must be pushed, perhaps by not letting him accept any help or mediation from Octavian.

She went down to the Hall of Audience. For this, she always dressed Egyptian-fashion and wearing her crowns, with her hair swept back and gold-dusted until it looked like a wig. Her advisers here were all Egyptian, since often she had to judge in cases of land or inheritance or custom going back centuries and in many different parts of the country. And yet, by now, she knew almost as much as any of her advisers. She was well aware that, before her time, people had gone for justice and help not to the ruling Ptolemies, but to the priests of the greater temples, who seemed more nearly successors to the Pharaohs. She was also aware that, because of this, she was not altogether loved by the priesthood, though most feared her. Only, as she knew, certain of the priests of Isis had passed beyond that. But she knew too much. She knew of times when there had been other thoughts about the gods; she knew that gods could be made and changed by human thought, as Aton had been made, and that they could also perish, though not entirely, since some worshippers will always be found, far separate perhaps in time and space.

As she leant down from the light stool, a stretcher of lion-headed gold, threaded across with panther skin, her head close to the head of the kneeling suppliant, she heard the murmur of her name. And the name was not Cleopatra but Isis. To be designated by the people: what did that mean? What did it make one? As one becomes older, one becomes less mortal, more aligned with the eternal things. Once she did not think of death except as something to be inflicted on others, a punishment. Now she knew it growing and ripening within herself.

Often people came to her who were merely and only poor, desperately poor in rich Egypt. Perhaps the breadwinner was sick and might or might not recover; perhaps the crops were gone, the beasts dead, the children starving; perhaps the suppliant was struggling in the grip of the village moneylender, perhaps only needing the little for a decent funeral for father or mother. These problems could be solved from the purse at her side. Sometimes there would be a quarrel, and she listened to both, trying to pick up the points where they might be reconciled, cooling down the angry, rebuking the greedy. On the whole people did not lie to her

47

much; one does not lie to the gods. It was hard work and yet she loved it. The dirty and rough hands of the people fell on her smooth ankles and toes like blessing, like a sweet ointment. The dusk fell. Lamps were lit. The audience was over. Here, without swords or spears round her, here where she was Isis, clear daylight was best.

She rose and faded from them into the dark of a narrow doorway. Beyond that was a long corridor painted with figures. This was not something which Antony would understand. Or any Roman. Or, for that matter, any Greek.

She turned across a hall and past a hanging into dim light and the children sleeping, curled on their mats. One of the nurses started to her feet, wide-eyed, saying the name: Isis. Making the gesture of worship. Then saw it was the Queen, the mother. The nurses drew apart and the Queen knelt by the children, now three-year-olds, watching them breathing gently away in their own world, the fair curls springing softly from their heads, the boy and girl still alike, still one another's best playmates. The girl stirred and threw off her cover, embroidered with her own moon symbols. The mother knelt down and drew it over her again. Selene half opened an eye, closing her fingers over her mother's big finger. 'My little Moon,' the Queen murmured.

But the weariness caught her again, partly of the body but mostly the weariness of decision, the many small decisions of the Audience, the main decision of the Council. She took her way through lamplit and moonlit balconies, to which the harbour sounds rose faintly. Iras came to meet her, to say that her bath was ready and here was a new perfume, just come to town—would she try it? Hardly answering yet, she stepped down into the bath, into the comforting warmth and scent, the wet that covered any tears which might squeeze themselves out of her. Could a man help her, could Antony the father? She remembered, in detail and critically now, his lovemaking. Yes, one slept well after it. One was vastly refreshed. Though it could lack novelty now. He had probably learnt little in the interval; he was too sure of himself, not really the perpetual learner that a lover should be. One wanted, sometimes, the touch of a stranger, a shape-changer, a god. Osiris—Osiris dead and cut into small pieces, as she had seen, unflinching, at executions. Osiris punished for the sins of mankind: for the winter and the darkness. Yet also the Judge, the weigher of souls, towards whom there could be no bribery. Antony? Antony the easy taker and giver of money? No, she knew him too well. And perhaps she would have to destroy him. For the sake of Egypt.

Now the women were drying and powdering her. She lay back, her hair swept aside, for the massage which kept her skin unwrinkled, her belly and thighs smooth and receptive, her breasts upswept. Gradually it drove the tiredness out of her muscles, freshened her blood. Traces of oil were wiped carefully off, an errant hair or two plucked, a sharp dab of perfume here and there. Then, her head on a pillow, she surrendered her hair into the ministrations of Iras. She shut her eyes during the rubbing of the scalp and upper neck; the music of the girl harpists at the far end of the room helped to untwang her stretched nerves.

Her face felt more itself now; Iras found and removed the occasional white hair, not many, not more than a year ago. Then the combing began, lifting the weight, lightening it. 'Iras,' she said, 'I think it must be a marriage this time. I must allow myself to be tied so that later there will be a great un-tying.'

'Marriage will be a change,' said Iras, 'but, even for a great Queen, in a marriage, the husband must take all.'

'I think not. Not this time. It will be marriage between Gods. Am I a God, Iras?'

'For me, my lady Queen, and always will be.' Iras, sweet-breathed, stooped over and kissed her lightly.

'And Antony?'

'Antony is a Roman. I do not know what the Roman gods are like.'

'They are like men and women, very large. Venus is a woman with breasts like great bath sponges. Caesar put a statue of me in the temple of Venus Genetrix, whom he called his ancestress. I was quite embarrassed to find myself in the same room with her! Mars is a Roman general, always victorious. Jupiter is an old man who found a thunderbolt under the bed and doesn't know what to do with it. But Antony at least is Dionysos. He is getting too old for Apollo, though he still likes to have all the muses in attendance. Especially Terpsichore. Give me the mirror, Iras. My poor Charmian, I miss her so much.'

'As she does you. When I saw her she was crying for you.'

'What did she say?'

'That nobody else was interesting. That's what we say, love.'

'You are sure the illness is nothing?'

'Quite sure, my lady Queen. And when she hears there is to be a wedding she will become entirely well.'

'How I hope so. Most of all now that her sister is married and has a fine son. Is Charmian jealous?'

'Charmian and I,' said Iras, with the least, tiniest quiver in her voice, 'so long as we have you, we want nothing else.'

'All the same, send word to Hipparchia that I want Charmian to attend me. And her brother.' Iras nodded; it would be done. That was a good Macedonian family, entirely trustworthy. The Queen smiled to herself, making a few wild plans which would come to nothing but were pleasant in the imagining. A wedding. Her first. A shrinking virgin—could she remember...? Most Queens were betrothed as babies, married as girls. She remembered her Indian. But that would have been different. 'I shall send my envoys first,' she said, 'to see what a state it may throw him into when he hears that a wedding is intended. Who will bring me the most amusing report? I shall want details. Perhaps you should go, my Iras. I think I know how it will be. But I must be sure. My lion must be well netted.'

'Oh, lucky lion!'

'Will he be? Perhaps. Or perhaps not. At least he will not be bored. Sometimes I think that what my poor lion needs most is something to sharpen his wits—shall I say his claws?—on. Not soft wood. We talk and talk. Yes, I like that too, for my own claws. There is another report I shall need. Just what Octavian says when he hears.'

Iras, watching her lady's teeth bare ever so little, said quickly: 'I shall certainly not be the messenger there. We know exactly what will be said. Octavian and his gutter poets!'

'Yes. It is curious to be so hated. It makes one feel powerful. But one must not forget the Gods.'

'And you will not forget—Egypt?'

'No. Never.'

The wedding preparations were beginning to be more clear-cut by the time Charmian came back from her parents' home, not entirely herself yet, but for all that the Queen's true mate. She had left Elpis at the farm with her grandmother and her foster-mother, to run and swim and grow strong before her education needed to start. 'Will you take the children with you when you go?' she asked. And suddenly she knew that the deep anxiety which she had felt fluttering ever since she had heard that this time it was to be a marriage, was simply lest the Queen allow the passionate love she felt for her two children to overflow on to their father and enmesh not only herself, but Egypt.

'Perhaps Caesarion. It is time he saw something beyond Alexandria. And he should learn how to speak and act towards those who have power.'

'The new men whom Antony has put into the old kingdom?'

'I think we shall see them. Yes, I think there may even be some bargaining. But I confess I would not care to eat with Herod the Idumaean.'

'Nor he, perhaps, with you, Ma'am!'

'I doubt if I shall even take my poisoner. Though occasions might arise. No, all will be omened for good. Yes, for good. You will see, Charmian. For a time the world shall be as it was under Alexander and afterwards when Ptolemy Soter became King. His kingdom shall again be mine. All of it. This is promised. But I shall have more power than ever he had. In time, in time. Alexander will smile in his deep sleep to know of me.'

'You are sure your Antony will keep his promise?'

'Yes, yes, this is my marriage portion. Without which— Charmian, he is mine.'

'I believe you, love.'

'And he will see his children when he comes back. His little golden sun, his heir, Octavia can only give him girls.'

'You are sure, my Queen,' said Charmian, 'that he will be walking into your net, not you into his? You are utterly sure?'

'I think I can keep my balance on a thin rope still, my Charmian. Rome does not know this; they think I am a common queen. Let them go on thinking it! Antony: yes. But I will go this far. If things had turned out otherwise, so that Antony was the stronger of the two and Octavian the weaker, and, in order to destroy the rule of Rome, I had to buttress the weaker, I would not care to have Octavian in my bed. And yet I would do it. He may not think so now, but it would happen nevertheless. And he would not know that he had been trapped. Yes, I would do even that for Egypt.'

CHAPTER SEVEN: B.C. 26

Tahatre held the mirror for Aristonoë to look critically at her hair-do. The bronze surface had been polished and polished. This was Tahatre's first duty every morning. If Aristonoë woke early, as she often did on the farm, hearing cockcrow from every side, the dogs barking and the men going to work, laughing and shouting and spitting, the first thing she would see would be Tahatre squatting on the floor in the corner, polishing the mirror with the finest sifted sand, and then a few drops of oil, wiped off and off, again and again. She would blink at her and Tahatre would smile quickly back. On the other side of the mirror was a Greek scene, lady or goddess. It was an old one that had belonged to her mother and indeed to her mother's mothers, for a long way back.

While she had been washing, Tahatre had laid out two of her prettiest dresses, with deep patterns woven into the borders. But today was a philosophy lesson: better keep everything plain. Zenon preferred it. While she was still at home, let things go on normally and quietly. She might need this to look back on: to know it had been her life. Perhaps it was time to speak. 'Tahatre,' she said, 'I am going to Rome.'

'My mistress! But not—not to marry?'

'A Roman like Lucius Mindius? You would not like that, Tahatre?'

Tahatre shook her head violently. She was such a sweet, clean girl with her clear-cut Egyptian bones, her face softening to the chin, not jutting out in the heavy Roman way. Her hands were narrow and clever. Now that she was learning to read and write, she got on surprisingly fast. 'Why not?' Aristonoë asked.

'They have other gods. And these gods are devils. They make only pain. They tell nothing, they lead nowhere.'

'But, Tahatre, my gods are not the same as your gods.'

'They have other names, that is all. It is only shape changing between the same god. The Queen knew that.'

I must follow this up, Aristonoë thought, and asked, hesitating a little: 'Tahatre, do people remember the Queen? I mean not people like my father and my aunt, but ordinary people, shopkeepers and farmers, the girls beating the washing on the stones, the old women who come in with the baskets of dates, fishermen, beggars, everyone?'

'They most certainly remember. The fishermen call their boats for her, even quite little boats. They paint her eyes on their boats. They put her sign over their doors. The Romans do not see this. My people believe she will give them justice and mercy. But, my mistress, you say you are going to Rome. Is that true? Shall I lose you?'

'Yes, it is true. But not for marriage. No! But I am taking you with me. Do you come willingly?'

'I must tell my brother and my uncles. They will say yes. But, my mistress, why are you going to Rome?'

'Do you remember, Tahatre, that the Queen had children and that the conqueror, Octavian, seized the children and took them to Rome? All except poor Caesarion.'

'You know the story of Caesarion, my mistress?'

'I only know he was killed because there could not be a second Caesar. Is there more?'

'Oh yes, there is more. We know because he passed through. Three days before the end, the Queen sent him secretly South with his tutor, a man called Rhodon, out of reach of the Romans. She knew he would be safe with the Queen of Punt. He was meant to be the one to build the trade between Asia and Africa. He was to found the new Alexandria. You understand, my mistress?' Aristonoë was deeply surprised, but said nothing. Was this something her aunt or her father would have known about? Tahatre, kneeling back on her heels, fixing her dark eyes on Aristonoë's blue eyes, went on: 'They rode fast. A boat would have been too slow and easy to catch. Always, always, the villages welcomed them in her name, gave them fresh horses, lied to the Romans if questions came later. They came to Meroë and stayed there for a while. There also they were welcomed. The people of Meroë did not fear the Romans. But they stayed too long. It is said, and this, my mistress,

53

is true, that messengers from Octavian, the new Caesar, came to the palace of Meroë and had secret words with this tutor, Rhodon.'

'He was—not a Macedonian?'

'A Greek, my mistress. But the boy trusted him. They had been bidden to go on to the Land of Punt. It is a long, long way, but the people of Meroë found guides for them. But it is said that they were much frightened by wild animals and devils that came at night. Perhaps this tutor made things seem more bad than they were.'

'The Queen's son should not have been afraid.'

'He had his mistress with him, a young girl. She was certainly afraid and in the end she became ill of fear and died. She lies in the deep forest far from her home. We who have heard this do not think that Caesarion ever got as far as the Queen of Punt, since she would by all means have stopped the thing which happened. For this man, this Greek, spoke cunning words to the boy, persuading him, sad and discouraged, that the Romans had promised him a kingdom if he returned. There would have been lying letters to show, do you not think, my mistress? They came back. The boy was killed by the Romans.'

'And the tutor is—where?'

'The boy's mother is Isis. Her spirit came to certain priests with instructions. It was clear. The man Rhodon is no more, either in this world or in the next. The boy is with his mother, having crossed safely in the Boat of Isis.'

'You believe that, Tahatre?' Aristonoë took the girl by the shoulders, feeling under her hands the delicate bones, and suddenly, so much, wanting not to hurt her. And oh, wanting to be able to believe the same thing!

'Surely I believe it,' Tahatre, wide-eyed, answered. She twisted her hands in a gesture of uncertainty—whether to speak the next thing. Then said: 'There is a new star. Since then. I myself have seen it. My sister Shepenese has seen it. It is *her* star. It is she, the Queen. But it is said that Romans cannot see it.'

'Could I?'

'Yes, my mistress. But I have not yet been told, what do we do in Rome? You said, I think, yes, my mistress, you spoke of the children.'

'We shall see them, somehow. You and I. And also Charmian's daughter, Elpis.'

'And then, my mistress? We take them away from Rome? We bring them—home?'

'I don't know, Tahatre, I don't know. But I want you with me. I shall need all the help I can get. I shall need someone I can trust to the hilt.'

'To the hilt, my mistress. I will bring a very sharp knife which my brother will give me.'

'Oh no, it will not come to that! At least—Tahatre, let no knife be seen.' She began to walk about the room, aware that Tahatre was watching her. She picked up a book roll and then dropped it again. Once, not so long ago, she had wanted to go on reading and reading, it filled her with happiness to think of so many books, so many plays, so much poetry, waiting to be read. Soon it would be time for her tutor to come. There would be comment on the tragedies of long ago. The actors died off-stage; there was no blood. Medea's children were not killed where you could see it happen. Tahatre was folding and putting away the two pretty dresses which she was not going to wear, with the kerchiefs and belts that went with them. From the far side of the room Aristonoë said softly: 'You do hate the Romans, Tahatre, don't you?'

Tahatre, kneeling beside the opened chest, answered, equally gently, the obvious and truthful answer: 'Yes, my mistress, I do hate them.'

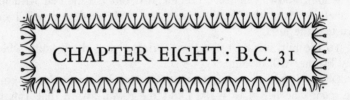

CHAPTER EIGHT : B.C. 31

They waited and waited for news in Alexandria. Sometimes a rumour would start, and first a few people, then dozens, then hundreds, would tear through the streets shouting and demonstrating. Mostly, they finished up at the palace, screaming under the balconies. If they were lucky, the nurses brought out the royal children and everyone cheered. Sometimes they would surround and shout at a squad of Roman soldiers, but when the words of command barked out and swords were drawn, the mob melted away.

But it was bad for everyone. Today there were more than a few who went out across the causeway to the Pharos island at the far side of the great port, watching out to sea for a sail till their eyes tired in the blue dazzle, climbing to the top balcony of the great Pharos itself, to see further. But they only saw the port busy with shipping or, further out, the little fishing boats from the island. Pathrophis and Kleanthes came down the steps of the lighthouse, walked through the square, colonnaded courtyard with the piled fuel and tired donkeys, and took the path back between the fishermen's houses. There was always a stink here, of fish and dirt and rotten vegetables. Close to the water line there were brothels much used by the foreign sailors and a brood of queer-looking children playing in the mud. One or two women shouted after the two councillors, but knew there was no money there.

Pathrophis was biting his nails with anxiety. 'I think back, you know, to that Council we held before the marriage. Did we judge wrong? Were we simply cowards, not able to see further than our own comfort?'

'It begins to look like that now,' Kleanthes said sombrely.

'If we had encouraged the Queen to follow her vision: to vanish

into Upper Egypt, to the far reaches of the river and a new city—
to leave the Romans to rule the world and gather in more and
more tribute and become more and more hated?'

'I doubt if it could have been done,' Kleanthes said; 'it would
have taken too long. For a time we would have been weak.'

'If she had forced us—'

'And besides, would the Romans have been so much hated?
People get used to anything. At least the rule of Rome gives them
corn and oil and a few shows. A Triumph or two. They will soon
learn to hold these disgusting games of theirs beyond Rome. In
all the capital cities. And everyone will fall for them. Even in
Athens. Or here. The Romans can hold their Empire for a long
time if they are clever. And they are certainly clever when they
have to be.'

'But her other plan?' Pathrophis said. 'That the East and West
Romans who are hated now by most of the world were to fight
one another to death?'

'Yes, that plan was accepted in the end. But I do not think that
the rest of the world are joining in. Unless they are paid. And
we have spent almost all we can already. In fact they are not
hating. They are only waiting to see who wins in this war.'

'Which is happening now. I hope very many of these Romans
are dying and going to their own hell,' Pathrophis answered
harshly.

'Have sense,' Kleanthes said, pulling his cloak tighter, 'Marc
Antony was not much hated. Did you hate him, Pathrophis? No,
be truthful.'

After a pause Pathrophis said: 'Personally, I hate Romans.
Though not every individual. No. And besides we knew—yes, we
did know—that Antony was loyal to the Queen. For most of the
rest—they were Romans. It would have been a pleasure to see their
blood in the streets. But Alexandria did not hate Antony.'

'That was not all. He was not really hated anywhere. Certainly
not in Athens! All our letters proved that. In fact, many people
thought he was the best thing that has happened in the Eastern
world. The best certainly since Alexander. After all, Pathrophis, he
made peace, which is what everyone wants most. Right?'

'But their peace, not ours!'

'Come, he sent away the Roman tax-gatherers from what had
been the provinces of Asia and put in princes of their own noble

57

houses who were likely to govern justly and wisely. Not bad for a Roman.'

'Yes, yes, he did all that. We don't know, but I suspect that the Queen advised him. Yes, you may be right to say that Marc Antony has not been hated. Naturally, not here. Perhaps in the end it was the Roman tax-gatherers and businessmen who hated him. He took their profits. But is that going to help to destroy Octavian? No.'

The two councillors walked slowly back towards the head of the causeway. Almost the whole island was built up, except for a low ridge of rocks and salty shrubs. Someone shouted from up there, and both turned. Could it be news? But no, no, it was only a sailor shouting down to his chums who were unloading barrels. Although it was sunny there was a chill wind. How would it be blowing up there in the mouth of the Gulf of Corinth or down the funnel of the Adriatic? 'If only we knew whether the Queen still intends to let the Romans break one another into little bits or whether—'

'Whether she has taken her husband's side.'

'Just that. She is with him. That proves nothing. If at a certain moment she left him, he and Octavian might destroy each other and the rule of Rome would end.'

'And it might be our turn again. Would that be better, Pathrophis, better than Antony's peace? Did we never oppress people? Be honest!'

'The Queen has said it will be different. We shall live in friendliness, trading fairly with other nations, not forcing our will on them. When she called the little one Philadelphos, did that not mean brotherhood, the thing which Alexander hoped for and prayed for?'

'Or was she thinking of Ptolemy Philadelphos two hundred years ago when Egypt was at her greatest? He was a conqueror, not a lover of brotherhood. No, Antony and Cleopatra together might make an Eastern Empire which would hold Rome off. That is why we in Alexandria must be as loyal to Antony as the Queen is.'

'If she is. Kleanthes, I hate Rome!'

'You are not the only one. But Antony has been loyal to the Queen, in spite of the advice and counsel of many of his friends. Can she be less loyal to him?'

'She is more intelligent. And a woman. If she can keep her head and leave him at the right moment—'

58

'But that might mean Octavian winning. Surely that would be the worst that could happen? Stop biting your nails, Pathrophis! You are no more anxious than the rest of us.'

Now they were joined by Caius Laronius, in command of the Legion of the Roman garrison, he too desperately anxious. When the news came, it might be a case of making a quick decision. He had been Antony's choice, but what mattered was Rome. Yet for the moment he was loyal to Antony and to Antony's wife, the Queen. They got on with him well enough.

'No news?' they asked.

'None yet, Kleanthes. You know what it's like in winter. No, Pathrophis, no letters, scarcely a rumour.' He shook his head. The latest news had been bad. It had seemed, earlier on, that Antony and Octavian were matched in power. And in what they wanted? Antony for the Republic and the Consuls, and surely that was right; Octavian for—what? Caesarism? No, no, that was finished, surely. And it was not simply his own rule in Rome; somehow he had gathered in all Italy. Or so it was said. How? Through political cunning, or, if you like, supreme diplomacy, snatching away Antony's friends and allies. Money had certainly passed, and high offices, but this was nothing new. And added to all this Octavian, in spite of his alleged honouring of all Roman tradition, including the Eternal Flame, had forced the Vestal Virgins, in whose keeping it was, to give him Antony's will. He had read it out to a shocked Senate; the will made it all too clear that Ptolemy Caesarion was genuinely the son of the great Caius Julius Caesar, in the Macedonian sense legitimate, and by that a threat to Octavian, the nephew, or rather the great-nephew. The same will also showed Antony as acknowledging as his own legal children the other children of Queen Cleopatra. To them he left kingdoms and principalities—the property of the Roman people!

Caius Laronius had heard more and for the moment discounted it, but it was there at the back of his mind. This matter of Antony's will and much else had been meat for the pamphleteers and the poets. Out they came with horror stories and naturally the most powerful punch was at the foreign woman, the witch for whom once noble but now drunken and besotted Antony had deserted and divorced the virtuous Octavia. The fouler the story, the more readily it was taken up. Women with power were bad enough, but this one was the worst yet. The respectable were duly horrified to think that Antony intended to put his Great Whore of the East over all Rome to do what she liked with them and theirs! How could one adequately grasp such utter wickedness, such treason to all decency? Rome, lift your head, you have a noble leader, crush Antony, crush the foreign she-monster! Cut him off in his seditious guilt! As for the foreigner, catch her, burn her, torture her, give her to the soldiers, destroy her and her foul offspring! Yes, Antony would have given up Roman provinces to these Egyptian brats, given up the Roman people's corn and oil and money, their rightful due! Round went the stories and all the time Octavian was pouring out more money to the legions. Men who had sworn to follow Antony had come over to him, secretly or openly, among them Quintus Dellius, eager to prove himself to his new master and full of good Antony and Cleopatra stories, ready to be circulated. Caius Laronius had loyally told Kleanthes of one attempt to bribe him away. Kleanthes had wisely given him an immediate present from the Treasury. Yet perhaps it was not necessary. The father of Caius Laronius had been loyal to Pompey; the son felt impelled to be loyal to the perhaps equally doomed Antony.

He had stopped his troops from singing the fouler of the Cleopatra songs or chalking up words which might have set the mob on them. But enough drifted through to boil up into hate. Kleanthes knew that this was part of his friend Pathrophis's special hate of the Romans. And hate turns into war.

Over the last two years war preparations had been building up: war between East and West. There were sensible men everywhere who hated the thought of another civil war; they tried to avert it, to make the protagonists see reason. Antony, after all, was no menace to Rome. Indeed, he had done well. His conquest and pacification of Armenia was no small thing. They did not believe these dirty stories. Some were shocked that a poet as reputable as Horace should have let himself become part of the propaganda machine. But there, he was after all the son of a provincial freedman, even though he had been taken up, first by Pollio, then by Maecenas. Yet all the same there is no smoke without fire. Cleopatra the Queen of Egypt might be a danger and must be eliminated. If that meant Antony as well, it was just too bad. But war must be declared on the foreign woman, and so it was, in due form and ceremony, by the Senate and people of Rome.

When winter came, Antony and the Queen were with their army

60

and fleet in the mouth of the Gulf of Corinth, or spread along the coast as far South as the tip of the Peloponnese and as far North as the gulf of Ambracia sheltered by Actium point. The corn ships from Egypt had set up huge depots. Who would be the first to start the war?

It began tentatively with attacks on communications, both sides engaging and breaking away. When a ship brought news to Alexandria, it was apt to be the story of some one small fight, a ship rammed, a company cut off, all blown out of shape. There was nothing one could hold on to, and yet they talked the shreds of information over and over, trying to get some sense out of them.

Polemo, as restless as the rest, had walked over the causeway from the city and now joined them, his old scarlet cloak wrapped well round him, against the wind. 'How are the crops?' Pathrophis asked.

'The winter wheat is well on. Gods willing, we shall get a crop.'

'And the pretty little daughter?'

'Growing up like a wheat stalk. But sometimes I wonder if I have a boy or a girl. I take her out hunting with me; she has her own bow and is a good shot already.'

'A real Macedonian young lady.' Pathrophis noticed that Polemo was trying to catch his eye. 'By the way, there is a huge shoal of fish, close in. You should look. In fact, one can see them best from the Pharos end.' They walked away slowly in that direction. In the fishermen's little houses, the women were now busy cooking; they called sharply to their children or shouted to one another, not bothering about what was going on in the great world. Neither they nor their men had ever been able to do anything about it.

After a while Pathrophis said: 'What is it, Polemo? A letter from your sister?'

'Just that,' said Polemo, 'and by a sure hand. It has come quickly by way of Corinth. She warns us that things have been going badly.'

'Most of us have been thinking that, Polemo. It is nothing new.'

'This little swine Octavian, on to whom they are heaping praise, names and titles, is determined to destroy the kingdom of Egypt and make it into a Roman province to feed his supporters and cover Rome with his wretched temples and statues. He has a personal feeling against the Queen.'

'Because of his uncle Caius Julius—and Caesarion?'

'Perhaps. More and more people believe he will succeed. Char-mian is afraid that Antony's soldiers may go over to Octavian. Money and positions are changing hands; she gives details. Men I thought were safe. It is—extremely disconcerting. She warns us that it is possible that the Romans may not be willing to destroy one another. What do you make of that, Pathrophis?'

'Does that include Antony himself?'

'She thinks not. He is too deep in. If he does not win, he loses everything.'

'He will, however, be weakened,' Pathrophis said thoughtfully. 'And then the Queen holds the balance.'

'That is one reading of it. I hope you are right, Pathrophis. I hope desperately that you are right. But Charmian is very anxious about some of those whom Antony trusted. If only he had attacked earlier...'

Pathrophis nodded. They were climbing slowly up a stepped path. A boy hunched in an old cloak was sitting on a stone playing a flute, but the notes were blown away by the wind. 'All this seems only too likely to be true. What must the Queen's position be?'

'She must support Antony. If it is true.'

'Yes, I see that. Though it will be painful for us all.'

'Charmian writes that, even in Antony's camp, the men are singing these filthy songs about the Queen.'

'Once a filthy story is set going, it will be more successful than the truth. We all know that, Polemo.'

'The Queen is angry, Charmian says, angry and hurt. But she does not let her anger go in front of Antony or the Romans. Nor does she let him see how pained she is. I suppose she feels there is no Roman whom she can trust. Not even, entirely, Antony. That is a very terrible thing to happen to her. Our Queen. I wish there were more of us with her.'

'At least she has the ships.'

'Yes, Charmian says she is often aboard. Her cabin is always kept ready on the Admiral's galley. She has become very much interested in tactics. Whatever the soldiers may do, the sailors, even the Romans, cheer her when she comes out in her pinnace.'

'She has never been afraid of the sea.'

Polemo looked back at the harbour. 'The sea has always been our friend, in Alexandria.'

'I am glad, at least, that your sister is with her. Elpis, I suppose, is at the palace?'

'Yes, in attendance on Princess Selene. We have tried to keep the bad news from the children, though of course Caesarion knows. He is not reacting very well, but I blame his tutor for that, not the man I would have chosen myself. I think too that Princess Selene has some notion of what is happening. Poor child, I pray that somehow things may go well.'

They were coming up on to the ridge of the island now and suddenly saw that there were two or three men running from the great tower of the Pharos, along the sandy strip. They seemed to be shouting but the wind carried it away. Pathrophis stopped and stiffened. 'They have seen something.'

Both of them waited, breathing short and quick. The runners were near. They began to hear the shouting. The Queen's galleys sighted, coming in before the wind. Victory over Octavian? Or defeat?

CHAPTER NINE : B.C. 26

'You understand, Aristonoë,' Hipparchia said, 'if you can get them away, all Egypt will rise.' They were back in the town house now; in the next room were two heavy chests, roped and padlocked, with all that might be needed for a stay in Rome. For the voyage, another, smaller chest. Their ship would sail as one of a convoy to Ostia, the port for Rome; it was safer, for there were still pirates, whatever was said about Roman peace and order. The weather was set fair, as far as any of the professional weather predictors would say. It was evening and the lights of Alexandria were coming out. Soon the Pharos would be lit and show far across the sea. The Romans, who stopped everything if they could, had at least not stopped that.

In spite of the padlocked chests, Aristonoë still didn't quite believe in it. She couldn't really be going. Still less could all this which her aunt and her father kept on saying, mean nothing. She looked from one to the other. Wasn't it all a story in their minds?

'I wonder if we were right to speak to her,' Polemo said to his sister; and then : 'Oh my rabbit, my poor darling rabbit, what a burden we've put on you!'

'But all she has to do is to find out if they are willing,' Hipparchia answered. 'If so, her uncle makes the contacts. The horses are waiting and the ship. She is carried off with the children, apparently unwilling. No suspicion, even if, by any dreadful chance, it all fails. She is the messenger, the angel, that is all.'

'And if they are not willing, she will forget and come back.' Is that what my father really wants? Aristonoë thought. Grown-up people were always being torn between two kinds of love and loyalty. 'But you must never say that Egypt will rise, not even whisper it!' Polemo went on anxiously.

64

'You must only say that it is a visit of respect and love, and that they will receive the same. Only that. It is possible, even, that the Romans might let her go peaceably, though we do not think so.' Hipparchia looked at her brother, who nodded. 'They are in a sense still prisoners. But if she is Cleopatra's true daughter she will understand,' she said. 'This is mostly for Selene, you know. Your father has told me what they did to Alexander. Our Alexander. The little Ptolemy is too young. But if Selene is her mother's daughter—'

'You mean,' said Polemo, looking hard at his sister, 'she will expiate our guilt. Because we failed her mother. Besides, Selene may have been changed and cowed. She may not even wish to listen. My dearest, you must not press her!'

'I know, Father, I know,' said Aristonoë. It was getting to be as much as she could take: the worry, the instructions. 'I will be very careful. You must not be anxious.'

'I shall be anxious every moment you are away, rabbit.'

'No, no! But you do truly think it could happen—all Egypt rising? Is it possible? The Romans are everywhere. They have garrisons. You know, I went with Hellanike through the great camp. It was a city, waiting to pounce. Just one trumpet blast and it would all go into action. And so many spies telling them everything!' And suddenly she thought: they may have been listening all the time. One of the servants, bribed? But not Tahatre.

'They are not everywhere,' her father said. 'They are not, for example, in the temples. You remember my friend, Knemmose?'

'The old Egyptian with the shaved head? But...'

'You would be surprised at how much he knows, rabbit. No, forget it. Forget his name, please. I will only say that the temples have corners in them which the Romans do not know.'

'I thought they had stolen everything from all the temples, carefully and thoroughly. That is what was said.'

'They did not know everything. They were not a little afraid. Other people's gods can be very alarming. Nor shall I tell you. Nor, even if they tortured me, would I have much I could tell.' She bit her lip. It was all rather horrible. War? Getting rid of the Romans? Hellanike's husband. And perhaps Hellanike.

'But there are so many who wouldn't want the Romans to go. Here in Alexandria. You've said so yourself, Father. People who are making plenty out of the occupation. People who depend on it. They wouldn't fight, even if the Queen herself came back.'

Her father said nothing for a moment, but Hipparchia looked at him. 'What the child says is true enough,' she said. 'In a big city there are always people making money out of any situation. Oh, that's understood. But it will not be in Alexandria alone. People feel it worst in the corn-growing districts.'

'Yes,' said her brother, 'that's so. You'll remember what Kleanthes told us about his own estate. Something like five times the old tax. Equally so for his neighbours. But, money apart, people don't like to be insulted.'

'Even the way they call us Egyptians. As though they meant—dirt.'

'Fair enough,' Polemo said. 'We used to feel very different, we Macedonians of Alexandria. We never really joined with the Egyptians, did we? But I don't think we feel very different now. Of course, that was partly *her* doing.'

'I'm too old to take after these gods of theirs,' said Hipparchia. 'They put me off, whether or not the temples might be centres of resistance. Yes, yes, I know! But I daresay some of the Egyptian gods are popular now. My son Kerkidas tells me so, but students are always after something new. What do you think, my dear?'

Aristonoë was uncomfortable. She knew her tutor's answer. It was all superstition. Only the great poets of the Greek golden age knew the meaning of the gods. But at the same time she was well aware that the Egyptian Mysteries were much followed. Quite lately, some of her friends had asked her to come with them. One couldn't help being aware of the special robes, the musical instruments, the repeating of names. But would this mean anything against the power of the Romans? If the authorities said no and said it firmly enough, half the worshippers would run away. And besides, some of it was—yes, downright silly. The things they seemed to believe! As if there was any answer to someone running you through with a spear. That nasty, short Roman spear. She had once seen them dealing with a crowd, herself safe at an overlooking window. The spear came out at the other side of a heaving, collapsing chest. The yell cut off. Surprise, and then dead. Either you faced it, knowing death was entirely real, or you ran away. Religion didn't help. No. 'Everyone hates the army of occupation,' she said, 'but that doesn't prove that they'd risk their lives, does it?' She looked sadly at her father and aunt. 'I know you would, both of you, I'm not questioning you, but how many others? After all, look what happened at the end. When it could have been prevented.'

'It seemed to be hopeless,' Polemo said slowly. 'Of course, when I try to remember, I see all the mistakes. Everything went wrong. Ourselves included.'

'Could it be any less hopeless now? The Romans are here, after all, and they've got most people organised, their way. Mustn't it always be easier to—to crush a rebellion, for that's what it would be, Father, than to conquer a free city? And Alexandria was a free city then.'

'Yes, in a sense we were free. But when there has been a plan and it has failed as hers did and nothing has quite taken its place, everyone loses heart and then—'

'Is that how it was?' Aristonoë said. 'It's the one thing I have never quite understood.'

'I was there at the end. I remember it very well. And naturally your Uncle Eumenes, the man he was, before—before the sky fell on him. Yes, all of us.'

CHAPTER TEN : B.C. 30

Elpis ran in and across the big cool room, her tunic caught up to her knees; she looked round quickly and banged into her mother. too upset to be even crying: 'Mother—the Princess—she says she must come—'

'You've told her she mustn't? The Queen is sleeping—at last. Speak quietly, lamb.'

'She's frightened.'

'Aren't we all!'

'Not Father?'

'Perhaps not Father. Are the others frightened?'

'Alexander is angry. He wants to fight. He wants to be with Antony.'

'Who isn't fighting. Oh my dear. We must try and stop Selene. Have you seen Caesarion?'

'He's got that silly girl with him. And Rhodon said—'

'Forget it. Oh, there's Selene!'

'I can't help her coming, I can't help it!' Elpis wriggled with fear and misery. 'Oh Mother, are we all going to die?'

'No, my sweet. Selene dear, you can't see the Queen. Not now. She is sleeping.'

The Princess who looked so like her father stood solidly, all ten years of her. 'I want to see her. I want to ask her something. Why is she sleeping now? It's no time to sleep.'

'She didn't sleep last night. Please, Princess Selene, go back. There is nothing to fear. You must look after Alexander. Don't let him be silly.'

'Charmian, he isn't silly. He can fight horrible Octavian. He knows how to throw a good spear. Charmian, so do I, we are both going to fight.'

'It wouldn't do any good, Selene.'

'I don't care. And you're lying when you say there is nothing to fear, I can see you are lying. Are you frightened, Charmian? Are you afraid to die? I'm not.'

'Nobody wants to die. We can all die if it is useful. We can choose our deaths as we choose our duties. Your duty is to live.'

Selene disregarded her and pointed to the alcove with the golden phoenix over it. 'Is Mother in there?'

'You are not to go.' She caught the girl's wrist and Iras came over to help her.

Selene struggled quietly. 'I am the Princess! It is wicked to hold me, Charmian! I must see her, she has got to tell me—nobody says anything true! Oh let go, let go or I'll scream!'

'Please,' said Charmian, 'don't do that, whatever you do. Selene, she feels so tired. She must get rested before she can plan. Try to understand. Is there anything I can tell you?'

Selene suddenly caught hold of her. Yes, thought Charmian, and it is true, underneath she is frightened; as frightened as I am. When the house begins to fall. Now she had the two little girls, Selene and her own Elpis, who was still so young, too young for what was going to happen, only a little older than the Princess. Above their heads she looked at Iras, who said, 'Tell her. She ought to know.'

'Come over to the balcony,' said Charmian. 'Then we can talk and she won't hear us even in her dreams. The Queen loves you so much, Selene; she wanted everything to be beautiful and good for you—and your children after you.'

'And Alexander?'

'Yes, both of you. And Philo. She wanted her children to rule over a golden age when there would be enough for everyone. No wars. No famines. A kind of light over us all.'

'Like that King she told us about—Akhnaton. Long ago. But the Romans stopped it all. So if we want it we've got to kill them.'

They were together now on the balcony looking out over the sea, which moved gently as it always did. The beautiful sea which swallowed ships and sailors and was blue afterwards. Charmian went on: 'You see, Selene, your mother is a great queen, the greatest there has ever been. She could have been like the great Alexander and conquered the world, but not by war. By trade and friendship, by treaties, by justice everywhere. By using riches to buy allies. But the Romans will not have any rule in the world except their own.' Selene nodded, listening. 'Your mother planned for the two halves of the evil Roman world to destroy each other. They had almost done that in their civil wars and again after Julius Caesar was killed. But then his nephew Octavian got power in Rome.'

'And our father in the East.'

'Most of the power was at the Roman end because the legions came from there and the soldiers wanted land in Italy. Your father's side was weak. So your mother thought that if she took his side it would balance out.'

'Besides,' said Iras, 'he seemed to want the same things as she did. The Golden Age, the rule of love. She showed him that and he followed.'

'But Octavian wouldn't have it,' Charmian said. 'Perhaps he was jealous of Antony.' Should she go on? Yes. 'At first, perhaps the Queen thought that this would mean the two Roman armies destroying each other and the end of the Empire. But that would have meant Antony. That would have meant destroying your father, too.'

Selene was very quiet now, listening.

'He had been loyal to her when the other Romans and his Roman wife tried to drag him away,' Iras said. 'Yes, he could have saved himself then by betraying her.'

'But he didn't!' Selene said.

'No. So she could do no less. Being a great queen. Antony's soldiers would not fight at Actium. So he came away with her and the few who were loyal. She meant to rebuild her navy and fight again. But he— Selene, surely you have seen how your father has been like someone without hope? In an evil dream?'

Selene looked away and kicked at the bronze rail of the balcony. Her fists clenched and unclenched. Iras said: 'That was why there were all these parties, all this music and feasting. To wake him out of despair. To put hope and strength into him again. It seemed the only way, though some people thought it wrong. But it did little. And too late.'

'Not too late!' Selene cried and looked round as if she were going to run suddenly for her mother. But the two women were ready to stop her once again.

Charmian said: 'Too late for what was needed. Too late for us.

But not—not, we hope . . .' she choked and couldn't go on.

'Not too late for you,' Iras said, 'Princess.' For a moment Cleopatra Selene stood proudly and her mother's two ladies bent their heads a little in front of her so that they seemed no longer tall and grown-up and to be obeyed. And Elpis knelt clinging to her hand. Then there was a knock on the outer door and the sound of a spear grounding. Charmian ran across, not as lightly as she would have done fifteen years before, but well enough. She half opened one leaf of the bronze door and beckoned her husband in. He was wearing the full armour of the Queen's guard; the crest of his helmet towered and his breastplate shone but his face had grim lines. Only his eyes were still very blue.

He said, 'You must wake her. Now. Pathrophis is coming and some of the Egyptian leaders. She must give them the word.'

'You mean,' said Charmian, and flushed as though she had been kissed, 'to fight?'

'Nothing wrong with the Egyptians as soldiers,' said Eumenes. 'We've known that since Raphia. But they have always risen against us before. Never for us. This could be the right thing at last after all the nonsense and waiting for Antony.'

'You think,' said his wife, 'there's a chance?'

'Wake her!'

'And Antony?'

'They are not rising for *him*.'

'I see. Wait.' She went across to the alcove, Iras with her, and looped the curtains back and then touched her mistress on the humped shoulder. The Queen was breathing heavily and unevenly. She jerked away from the hand and then turned slowly, blinking open heavy eyelids. 'There is something happening,' Charmian said. 'My darling must wake and hear.'

Cleopatra looked at the water clock on the low table. 'They are eight miles nearer. I could hear their boots. Marching at us across Syria. Marching.' And then, 'Who is it? What is going on?'

Iras had brought steaming water and fine towels. As she wiped the crumby sleep off her face the Queen saw Eumenes, who knelt on one knee with a clash of metal and his sword drawn in salute. 'The Egyptian leaders are coming,' he said.

'I thought they would,' she answered half to herself. 'Yes, I thought they would. Very well, I will see them.'

71

Eumenes saluted and strode out. She smiled a little once more at Iras. 'The crown,' she said.

They dressed her quickly and skilfully. The gold net over her hair almost restored it to what it had been, but there was not time for much on the face. She put on her rings, as always the engraved amethyst with the figure of divine intoxication, that joy or knowledge which is so deep that those who have it do not need to weigh and consider but can come at once to the right conclusion. Blue wings were folded at her breast. A guardian serpent wreathed up her arm. As they clasped the last necklace and arranged the folds of her dress round the foot of her chair, they began to hear steps and then again the knock.

Pathrophis came straight to the point: 'Egypt has decided, Ma'am. We will rise for you. We think we can defend the line of the Nile. It has saved Egypt before. This is not certain, but we have said to ourselves after consideration that it is worth trying.'

'At least we can die for you, Isis,' said another man. He did not look at all like one devoted to a goddess. Suddenly she recognised him, though it was some years since they had met. He was a lawyer and had been defending the rights of a small town to withhold its taxes on the grounds that the government official concerned had appropriated half of what had been paid. She had hanged the official but made the town pay up. He had said very calmly and courageously that it was an unjust decision. She had told him to wait and see. The next year she had reduced their valuation.

She said, 'It is useless to die. Give me some figures.'

They all spoke; some were soldiers, others were officials, priests, town workers, even a couple of peasants. They came from Upper Egypt as well as Lower. There were Macedonians as well, mostly the older ones, Polemo among them. He glanced once at his sister but she did not notice. The Queen snapped her fingers for her tablets, wrote and rubbed out and wrote again. She saw the two girls on the balcony and gestured them to come in. Selene came and stood beside her, strong, solid, very troubled. Elpis behind her. There was more talk. Then the Queen stood up. She said, 'There is no possibility of your holding back Octavian's legions. None. The line of the Nile is useless because he can bring in legions from both sides. Cyrene has gone over to him. They would catch us in the back. If we try to fight he will only destroy Egypt. He can bring up the rest of the legions from all over the Roman world slowly and crush us without losing a man himself. Remember, the only Romans here who will fight are Antony's own bodyguards. Perhaps a few hundred others who used to follow him. If this had been possible I would have gone and led you myself. But I will not lead you into destruction. I love Egypt. I have made Egypt what it is now. I will not kill my child.'

Several of them spoke, arguing and entreating. She answered. But a few of them, Pathrophis among them, knew already that she was right. Octavian had all the legions. Almost all Antony's commanders had gone over to him. Apart from that, the old enemy Herod of Judaea would be delighted to act the jackal and pick up whatever pieces Octavian left. How little she wanted to say all this, how much she would have liked to let them convince her! But it must not be allowed to happen. 'Go in peace, my children,' she said at last, and hearing her own voice, knew she could not have taken much more.

'May Ra strengthen you, our Lady and Daughter,' one of the priests said, making a sign to which she responded, bowing her head a little, knowing that now she would need all the strength she could get from any source.

Pathrophis left last. 'If the Queen sees any way out let her call us,' he said. 'And we will be there.'

'I know,' she answered. 'I trust Egypt. But that will not be the way. I shall do the best I can for you all. But also I must bargain now for her and the others.' She put her hand lightly on to Selene's arm. 'You will remember, Pathrophis, I was always a good trader! Perhaps I can still manage. But I am back to the beginning and dealing not with dear old Caius Julius who thought I was a kitten, but with Octavian who knows I am a tiger and must be eliminated. If it comes to that I believe I can take it.'

'No!' said Pathrophis. But she smiled and shook her head and gestured him out.

When he left she turned towards Selene, who said, 'Mother, what do you mean?'

'I mean to try and save you, perhaps even to get you small kingdoms. If Octavian is wise. Caesarion will go to Meroë and then on. He knows what I want him to do. At least, I hope so.'

'But you, *you*, Mother?'

'It is very tempting to die in battle. Your father will think the

73

same. But if we do that they will revenge themselves on you and your brothers.'

'But, Mother, what will happen? Mother, you aren't going to die—or are you?'

'Perhaps it isn't very important, my sweet,' said Cleopatra and kissed her. 'Now go. I must tell Antony what I have decided.' Her voice dropped; now she was talking to herself. 'I hope he will not wish I had accepted their offer. I hope he will agree to bargain. Oh, my poor Antony. If only he hadn't loved me so much. I could have saved myself. And perhaps Egypt. Poor dear honest Antony. We must stand by one another now.'

PART TWO

Rome

THE NEW PEOPLE IN PART II

Romans in Rome

Pollio (Caius Asinius Pollio)
Antistia, his wife, sister to Antisteus Labeo
Horace (Quintus Horatius Flaccus)
Maecenas
Terentia, his wife, sister to Varro Murena
Propertius
Octavian Caesar Augustus, *dux et princeps*
Julia, his daughter
Octavia, his sister, widow of Marc Antony
Marcellus, her son, by her first husband, Caius Claudius
    Marcellus
Marcella, her daughter
The two Antonias, her daughters by Marc Antony
Agrippa
and others

Greeks in Rome

Madame
Lalage, a lute girl
Butas, secretary to Pollio
and others

Alexandrians in Rome

Callimedon

From Numidia in North Africa

Prince Juba

CHAPTER ELEVEN : B.C. 26

'Who do you say it is?' said Pollio. He did not at all want to be interrupted. He had come to a crucial part of his history. This mattered: to get it weighed up. To show what the Republic was, what it became and why. The latter part would be difficult. Perhaps he would never manage to write it—can one ever write without passion about events in which one took part oneself: history which one hoped to make? One's own misjudgments and mistakes. Maybe. Maybe not. He would see. But he had a decade to cover before he had to face this problem and he was beginning to wonder how much longer he had to write it. His doctor, as was to be expected, said there was nothing wrong which a course of cold baths and diet would not cure, but did he know? The doctor was a Greek of course: clever little devil, but too apt to say what he thought people wanted to hear. A Roman doesn't need that. A Roman can take it. And now he was being interrupted again! His wife knew better than to come in, but Butas always thought he had the right if it was someone important or someone he thought was important.

'It's a poet!' said Butas, leaning irritatingly over the table.

'Which poet—Gallus? I thought he'd found a new girl-friend and one wouldn't see him for a bit!' He chuckled to himself but he would have quite liked to see Gallus.

'No, sir. It's Horace.'

'The devil it is. Butas, don't touch my papers! What does he want?'

'He seemed upset like.'

'Always wants to be looked after if he is upset. Doesn't care if he upsets other people.'

'Said he was never going near Maecenas again.'

'A likely story! Well, I suppose I must see him. All right, Butas, show him in. Not a word to the ladies, by the way.' His sister-in-law was visiting; she was one of Rome's worst gossips and that was saying plenty. His own Antistia was not nearly as bad; she had gossiped once about one of her brother's legal cases. It had not seemed important to Pollio, but Antisteus Labeo, who was after all a great lawyer, was furious and told his sister exactly what he thought of her. It had quelled her entirely. In fact she did nothing but snivel for weeks, poor dear Antistia, an excellent wife and mother.

Butas showed in a rather dishevelled young man—no, not young any more, hair well back from the temples, wouldn't make much of a soldier today, Philippi and the lost shield a long way back.

'My dear Horace,' said Pollio. 'to what do I owe this pleasure—this unexpected pleasure?'

'You know!' the poet said, taking him by both hands and putting a kiss squarely on each cheek. 'I'm sure you know. I have been meaning to come, wanting to come, all these months, but it was too difficult, Maecenas expecting me every morning, watching me as if—as if I'd been his pet actor! And speaking to me—well, one has one's dignity. And I had to get away to write, well, I did at least have the run of the villa and a country life suits me, yes, perfectly! But I thought so often of the old days with you!' Horace looked at him with those big eyes and Pollio, who had not appreciated the embrace, now smiled just a little. 'He insisted that I write—well, the official line all the time—but a poet must be free, mustn't he?'

'Not too free, I think,' said Pollio; 'unless he doesn't mind seeing his poems burned.'

'I have always been for law and order and the Republic,' said Horace. 'I know what Augustus has meant to us all—peace, security, faith. But sometimes one wants to write from a different angle.'

'I am sure Maecenas understands that.'

'Not as well as you used to! And he has these dreadful favourites putting on airs. The things they said! And he encourages them. Laughs. One falls over them at the villa. Bought slaves!'

Pollio did not remind Horace of his own father, who after all had been an industrious and intelligent man who had bought his freedom with his own earnings and had sent his son to the best

78

schools. Besides, he was entirely in agreement about these little sweeties of Maecenas. 'So what were you thinking?' he asked.

'I was thinking that it was to you that I dedicated one of the best of my odes. My own favourite,' he said.

'Ah,' said Pollio, 'your friend Virgil also dedicated a poem to me. Perhaps he has forgotten. Those were the days before Maecenas and Agrippa were so well thought of by the great Augustus. But you poets live too high up for a small prose writer like myself.'

Horace sat down uninvited by the table. 'We admire you so much, Pollio. You are all the things which we aren't. You are as hard as a spear point. You won't have anything to do with uplift and all that: making things sound better than they are. Yes, I agree we let ourselves become entangled with it, but it's a temptation. No, not just money, though I like money as well as the next. Or rather I like what money buys: the wine and the girls and the singing, the fine clean linen and the elegant silver. But I could do without it. You don't believe me, Pollio.'

'No,' said Pollio, removing a book roll which Horace had hold of and was tapping against the table. 'I'm afraid I don't.'

'It's true all the same. Half true. What I couldn't do without is the sense that there is someone looking after us, working without respite, always there, sacrificing himself—'

'The Divine Nursemaid.' Pollio clapped his hands. 'Butas, some wine! And a little simple country cheese for the poet.'

'Pollio, I wish you wouldn't! This is real. The Princeps taking it all on himself, ill as he is, our father and leader, the just magistrate, the bringer of peace and hope! I see him bigger than life, Pollio, after all our troubles and struggles. You can laugh at me if you like, but as I see it he is my inspiration. Augustus is my muse.'

'Bad teeth and all. No Horace, I'm not laughing at you. But it's not the way it looks to me. And too many people are inspired. All these memoirs one has to go through, all seeing things one way. This Quintus Dellius, for instance; he was Antony's right-hand man. Did a lot of useful things for him before he deserted, not that I blame him. For instance it was he who persuaded Cleopatra of Egypt to visit Antony at Tarsus. You wouldn't think so from his book.'

'When people see the error of their ways—'

'When they see they've backed the wrong horse, Horace. Suppose Antony had won the Battle of Actium?'

'Impossible!'

'It wasn't much of a battle. Antony's men wouldn't fight. When she saw that, Cleopatra called off her galleys.'

'A piece of oriental treachery!'

'I wonder. I wonder. What I am saying is that Actium wasn't much of a battle. In fact it's mostly an invention, a piece of literature to buttress up the story of the Princeps. Indeed there are moments when I wonder whether all acceptable history is not a poetic invention. There is also history of the kind I hope my own is, which simply intends to present the plain facts. But it is not acceptable in the same way. Not to ordinary people. It is not part of a religion. What you and Virgil, and for that matter Livy, though I find him tedious, are making is a religion around the idea of this new foundation of Rome. Admit it!'

'You would not have me remain outside the events of my time?'

'It doesn't matter in the least what I think, anyhow. Take some wine, Horace.'

'And you?'

'No. My stomach is troubling me.'

'It's a pleasure to be drinking your wine again.'

'If you say my wine is as good as Maecenas's wine I can only call you a plain liar, my dear Horace. And I don't like to call you a plain liar. I call you an adorned and delightful liar. That's different. And I am quite sure you don't really want to change patrons. Maecenas, as you know, is one of the three most powerful people in the world. I am nothing. And the Divine Augustus would not like to think you had made an exchange. It would look too like criticism.'

'It might make the Princeps appreciate how Maecenas is treating us!'

'You are an innocent, my dear Horace. People at the top don't think this way. No, no, leave me Gallus, who is not much of a poet, but I like the odd bits of ivy he twines his lute with. By the way this Quintus Dellius is supposed to be in Rome. There is one point of fact I should like to see him about. Would you drop a word in his ear?'

'Of course! If there is any way in which I can serve you, tell me. Just tell me. Let me stay by your side, my most esteemed Pollio!'

'I have told you: no. But I am glad to have seen you again. I shall always welcome you as a friend, but not as a patron. You can pass on anything I said.'

'Surely you don't think that of me!'

'It might make a good story. And none of it will surprise them. They know what I think about *auctoritas* and all that. By the way, do you see Varro Murena?'

'No. Why?'

'Nothing, probably. He is, I think, a brother to your liege lady Terentia.'

'Yes indeed. And Terentia has always behaved most properly towards me whatever that husband of hers does.'

'You really dislike Maecenas at the moment, don't you? Never mind, my dear Horace, one day you will look back and say to yourself that a man who can write as well as you do can afford to overlook a few minor insults.'

CHAPTER TWELVE

Leaving Pollio's house the poet was undecided where to go: not surely back to Maecenas! No, he was upset, he needed company. Where was that place Propertius had spoken of? He hadn't paid any attention at the time, feeling it was probably another of Propertius's Alexandrian finds, girls reading poetry and all that instead of being—just girls. But it might be quite the thing in his present mood. In the street he hesitated. It was hot and there was a strong smell of donkeys. Overhead the strip of sky between the houses was too like a lid. Sensible people were taking an afternoon nap to get ready for the bath and the evening meal, though no doubt Pollio was back at work. Would the girls be ready to receive, he wondered. It was not as if it were a brothel. No, no, they set out to be like the Athenian *hetairae*, delightful companions for intelligent men. Of course such companionship might ripen, or so Propertius hinted, but this was not taken for granted. There were even virgins among them, at any rate in the technical sense.

Yes, he had the necessary. Maecenas was lavish in certain ways, at least. Where was the place now? He looked up and down the street. From the outside Pollio's house was uninviting: bars, a heavy door with metal studs on it. Would there ever be a time when people could feel safe in their town houses? Yes, perhaps. But the mob, the uneducated, was becoming no kinder, no more intelligent. Could the Princeps, even, reach down to that level and civilise it? Doubtful, doubtful. The rest of the street was mostly tenement houses, often quite pleasant inside where the main rooms faced over a garden court, perhaps with a little fountain. But the outsides again were uninviting. Rude boys had scrawled in chalk on the dirty plaster. A few street sellers dozed with their backs against the shadowed walls, their arms slackly guarding their baskets of unpleasing wares. At the corner there was a little shop which sold trinkets. He stopped and bought a small bracelet in good taste, silver gilt. Slipping on a bracelet might lead to—well, better things. A few roses? No, roses were really too cheap just now.

Propertius had given him reasonably accurate directions. The house was in quite a pleasant suburb with a high wall round the garden. The slaves who opened the door looked particularly tough, and one held back a large and unpleasant mastiff. There was the usual awkward wait and conversation; however, when he let it become apparent who he was, there was an immediate and welcome change. Yes, indeed, they had hoped so much that he would visit them. And how was his friend Propertius? He had written the *sweetest* thing—but of course Horace was far above that! But naturally he had his fans here. I must introduce you. I have one magnificent reciter; you shall hear her. I believe you will think she was your muse!

'Propertius spoke of a charming young Alexandrian—Elpis, I think.'

'Ah yes, a girl of good family. A sad story. And yet in a way a fortunate one. Let me have the pleasure of effecting the introduction. You will find an admirer there, too. Yes, a very well-read girl, a little moody sometimes, but there, I am sure you will have the cure for that.'

A couple of hours later the poet left, feeling vastly refreshed and superior to Maecenas or any other patron he might have. No, nothing indecorous had occurred; it was a true meeting of minds, or rather of spirits. The romantic Alexandrian touch, genuine as a ripe fig plucked sun-warm from the tree. One sensed the slight accent in her Latin but her Greek was flawless and grave and she had this marvellous sense of poetry. He had read her something of his own, half finished and jammed painfully on its way to birth. She had repeated one or two lines after him and now— yes, now, the rest of the poem was coming, the stresses were beginning to go into place. And was he perhaps allowing a faintly Alexandrian conceit? He who prided himself on being a Latin! Well, a small phrase for his new muse.

He had not even considered giving her the bracelet; it was too trivial. Perhaps one day he would give it to her maid. One day ... for her the gift must be something unique: either valueless, a single forest lily with the dew still sparkling on the leaves: or so valuable that she might gasp and change colour. What a find, oh, what a find! Doubtless Propertius had mentioned her first but he was too coarse-natured for Elpis. Utterly enchanting Elpis.

'Didn't he give you anything, dear?' said Madame, paddling through with her hair over one eye.

'No. He's a great poet, after all. It is a privilege for us to have a visit from him. And really a great delight to me. He should have paid you something.'

'Oh, he did, he did. He even tipped the gate slave! He'd have given a bone to the dog if he'd had one by him!'

'Then that is settled. What he had from me was not for sale.'

'Ah, Elpis, that's tone! Real tone. To think when you first came here—when that Octavia wouldn't have you—'

'Don't. I'm not hating Octavia: never. It wasn't cruelty. I won't have anyone thinking that of her. It was only lack of imagination.'

'It's the same thing, love.'

'No, no, it was only that she didn't want Selene to be reminded of who she was. Poor darling, she was to be just another child in that household. It couldn't happen with me there. No, no, I don't blame Octavia, she being what she is and her brother's sister.'

'Well, love, you go on enjoying yourself with your poet! That other one gets fresh, doesn't he?'

Elpis smoothed her hair casually with one hand, taking a glance in the mirror. 'Oh, a little slap and he's as gentle as a lamb. Propertius fancies himself of course—all those Cynthia poems! Not that he doesn't read them well. But I sometimes wonder if it was a genuine love affair. He wrote a stupid poem about Actium.'

'I expect they asked him to write it, love. Battles aren't really his line, are they?'

'No. He keeps saying everything can be settled by love. Which is plain nonsense of course, but nice in a way. I wonder all the same what did happen at Actium.'

'They say it was a famous victory.'

'I remember when the news came. It was a terrible blow. It was as though a great dark cloud had come over Alexandria. But it didn't sound like a big battle. It was so much worse afterwards—when my poor father was wounded—'

'And your poor mother—'

'Yes, yes. More than four years ago. I wonder if Horace has

written about it too. I suppose they have to. Horace, yes, he's different. Still, he came at an awkward time, as you know. I was just going to have my afternoon rest. I think I'll have it now. And perhaps a bath.'

'You do just that. I'll send you up one of the lute girls. You'd like Lalage, wouldn't you. And a nice bunch of grapes.'

She felt so proud of Elpis, all that tone! She was glad she hadn't even so much as suggested to Elpis to do—well, anything she didn't fancy. Poor little Elpis, lost and crying. Just a kid. Whatever she said now it had been downright cruel of Octavia.

Elpis lay in her bath, just warm enough to be cooler than the air, and thought about her poets and contemplated her own body and legs, pale under the water, very desirable. Her long hair darkening as it wetted still gleamed like a gold brown seaweed as it clung and swung. She had gone further with young Propertius than Madame quite knew and better if she didn't. There had been a moment when they both felt bursting with it. She stroked a hand over her own belly, admiringly, and lower. His hand— Well, as she said, Horace would be different. But how, she wondered, did all this mix with the notion of a noble antique Rome reborn, where all women were chaste and none of the men went in for disruptive politics? Had it ever been true? Well, it didn't include herself: foreigner, Egyptian snake. Oh, she knew what was said. So who hates who? And what for?

She dried slowly with an occasional yawn, having a joke or two with Lalage, no beauty but a sweet girl and loyal.

'You'll be receiving this evening, love?' Lalage asked.

'Yes, if it's anyone worth seeing,' she said. 'Not a new rich senator!'

'Not old Paws-Off!' said Lalage, helping with the big hair towel.

'You know what he wanted last time?' said Elpis, her lip twisting up, and whispered.

'No!' said Lalage, a little shocked. 'From you!'

'But he did. Because I am Alexandrian,' he said, 'and all Alexandrians know how. He had the impudence to mention Corinna. No, I'm not seeing him again. However much he chooses to give anyone. Just spread my hair in the sun will you, Lalage? And give me the neck pillow. I'll just shut my eyes for a few minutes.'

Out of a half sleep Elpis heard Lalage not any more tinkling softly on the repetitive lute, but speaking in a rather scared, defensive voice. A man's voice answering. Who? Not Propertius, not Horace. It was difficult to wake up, she had an idea that she was somewhere else, someone else, no, herself but—with an effort she opened her eyes, travelling up from a man's feet, knees, cloak and, unbelieving, to his face. 'It can't be ...' she said, and then softly, 'Father.'

He didn't answer at once. He was looking round. Well, one thing to the good, she was wearing a wrap. As often as not she had her afternoon nap without and that would have made things difficult. She got to her feet quickly, pulling the wrap tight round her; it was an island silk, thickish, a pleasant honey colour. Now they were almost on a level. Her eyes dropped to the wounded hand, two fingers off and the others curled up and a bad colour. 'How did you find me?' she asked.

'My host told me. Apparently—he knew.'

Still her father was looking round. His voice was cold; nothing was being allowed to happen. No affection. Menander in the *Comedies* did it better!—the stock scene, father finds daughter sold as slave or what not. He'd better get that out of his head.

'I hope you realise, Father—' and then, to get rid of her—'Lalage, bring some wine and fruit—this bunch is half eaten!—Father, I hope you understand that I am a hostess. Not—not anything unbecoming.'

'A hostess—to Romans,' he said.

'Come, Father, this is Rome. You let me come. Indeed you sent me. Sit down, Father.' She took his hand, the unhurt one, and sat him on one of the light chairs.

'You came as lady-in-waiting to Princess Selene,' he said.

'Yes. But she was a prisoner. And—I was not wanted. Leave it at that.' He looked at her long and hard. When she had seen him last he had been in a fever and barely spoken. Everything had been in ruins. She had managed to rebuild her life. Had he? 'You are alone, Father?' she said.

'No, I have Aristonoë. Your cousin, Polemo's daughter, almost your age. I did not bring her—here.'

'Come, Father, this isn't a brothel.' Lalage was bringing wine, Madame of course the fruit. So long as the old girl said nothing—well, stupid.

'What is it, then?'

'A place of intelligent relaxation. Thank you, Lalage. Yes, we have everything we want.' She frowned quickly at Madame, who got the message and retired.

'You had better come back with me.'

She said nothing for a minute. This strange man. Her father. Yes. But— 'You are here with some purpose, Father?'

'We shall speak about that. Do you see the Princess?'

'Poor little Selene. Hardly ever.' In fact, never, she thought. But could not say so to her father. Not yet. 'She is part of Octavia's household,' she went on, 'and—somewhat guarded. You must understand that. With whom are you staying?'

'The merchant Callimedon, in the Alexandrian quarter. Are you coming—my daughter?'

'Not immediately, Father. I shall see. I would like to meet my cousin.' He sat there not moving. It was not exactly cheerful. She must find out later from Madame what he had said when he came in. So long as the old dear had been tactful. Which she usually was. Would any of the poets be coming this evening? 'Now, Father, give me a kiss and go back and think about it. Tomorrow is another day.'

CHAPTER THIRTEEN

'So we meet again, Horace,' said Pollio. He had been quite prepared for Horace to have had a grand reconciliation with Maecenas and in consequence to cut him. He could have done it so easily if he'd wanted to, without seeming to give offence, in the crowd. The Forum as usual was packed and there was a smell of people almost like a slave market, except that now and then there was a whiff of something extremely expensive. Why did one come? Well, it was the centre of things. As Athens had been once. But—of course—differently.

Horace began to ease him gently into a corner out of the sun. It was close to a fashionable jeweller's; one could amuse oneself endlessly watching slim, well-cared-for ankles and toes feeling their way down from smart litters. A dislodged drapery might even provoke a better view. If one preferred to watch young men there was also a barber's and a constant coming and going of smart clients. Waves were definitely in and beards completely out; in fact they might be thought a mark of wrongly directed thinking. But what agonies of depilation! What gingerly patting of newly smooth cheeks! Or if one looked in the other direction there were the lawyers and their clients. There were the country cousins and there were the Roman politicians, the live ones; most of the statues were to dead ones, though a few were still among the successful living. Yes, yes, there was *Dux et Princeps* large as life and gilt. And made to look grave and noble and all that, with a good head of hair. Now Horace was talking away and very nicely too. 'My dear Pollio,' he said, 'let us always meet! Yes, Maecenas has behaved suitably. And that verse I was stuck with, yes, it came away nicely in the end.'

'Is this possibly the main difference between prose and poetry?

That one can always go on with a prose piece. It merely means forcing oneself to do it, hammering. But verses cannot be hammered. What do you say, Horace?'

'Some poets hammer.'

'I'm afraid my dear Gallus does sometimes. Virgil now, occasionally when he wants to get on with the story? Or do the noble hexameters always flow?'

But Horace was trying to see over the heads of the crowd. He was suddenly excited and so from the change of noise were other people. 'Look!' he said. 'There he is!'

'Ah, *auctoritas* in person. Doing us citizens the honour of a face-to-face encounter. No, Horace, it's no use hissing and hushing. If I speak seditiously I am less likely to act seditiously. You agree?'

But the poet was upset. 'Pollio,' he said, 'you don't mean it. This is just a hangover from the days of—'

'The proscriptions,' said Pollio into the other's face.

'Forget, forget! It was something that had to happen before we could get peace. It was the very end of the civil wars. Surely, surely, my dear friend, my first encourager, what we have all longed for was peace! Now Rome can be herself again, the centre of the world to whom all the nations come in worship, the example of conquest with mercy!'

'Yes, yes, almost an ode already. I'm not sure the Spaniards would agree with you. The conquest there has been—somewhat lacking in mercy. Wouldn't you say after consideration?'

'But they're impossible people! Such arrogance. Such inability to appreciate where their true interest lies.'

'Yes. Sad for them, isn't it? One wonders what their version of recent history would be.'

'Well, one can always say that about any history. But surely one must be on the side of the future.'

'Meaning the winning side?'

'Not always the side that seems to be winning.'

'As Antony seemed to be at one time when after all he was almost Emperor of the East. Ah, well, one could always make up hopeful stories about the future.' Pollio glanced at Horace and then looked away at the group which surrounded the Princeps. Among the elderly and tough-looking and balding, of whom one was Agrippa, there was one young slenderer figure, his hair certainly with a

89

natural wave. 'Marcellus is a pleasing young man. You know him well, Horace?'

'A little, a little,' said Horace modestly, pleased to be asked. 'A very gentle person and intelligent. One hopes that Julia will make him happy.'

'Augustus was wise to choose him as a successor. He was a nephew himself and perhaps it runs in the family. By the way, Horace, what made you look uncomfortable when I mentioned Antony just now? Yes, you did! That's all past anyway. Or isn't it? Of course there's Octavia, but she was always more her brother's sister than his wife. It must have been a relief to her in a way to be his widow. Easier. You're not in love with Octavia, Horace?'

'Certainly not!' Horace was shocked. 'Nor with either of the Antonias. You are imagining things, Pollio.'

'I don't imagine easily. But I have eyes.'

'Well, then, I have been through a curious experience which gave me a slightly new impression of Antony. There is a girl—'

'Not at least an uncommon experience for Quintus Horatius Flaccus?'

'I thought—well, she is a charming young Alexandrian, well read, nice voice, nice manners. I realised she had been well brought up. It was only recently she told me the rest.'

'She knew Antony?'

'Had seen him often. Actually she is the daughter of Charmian, one of Queen Cleopatra's ladies-in-waiting. You will remember, Pollio, that Augustus put up statues of the two who died with their mistress in front of the tomb.'

'Yes, he had the decency to bury Antony and his Queen together. It is certainly not every queen whose ladies decide to die with her. Had the girl seen the statues?'

'No, she left Alexandria with the Queen's children, the three by Antony. She was lady-in-waiting to the little Princess. But it seems that Octavia refused to have her in the house. I find that a little hateful.'

'Yes, our celebrated mercy barely extended to Egypt. People were very frightened of Queen Cleopatra. So frightened that they even accused her of cowardice at Actium.'

'That at least I never did! You remember my ode, Pollio? You do. Good! It has been so queer listening to my Elpis speaking about the Queen. As if she were a god.'

'You could have contradicted her like a true Roman, Horace. We have our own divine leader after all. And it is well known that too many gods spoil the pudding.'

'But I love her.'

'You shouldn't say that, Horace. It's most rash. What does she want out of you?'

'She wants—well, it's a strange story, but her father has come to Rome. He was apparently captain of the Queen's guard. He wants to see the little Princess. I could arrange to take him to the house.'

'Would that be wise?'

'Probably not.'

'Would she be sufficiently grateful?'

'I'm afraid she would take it as a matter of course. She simply asked me.'

'And you simply said yes. I see!'

'If you had heard all she told me ... and *how* she told me— Pollio, I must go!'

'Be careful then, a little careful. One may take risks for a principle, but hardly for a girl.'

'This one is different, Pollio!'

Horace went rushing off, every inch a poet. And how often had that particular remark been made! I suppose, thought Pollio, that he wanted to tell someone; but if so, why me? I don't like being told, he thought, and his mind went back to Varro Murena who had come to see him the day before. Naturally it was the moment when he was trying to keep his mind firmly on a difficult historical point. But Murena had talked and talked, couldn't stop apparently. Pollio had got the smell of conspiracy. He had warned Murena that the powers at the top would stop at nothing. It was no use his relying on being the brother-in-law of Maecenas. A mere brother-in-law was expendable. Nor could they count on Augustus being a sick man; he had never been strong but he had this immense will-power which pulled him through. He might live another twenty years. No, they had better give it up. Whatever it was. But would they? No more than Horace would give up his new girl.

CHAPTER FOURTEEN

'I have found it,' Tahatre cried, 'my mistress, I have found it! If you will come with me you will see. You yourself. Just as you saw the new star when we were standing together that night on the front part of the ship.'

'You think,' Aristonoë said nervously, 'that it wouldn't matter —that I'm a Macedonian?'

'*She* was a Macedonian,' Tahatre said, 'and you begin to speak the old tongue so well, so well. You will be safe. But you must not, I think, tell your uncle.'

'It's not as if he told me everything. He's not like my father,' said Aristonoë, and twisted uncertainly at her necklace. They were sitting as always in the back room of the Alexandrian merchant's house where they were lodging. There was a small window to the street on one side, to the courtyard on the other. The house was in fact the bottom floor of a big tenement building; this meant that they had water laid on, whereas the upper flats had to carry all theirs up. You could also walk directly into the courtyard at the back where there were one or two trees and bushes and a few tubs of kitchen herbs and flowers. The bottom-floor people rather looked down on the others, though Aristonoë tried to make friends and sometimes played with the children. The two ends of the house were solid locked storerooms with separate entrances on to the street. Callimedon was proud of his apartment in which the two best rooms had a couple of marble pillars each and nice inlaid floors. There were a good many Alexandrians in this part of Rome. They had their own public buildings where they met one another and discussed their own affairs, trading regulations, marine insurance and who should be placated this time and at what expense.

But apart from the baths, Aristonoë hardly saw anyone. It was so unlike Alexandria! Nothing happened except uninteresting meals. Eumenes went out from time to time. He seemed to be trying to find some way of getting to see the Queen's children, but nothing had come of it yet. How Aristonoë longed either to go back to Alexandria or into some kind of action! A little danger would not come amiss. Boredom did.

'Our master Polemo would not have left my mistress like this, saying nothing, with great Rome all round. But now after supper we shall go. Make your excuses, my mistress, and leave early to bed. I will be there.'

'Very well,' said Aristonoë. 'I'll come. It might—it might lead somewhere.'

'It will do that indeed,' Tahatre said.

Heavily veiled they slipped out of the side door. Clearly the slave was not aware that one of these figures was the visiting lady. Tahatre began to hurry along the narrow streets. A woman did better to hurry than to loiter in Rome. Then at a corner they saw lights ahead, moving. 'It is them!' Tahatre said. 'Now—we will join them. Do not be afraid at all, my mistress. I know the words.' In a little they caught up with an irregular procession, mostly women, with an occasional torch-bearer. The light of the torches showed little except bare plaster of house walls or now and then a shuttered, light-chinked window, past which the smoke drifted up. Tahatre said something to the woman next to her and was answered. They were speaking in Egyptian; Aristonoë got the hang of it. Tahatre was saying they were newcomers but had their feet on the way. What did she mean?

The faces glimpsed under the veils seemed mostly to be Egyptian, but one of the boys who was carrying a torch looked more like a Mede or Parthian. Who were these people? Free or slave or what? She should have asked Tahatre. Then Tahatre spoke to her in Egyptian slowly, so that she had no difficulty in following it, saying they were near the place. She answered also in Egyptian that this made her rejoice. The woman one beyond Tahatre looked across and nodded with a quick smile.

Ahead of them was a small temple, the double doors flanked with two pillars, Egyptian-shaped but a little clumsy. They went through and there was a recognisable kind of music, the plucking of a metal tongue sounding a few notes only, but repeated over and over, and the smell of incense burning on a cedarwood plate.

They seemed to pack closer and closer together. Aristonoë felt Tahatre's arm around her, thin but reassuring. She looked back and as she did the doors folded shut, blotting out a few house lights and many stars. It seemed suddenly very hot, very stifling.

They moved slowly forward. Aristonoë felt those in front of her were stepping downwards and reached her foot out till it touched an edge. Down and down they went. How far? She couldn't tell. There was a curtain suddenly in their faces; a rough fold brushed her; it seemed prickly but perhaps wasn't. The people ahead must have gone through beyond. Tahatre leaned forward and breathed a word against the curtain, then nudged her. She too spoke it, she hoped correctly. The curtain pulled back enough to give them a space. Ahead of them was a lighted wall with the figure of an upright serpent on it, but a shaved and white robed priest—or was it a priestess, who could tell?—took them round to the left of it. And suddenly they were in a large and better lighted room with the sound of low singing through it, and there, there was the Queen. Clearly it was no one else. It was Cleopatra made God by the asp, the protector of Egypt, which had reared above her crown and now had taken her out of the hands of her enemies; her face was painted dead white and her diadem gilt. Her jewels were glass, since her worshippers, over whose heads she stared from blued eyes, were poor people mostly. On her knees was a dead man-child, the not-risen Osiris, her man-child by a mortal Roman, Caesar or Antony. And there at each side of her two standing figures: 'It is your aunt Charmian,' said Tahatre simply.

But could one's aunt, one's father's sister, become a God? Yes apparently, though through the same asp. Her aunt Charmian saying to the Romans as they burst in that all was well accomplished and so dying. One after another knelt at the feet of the Queen, the Macedonian, last of the line of Alexander. They were praying to her, gathering strength and making their petitions. A priest stooped towards Aristonoë for her asking; warned by Tahatre she had brought a small gold coin and now gave it. She spoke in Egyptian: 'I ask help to find the children.'

The priest looked at her as she knelt, saying, 'These are not your own children.'

'They are her children,' Aristonoë said.

'All children are her children,' the priest answered. 'She will

94

help you.' The singing grew all round them into wave after wave. Light seemed to float in it; there was one pale light, crescent-shaped. Was it Selene the moon princess, the one they were seeking for? Was it right to think so or was this superstition, irrational, something that should be disapproved of? Tahatre's hand in hers was wet with sweat—or was the sweat her own? But then they were moving again, they were part of the procession and in a little while there was cooler air and far above the unregarding stars.

Where were they? Tahatre in a small voice asked a woman; there were directions, a finger pointing. People dispersed quickly, in different directions. They were alone again, in a long dark street between high tenement houses with no windows on the outside. Aristonoë was thinking about the worshippers, Egyptians but what else? Could there have been Romans among them? It would have been nice to be in the crowd again, the street seemed very dark and the cobbles tripped one. Again they were hurrying, and then unpleasantly heard footsteps behind them but catching up. Was it one of the worshippers? Or not? Tahatre turned, with an indrawn breath that was half a scream. 'Run!' she said. 'It is a man! If we get to the square—' Both of them ran, their skirts picked up, the cobbles hurting their feet; but the other steps ran too and faster. There was a man's voice laughing juicily: 'Ah my little worshippers—all het-up, are you!'

'Get away!' Aristonoë shouted, stamping, first in Greek, then in Latin. 'Out! out!'

'My little Egyptians,' the man said, 'little Nile pussycats, come and be stroked!' He seized Tahatre and began to kiss her wet-lipped as she wriggled her head frantically.

'Stop that!' Aristonoë yelled at him. 'Dirty coward!'

The man looked up grinning. 'Oh, you want some too!' He let go of Tahatre with one hand and reached for Aristonoë, who hit out with all her strength and all her anger and got him on the point of the chin. Surprisingly he toppled over, dropping Tahatre. Aristonoë pulled her. 'Run! We've got a chance!'

They got to the square, where there were still a few lights over the stalls and some respectable people still about. Their veils were flapping loose, but there was no sign of the man. Neither said anything until they were safe back in the house past the door that the stupid slave shut behind them, back in their own quiet room with the lamp lit. The curtains were drawn. Everything was

95

as it had been. Or was it? Tahatre suddenly dropped to her knees and began to kiss Aristonoë's feet. 'You saved me,' she said, still panting and trembling, 'my mistress.'

Aristonoë sat down on the floor too; now they were on a level. 'You didn't have your knife with you, Tahatre, did you?'

'No. Not there. I trusted.'

'Just as well, perhaps,' Aristonoë said and grimaced. 'Did you look back?'

'No.'

'Well, I'm sure I didn't kill him.'

'I wish you had done that,' said Tahatre.

Aristonoë was rubbing her elbow. 'You know, it's sore. And I skinned my knuckle—look! It was like hitting a brick wall.'

'You were given strength,' Tahatre said. 'That's true isn't it, my mistress?'

'I just hit out,' Aristonoë said. 'I never thought I'd get him on the jaw.' She giggled. 'I was just being a Macedonian.'

'As *she* was. But your hand was guided.'

'Tahatre, it was an accident that I hit him on the right place —just an accident!'

'Nothing is just an accident,' Tahatre said. 'We thank her.'

CHAPTER FIFTEEN

Octavia leant forward, letting her spindle lie on the floor. Horace, in a moderately businesslike way, was assessing the quality of the thread—reasonably good? How much did she really spin herself, he wondered, she, Octavia, sister to the Princeps? Quite a lot probably, making herself do it as an example to the maids to whom she weighed out the day's wool supply early every morning, and of course the girls. He wondered if the two Antonias were completely domesticated. And Selene? She hadn't had to spin as a child. Selene the moonchild whom he had barely seen.

'I wonder if you know what you are asking, my dear Horace,' Octavia said. 'I know it may seem little or nothing to you. But if you understood how I tried to protect my poor little stepchildren you would not ask so lightly. Let me tell you. They came here, you know, five years ago, prisoners, enemies of Rome, but—Antony's children. They were utterly unused to the ways of a respectable household. They had the most unsuitable clothes. Selene—oh, she was bright enough, spoke good Latin as well as Greek and the local language, I believe, though I hope she's forgotten it now. She was forward in mathematics. But she had no idea of the ordinary womanly things.' Octavia shook her head. Yes, thought Horace, I was right. She has had to learn to spin. 'Just once,' said Octavia, 'I whipped her. Myself. Once was enough. But she had to understand that she was my child, under my care. The little boy was no trouble, hardly more than a baby after all. But I took care that Selene should not have any bad influence about her from the old days.'

'I see,' said Horace, and remembered that this meant Elpis. 'Did the child—miss her mother?'

'Her mother was a witch, a witch!' said Octavia, and suddenly her voice was different and she beat her hand on her knee. 'She took Antony away from me. She told the children they were kings and queens. Horace, she would have destroyed Rome! I was so happy with Antony—at first—in Athens—then—a witch, a witch! I wish they had burned her wicked body into smoke!'

'So naturally you wanted the children to forget.'

'Horace, I love them! And then—the boy—Alexander—began somehow to have the idea that he was something different, you understand, a king. You remember how he had been dressed up and given Media and Parthia, yes, and betrothed to a princess.'

'Iotapé,' said Horace. 'A lovely name.'

'Perhaps. If you care for these foreign names. I kept telling him that this was all nonsense, part of something he must forget. He must only remember now that he was the son of Marc Antony, a noble Roman, led astray, but my husband before all the gods! Marcellus, who had some influence with him, as I was always glad to see, told him the same thing—but it was no use, no use. Her witch marks had gone into him. Poor boy, poor Alexander.' She dabbed her eyes.

'It must have been very sad for you,' said Horace sympathetically. He remembered that Antony's eldest son, Fulvia's boy, had also been got rid of, in Alexandria, during those few days when anything went. He too could have had the idea that he was different. The younger one—was he here in this house? He wished he knew. And then he noticed that the girls had come in, the two Antonias and the young Marcella; they had brought their spinning and were sitting together on the broad step which led down to the garden. The younger Antonia had her parrot with her, sitting on her shoulder. The elder Antonia gave him a look and a giggle. He found her strikingly handsome, and wondered who she would have to marry.

Octavia went on: 'He was taken away. We were never told, of course, but—what could be done? He might have been a danger. I spoke to my brother, most certainly I did! And to Agrippa. But by that time it was out of their hands. The inexorable processes had started. It was *her* doing. Even dead! You know, Horace, I dream of her sometimes.' Her voice dropped and she stared in front of her. And this, he thought, was the Octavia who had twice, mediating with love and intelligence between her brother and her husband, averted civil war. But not the third time.

'Did you ever see her?' Horace asked, and suddenly longed to know, and could not help imagining the confrontation, in a swirling of images. Almost, the words of the poem were beginning to come.

But she shook her head. 'No, no. Not in life. But dead she—she comes between me and my household gods. *His* gods. I almost see her hissing with Nile serpents. But I think—yes, I think and trust that Selene has forgotten her. That is why I do not wish you to bring this man from Alexandria into my house.'

'Naturally, I understand,' said Horace. But what was he going to say to Elpis? A flat no was out of the question, and she was too intelligent to see through a half lie. Elpis. Had she and Propertius...? Propertius gave himself these airs. No, no, she was not like an ordinary, easy girl.

'Now,' said Octavia, smiling again. 'I must go and see my secretary. So many arrangements to make. Settling the dear girls. One hesitates. Sometimes my brother seems to think almost too much about the political side. I want them to be secure and happy. So much more than politics to weigh up before settling on a match!' She put her spindle back in the wool basket and rose, graceful still. 'I have neglected my spinning but I shall manage later on. Stay, Horace, and amuse the girls while they spin. Poetry twists a spindle better than gossip.'

She waved Horace over to them. 'Bite him, bite him!' young Antonia said to her parrot, shrugging it off her shoulders. It fluttered about but Horace warded it off. It flew into the garden but settled on a small tree in a pot and began to bite at the branches. 'Oh, stop it doing that!' young Antonia said. 'That's one of the new apricots! I'll be smacked!'

Horace rescued the apricot tree from the parrot with only a small peck. 'Two leaves off,' he said. 'I fear that deserves a smacking. May I—?' Both the Antonias threw balls of wool at him.

'Mamma would like you to recite us a serious poem suitable for our young ears,' the elder said. 'Or don't you know any but your own?'

'Stop being silly,' said Marcella. 'What have you done, Horace, to make Mamma cry? What were you talking about?'

'We were talking about Selene,' said Horace, watching them.

'Poor little Selene,' Marcella said.

'You're always on her side!' the elder Antonia said; 'but after all she's going to get a king to marry. I don't see why you need to be sorry for her.'

'A king!' said the younger Antonia. 'That sad little bookworm. I wonder what sort of king Juba will be allowed to be—or want to be. She'll want to be a queen of course! Numidia! As though it were somewhere. But what was it all about?'

'There was an elderly Alexandrian, who was once at Queen Cleopatra's court.' There, that sounded respectable, didn't it? 'He was anxious to pay his respects—'

'To Cleopatra's daughter, no doubt!' snapped the elder Antonia. 'No wonder Mamma was upset.'

'It would cheer Selene up,' Marcella said. 'You know she hasn't been herself since—well, I suppose twins are always closer to one another.'

'He couldn't really do any harm,' Horace said. He began to wonder if Marcella could be an ally; she wasn't as handsome as either of the two bright-cheeked, curly-haired Antonias. She was more like her brother Marcellus, slender with gentle dark eyes and an oval face between straight hair drawn back. He looked at her. 'There's a girl too, his niece. She couldn't possibly worry Mamma, could she?'

'What's she like?' the younger Antonia asked. She had twisted a thread round the parrot, which naturally broke it. Then she slapped the parrot and it flew off squawking, but beyond the apricot tree.

'Now look what you've done!' her sister said. 'Even your monkey wasn't as much trouble as this wretched bird!'

Marcella said: 'Now girls, don't quarrel, stop it! We've all got our work to get through. Our dear poet will kindly chase your bird for you. Now let's all pick up our spindles again.'

'Silly old spinning!' said the elder Antonia; 'when I'm married I shall see that my husband doesn't allow me to spin. Hurting my lovely fingers!'

'They say Ahenobarbus is rather a one for the old-fashioned virtues,' the younger one said, making a face at her sister.

'Yes, if it is him! But you never know till the last minute of a wedding, not in our family! And if he isn't very, very nice to me I shall divorce him. So there!'

'You mustn't talk like that,' Marcella said.

'Why not? Everyone does.'

'Mamma would be very, very cross,' her sister said. 'And what's more she might blame me. Oh, Horace, you've got him! You are sweet. Let's give Horace a dance before we settle down again, shall we?' She jumped to her feet and clapped her hands. A slave girl ran in. 'Take that parrot and give him some grapes, and see you don't let him fly!' The girl nodded vigorously. 'Now be off!'

The three of them were standing round Horace now, three Graces, he thought, three nymphs. They began to sing, a grave ancient-sounding song and the movements of arms, bodies and heads that went with it equally grave and gracious. Marcella suddenly beckoned and smiled and now there were four in the dance. Yes, thought Horace, this is the moonchild, this is Selene.

She was not somehow moonish, not pale and slim, but a strong solid girl, rather unbecomingly dressed—was that, he wondered, deliberate? And was she in face like her mother, the witch, the serpent? Because if so, it was not how he had thought of Cleopatra, the enemy of Rome. She was not dancing as well as the others, but Marcella was encouraging her.

They finished, laughing a little and tucking their hair back, then went on with their spinning. Selene had brought her wool basket and spindle with her and sat down beside Marcella. 'Now,' said the elder Antonia, 'our reward; an ode at least!'

Horace performed. It was a pleasant audience. They went on spinning quietly. He remembered times when he had recited at a dinner party and guests had even vomited. At the end they thanked him nicely. The elder Antonia ran down into the garden, quickly made up a wreath, and put it on his head. Marcella accompanied him to the door. 'I think you should bring this Alexandrian girl,' she said, 'or better—let her come and ask for me. I can say I sent for her. It might help Selene.'

Horace thanked her warmly and went out into the street. Halfway down the wreath came adrift and he had to pull it off and throw it away. At least he would have something to tell Elpis.

CHAPTER SIXTEEN

Aristonoë, with Tahatre walking close behind her, quick and quiet, followed Horace out of the Alexandrian quarter and across to the fashionable world where she had never been. Her uncle had gone halfway, then at a whisper from Horace had turned back. She had first put on her best tunic of embroidered muslin, then decided instead on a crisp linen, turquoise colour with a deep hem woven with formal reeds and fishes. Over it she wore a heavy veil which covered her from head to heels, of undyed linen, soft from much washing. She felt extremely nervous and yet glad to be out of Callimedon's house and doing something at last. And was it, possibly, due to her prayer? Could the Queen be guiding her? Or was that superstition? She knew what Zenon would have said. Equally she knew what Tahatre was thinking as she followed; sometimes her lips moved in gratitude. Her guide, they had said, was one of the best poets, but nobody had explained why he was doing it, not even her cousin Elpis when she had come over to the house. Elpis...? People kept on hinting. She couldn't quite understand, but things were different in Rome, dreadfully, boringly different. Whatever was happening it seemed to be making Elpis angry and sad.

Marcella, whom she was going to see, the sister of the heir to the—no, not kings in Rome but Heads of State, always in big letters in people's minds—she was a kind of princess and must be approached as such. It seemed then that Selene was in a kind of royal household. But when she had timidly questioned her guide along these lines he had laughed. So where was she?

It was interesting to see the sights of Rome, even if they could not stop and look. Every now and then Horace would turn round and drop a few words of explanation. Comparing it in her mind with Alexandria, she missed the sea seen at the end of so many streets and sometimes a glimpse of the Pharos. Was there a library here? If so, it had not been pointed out. But there were certainly more temples, more statues and more inscriptions. Some of the statues were very beautiful and these, she began to realise with a certain shock, were the loot of Greece and Asia Minor, brought here so to speak in chains. Later she would think about this.

They came out of the heavily built-up central part and on to a hill and terraced gardens with hard brick walls which hid all but the higher terraces. There was a gate in one of the walls. Horace took them through and the gate slaves gave him a deferential good morning. There were shallow steps with small trees planted at each side. Horace stopped and pointed. 'Up there and say that the Lady Marcella is waiting for you. No, I'm not coming.' He had suddenly felt an urgent need which he could not entirely identify. To tell Elpis he had done what she wanted and expected immediate practical gratitude? Or not to have anything at all to do with foreigners? To go down to the Forum and be completely Roman, part of the Top? To have a boy instead of a girl? Or just to write a poem?

Aristonoë squared her shoulders and asked, perhaps a little aggressively, for Marcella. But the door slaves seemed to expect this. In a short time an elderly woman who seemed to be someone in some kind of authority came through, looked her up and down and beckoned her to follow. It was quite a long walk, partly through galleries and halls and partly across two garden courts. Yet there was nothing very grand, no beautiful statues, only a few bearded family busts, no pedestalled vases, no leaping fountains, only a square fish pond. In fact it seemed to be several spacious but not very luxurious houses. The elderly woman said nothing. Tahatre pattered after her. Aristonoë tried to memorise her way back but gave it up. And then the elderly woman stepped aside at a curtain and drew it. Now she was in a room pleasantly furnished with light couches, stools and cushions and a good-sized loom with some heavy woollen material with broad purple stripes across it, half woven. 'I am Marcella,' the girl who came to meet her said.

'And I Aristonoë from Alexandria.' She spoke in Latin.

'And you have come to visit our little Selene.' For a moment Marcella said nothing, then: 'Sit down. I am glad you have come.

Try to cheer her up a little.'

'Is she—sad?'

'I'm afraid so. You know, when her brother Alexander was—taken—she—well, she reacted badly. We did all we could for her. And then there is little Philadelphos, a sweet child, you'll see him I'm sure, only he is too young to be much help. But she has not been like her old self.'

'Was she, then, happy here before that—was done?'

'Oh, yes, she was one of us. We are a big family, you see, all related. Sometimes we all used to go to the country together. Father had estates, quite big estates in fact. We used to have fun helping to gather the grapes and tread them or getting baskets of chestnuts and walnuts. Do you do that in Egypt?'

'Yes, indeed, I always enjoyed all that on my father's farm. We have most of your fruit and date palms as well. I've brought a few dates, I thought perhaps Selene might enjoy something from home. We make wine just as you do. And we go fishing a great deal.'

'I think Selene would like to talk about all that. But not, you understand, don't you?—too much about her mother. We hope that —there is much she has forgotten. It was all so dreadful. Better not to think of it. Ah, here comes Selene! Now I am sure you two will want to talk Greek. I know it of course, but my accent is bad. Or so they say! You'd make me feel shy.' Selene came in slowly, a little awkwardly. Aristonoë got to her feet; it was all unexpected. Suddenly she felt tears prickle in her eyes and knew that underneath she was intensely moved. And then Tahatre ran past her and fell on her face in front of Selene who drew back startled. 'Tahatre!' said Aristonoë quickly in Egyptian. 'This is not allowed!' She had told the girl she mustn't speak but hadn't thought of forbidding this. It brought her to herself; one must be sensible. Or else—

Marcella said: 'This lady has come all the way from Alexandria. I'm sure she'll have news for you.'

Selene said, 'Did I ever see you? Who was your father?'

Talk followed a little awkwardly, both shifting round the thing which they both had in mind. The dates, sprinkled with sesame seeds and well pressed together, were eaten and the slave girl brought watered wine with honey to drink with them. Marcella explained that her mother liked to have all the formal dress for the men of the house woven at home. This piece on the loom would be for her brother Marcellus. Yes, the toga was not very practical but it had great dignity and set apart those wearing it. Had Aristonoë seen the Forum? No? She quite understood. Rome was no place for an unaccompanied lady but she would try to arrange something for the two visitors. Aristonoë would come back? She glanced at Selene, who nodded vigorously. 'Come,' she said and walked back with Aristonoë towards the main door. Tahatre, following, looked back at Selene who saw what she wanted to do and shook her head. In one of the courtyards there was a young boy lying on his front and drawing on a big wax tablet. 'That's Philadelphos,' said Marcella, 'he's always doing mathematical problems. Mother bought a very good tutor for him, a Syrian who says he is far ahead of his age. Philo, dear, come here! But he isn't much of a companion for Selene.' The boy greeted them politely enough but clearly wanted to get back. At the door the elderly woman, warned, had a litter waiting. 'We shall send for you,' Marcella said; 'it has been good for Selene. And you behaved with great sense. Go on doing so and you will be welcome.'

As the litter jolted back Aristonoë thought this over. It would take time and so she told her uncle. 'No, Tahatre,' she said, 'we know that she is the Queen's daughter but we do not show it. You can honour her in your heart but not otherwise.' Meanwhile she must manage to see more of Elpis, and without her uncle Eumenes, whose disapproval had seemed to go with him like a shadow. Only, what did Elpis think?

There had been one awkward discussion when they were all together, speaking, to begin with, about the rest of the family. Eumenes had been looking at a necklace which his daughter was wearing. Aristonoë had simply thought it was very pretty and very becoming and must be valuable if it were real gold—but of course it was, you wouldn't put anything but pure gold with those pearls, not very big but so beautifully matched! But Eumenes began to nag her about the necklace—where did it come from? 'I have admirers, you know, Father,' Elpis said gently. 'People who appreciate my knowledge of the classics.'

'Men!' said Eumenes breathing heavily.

'Oh, perhaps,' Elpis said. 'But you know I give song recitals— ancient and modern.'

'And have pearls thrown at you!' her father said ironically and gave a sudden snatch at the necklace. One string broke. Aristonoë got down on her knees and picked up the pearls, holding them in her palm, the pretty things. Elpis had shut her mouth on her anger. Eumenes walked out.

'What a lot you must have learned!' Aristonoë said; then seeing that Elpis was taking it badly, added, 'I mean all those songs! However did you manage?'

'I'm reasonably intelligent,' Elpis answered softly, and then: 'or so they say.'

'You are quite right not to get cross with Uncle Eumenes,' said Aristonoë, 'but you'll come back with us, won't you? You'd like Salampsio, Aunt Hipparchia's daughter. Of course, she's younger, but she's full of life. And it would be such fun to have you!' But would it, she wondered to herself, was she certain that Elpis would fit in?

'I don't know,' Elpis said.

'But there's nothing to keep you in Rome.' Elpis smiled. 'Or—is there? Oh, Elpis, I don't know about customs here—I mean—had you thought of getting settled in any way?'

'I'm a foreigner,' said Elpis. 'It's always awkward being a foreigner. But by now I might have become a kind of foreigner in Alexandria. Perhaps I wouldn't fit in there. Do you like pearls, Aristonoë?'

'Oh, yes! My other cousin—not as close a cousin as you—my cousin Hellanike was given pearls. She's going to marry a Roman with lots of money. But—are you?'

'I doubt it very much,' said Elpis, and laughed, but in a way that worried Aristonoë, and then: 'So you've seen Selene. I wonder what stories they've told her about her mother. And mine.'

'We weren't able to talk about that—yet. But I mean to tell her the truth.'

'The truth. How it looked in Alexandria?'

'Of course. That's the truth.'

'You believe that. They believe something different here. They wouldn't thank you if you said it was lies.'

'You know this poet, Elpis. Does he believe the lies just because she was an enemy?'

'Poets never quite believe in anything,' Elpis said, remembering one evening. They had all been to the theatre; there had been some good chorus work, but she could not bear the principal actor, a dreadfully tarted-up young man but apparently a great success. Several of them had come back with her, including a bright young lawyer, Ovid they called him, a country boy as many of them had been, but already, they said, writing promising verses. What did they really believe? Horace was talking about the countryside and his Sabine farm. Virgil was talking about *his* farm and the splendid peasants. Then this lad Ovid made one or two remarks about country life—oh, catty as you like!—which undercut them, withered their belief. But all the same they'd go on writing their poems about the country and no doubt believing what they wrote.

'These stories are extra nasty because the Queen was a woman, aren't they?' Aristonoë said.

'Of course. Just as my father always thinks the worst of me. I think perhaps the Queen would just have laughed at the malice and stupidity of the people here who make up these stories.'

'Or had them crucified. I would! All these little inventions that make her out cruel and treacherous and—and not chaste.'

'Perhaps she didn't care about that. Chastity is only a notion that men have.'

Aristonoë coloured and took a deep breath: time she got that small truth into her head! Poor kid. Elpis went on about Cleopatra: 'Certainly she wanted to rule the world. And destroy Rome. Who wouldn't?'

CHAPTER SEVENTEEN

The border of bee plants and kitchen herbs, the thyme and savory, rosemary and balm, pink marjoram and tall yellow-flowered fennel, had suddenly been visited by a crowd of butterflies; the two Antonias had rushed down to catch them. The parrot had been put down in the middle of them and was squawking and snapping in panic. Octavia had left with Marcella; clearly they were going to have a long, serious talk. It was probably about her future marriage. There were several possible candidates, all considerably older than she was. One was married, with two children, but his wife was sickly and might die fairly soon. Marcella knew that she had little choice; this was the penalty for belonging to a great family and having Augustus as an uncle. He would decide, and of course he was wise and did everything for the best. But Marcella sometimes dreamt about a young husband, someone, perhaps, like her brother Marcellus, and sometimes she cried at night.

So now Aristonoë and Selene were alone—for how long? On this last visit, Aristonoë had spoken, cautiously at first, about Alexandria and how people there longed for the Princess to come and visit them. Selene had shaken her head, and yet she wanted to know more. Aristonoë suddenly felt that now was the moment. It was a risk, but must be taken. 'Selene,' she said, 'Princess Selene, do you want to escape?'

Selene looked round; if she had been smaller, a delicate moon crescent, one could have packed her into a basket. Or something. 'With you?' she said.

'With me. Everything is ready for you. Horses and a fast ship. To become—a new Cleopatra. In Egypt.'

'Back in Alexandria?'

'Perhaps: to start with. But they might chase you. When people began to call you Queen. We could take you away up the great river, the Nile—do you remember the river rising? Beyond Thebes. Beyond where the Romans come.'

'You want me to do—what?'

'First, you would visit your mother's tomb. Yes, your father's tomb as well, they are there together. To give them respect and remembrance. To get honour and love from many, many people.'

'Why? Aristonoë, why would I get that?'

'Because you are her daughter.'

'But did they honour and respect her? I didn't think—'

'Yes. Yes! Come back to us, come back to her and look. Selene, look towards India and deep into Africa. *She* did.' Aristonoë came close and began to whisper, urgently, remembering all that Aunt Hipparchia and her father had told her. What did it mean to this young girl? She was listening, very still, her head bent. Was she fired? Could she be the new Cleopatra?

Suddenly, in the middle of it, Selene laughed and clapped her hands. 'That was a good story!' But no, not mockery, she had heard a step coming. Yes, she was wise, as her mother had been. 'You must tell me some more!' she said, as Marcella came in, and then the younger Antonia. 'Oh Marcella, it was a lovely story, an old, old Greek story, wasn't it?'

'Yes,' said Aristonoë, 'it's an old story.' Then she felt she must do a build-up. 'They say it's the same time as the *Odyssey*, but not so well known.' And Princess Selene is a diplomat, she thought, yes, she can lie, she is quick!

'You'll tell me the rest,' Selene said, 'oh please!'

'Indeed you must!' said Marcella, 'but now we are going to gather rose petals to dry.'

'There are hundreds,' said young Antonia, 'here's a basket, Selene. Will you help, Aristonoë? It's better than spinning, anyway!'

'I'd love to,' Aristonoë said, catching a thrown basket that still smelled of the last crop of roses.

'We dry them in the sun,' said Marcella, 'to stuff the cushions. They don't last for very long, but Uncle likes them. He says they were used in ancient Rome, an old custom, something the priestesses did. This is the second picking. We did the first in May, but these rose bushes that are always being watered and fussed over, flower twice in the year.' They went down into the garden and began to strip the small dark Persian roses, an early introduction to

109

Italy. Then they tipped the baskets out, spreading the petals along the step where the scent came stunningly off them. It was hot but enjoyable; they moved to another rose bed.

But in a little the elder Antonia came out of the house and called to Selene: 'Your Prince wants to know if he can see you, Selene. Here, let me comb your hair! A petal or two won't do any harm, but you've got real birds' nests!' She tugged and Selene bit her lip and submitted. 'There, that's better! He probably won't notice whether you've got hair or hydras if he's in the middle of a composition, but you must do us credit.'

Selene went into the house without a word. You could not tell from her looks what she thought or felt. The elder Antonia made a little face: 'Juba won't make much of a husband!'

'It depends on what you want,' Marcella said sensibly. 'We can't get married like slave girls by just falling in love. Of course if you want a husband like a lover who'll make scenes if he thinks you are having a flirtation and then goes in for wonderful reconciliations, that's not Juba's line.'

'What I want is someone strong—who'll never get tired. Like my father was,' the elder Antonia said.

'I want someone I can respect,' said Marcella, perhaps a little reprovingly. It was what Octavia had been telling her and she had made up her mind to accept it.

'My father was respected by his army,' said the elder Antonia. 'He'd have been Emperor of the East if he hadn't been betrayed by that woman. And now you like Selene better than us!'

'Don't!' said Marcella, 'I'm tired of it. And I'm sure our guest doesn't like it either.'

'I don't quite understand,' said Aristonoë, though of course she did. 'You, who are so happy and fortunate to be Roman citizens, while poor little Selene is only an outsider!' But don't they see through it when I say that? Doesn't Marcella at least? No, they don't, because this is the proper attitude and they really expect it, even Marcella who is so much kinder than the others. But did I say too much? What did it mean to Selene? What had she been told about her mother? It seemed, from her surprise when she heard the truth, that she had been told, and believed, that her mother was a luxurious tyrant—the stupid old story—not someone honoured and loved by her people.

As usual, a litter was called to take Aristonoë back, and also, of course, her maid, who had been with the other servants of the great house of the Julio-Claudians. 'How did you get on?' Aristonoë asked.

Tahatre was flushed and angry, too angry to cry. 'They called me ... they called me ...'

'An Egyptian, I suppose—like me!' said Aristonoë, to break the tension.

'They said, oh—such horrible, horrible things about the Queen! But my mistress said I must not speak. So I was dumb.'

'That was right,' said Aristonoë. 'And remember, these stories were invented just because they were so much afraid of her. People who are afraid are always cruel and wicked, and what they can't do themselves, they shriek out loud! Perhaps we ought to be sorry for them.'

Tahatre held tight to Aristonoë's hand: 'But it will be believed— many, many years from now—*that* about the Queen!'

'They'll believe whatever the poets say,' Aristonoë said. 'Look, there's Horace. In his poem he called her fierce, implacable. That's not so bad.' She reached out and tapped the shoulder of the front litter bearer: 'Stop!'

Horace quite liked being beckoned over. From the uniforms and crested curtains it was clear to the gossips that this must be one of Octavia's litters and not clear that the inhabitant was only an alien visitor. No doubt it would appear that he had been summoned by a person of quality, instead of—but yes, a nice girl, pretty hair, good eyes, would look very well with a bit of make-up and some modern earrings instead of those queer old things she mostly wore. She must come from a rich family. However, Alexandrian families were not as rich as they used to be: tribute must come down on them quite appreciably. And a good thing too. But she was a nice girl all the same and a little bit like Elpis.

She asked him about the poem which he was currently writing. Yes, these Alexandrians were certainly civilised. She appeared to be genuinely interested: unlike some. He in return asked after the lady Selene. However, she was not a sparkling conversationalist and could be shocked—embarrassingly easily. He suspected she was a virgin. So, quite soon, he was on his way again. He was going to visit Pollio and ask after the history. Pollio would be pleased. He had not been seen about much lately.

But when dear old Butas showed him in, Pollio looked ill. He was sitting there shivering. 'What is it?' Horace asked, genuinely anxious. 'A touch of fever?'

But Pollio shook his head, waited till Butas went out, then said: 'Varro Murena has been arrested. I don't think he has much chance.'

'But—what happened? Nobody tells me anything! Has there been a conspiracy?'

'Probably something of the kind if you like to call it that. He said publicly that the Proconsul of Macedonia had done nothing wrong—'

'But had he?'

'You are out of date, my dear Horace. Our good Princeps had decided he was dangerous. He had thoughts beyond his station. Unlike Quintus Dellius, who has always subordinated his thoughts to his career. Yes, Varro Murena opened his mouth a little too wide to defend someone who, it had been decided, was not to be defended. Yes, Horace, you may well look as if you were going to be sick. Such things make some people vomit. While others swallow them. Varro Murena was, unfortunately for himself, not a swallower.'

'But surely there must have been evidence?'

'Evidence is easy.' Pollio looked at him hard. 'I notice you are swallowing, Horace. How's the stomach?'

'I feel—oh, upset! I know I shan't be able to write what I'd intended...'

Butas came in and whispered to Pollio, who nodded. 'Yes, ask them to come in. Someone else is upset, Horace. Your lady, Terentia.'

Then two ladies came in, neither of them exactly young, though both were handsome and, at the moment, very agitated: Terentia, the wife of Maecenas, and Antistia, Pollio's wife. Terentia rushed to Pollio: 'You have heard! What shall I do? My poor brother, I'm sure he never meant any harm to Augustus!'

'What does your husband say, my dear Terentia?'

'He keeps avoiding me, ever since we heard. Oh, I can't believe they really mean to kill him, not my brother! Horace, will you speak to my husband? I beg you!'

Horace looked helplessly from Terentia to Pollio who looked back at him, expressionless. It was a bare room, without small comforts or cushions or anything to rest the eyes on. He had never before seen his patron's lady, Terentia, ceasing to be calm and dignified. She had been a beautiful young woman, with a certain reputation for wilfulness, a lively and exciting person to be married to. She had aged, but her features remained noble, her eyes brilliant and skin clear. Only now her hair was loose and her face blotched with crying. Antistia, behind her, said: 'We must try and do something, we really must! Would my brother take his case?'

'I doubt it, my dear,' said Pollio with a certain kindliness in his voice. 'The charge is treason. He probably won't be allowed a lawyer. They will want to finish it—quick.' He looked from her to Terentia, who gulped. Tears began to ooze down her face again.

'I'll see if I can help,' said Horace, 'of course I will! You mustn't despair, Lady Terentia, please not!'

Pollio came over and laid a hand on her shoulder: 'Nor must you hope too much.'

CHAPTER EIGHTEEN

'Philo!' said Selene, 'Philadelphos, listen. Do you remember your mother?' He looked up frowning, swinging his wax tablets by the string. He had been working out a geometrical theorem and it had come out nicely. He was puzzled by his sister. 'Your real mother, I mean,' said Selene very low. 'Your mother in Egypt.' They were standing together on one of the garden terraces. There was nobody about. The boy was almost as tall as she was, and growing fast, but slight, not strong like her twin, Alexander. Who must have struggled—no, stop! This was what mattered now. Look round. Still nobody. Across from their own there was another hill but they could not see it properly; the big old olives blocked the view.

'I'm not to think about her,' the boy muttered. 'Mamma told me so. And she was bad. That's why I mustn't think of her.'

'But perhaps that's not true,' Selene said.

'If Mamma told us—'

'But perhaps it's only a story. Mamma isn't really our mother. You know that, Philo!'

'I don't know,' he said obstinately. Then two tears began to ooze down his face. He said, 'I won't hear you! I don't want to know anything new. Not about...' He screwed up his whole face.

'Egypt,' suggested Selene.

He jumped. 'Alexander was taken away. He asked about Egypt. He asked about—her. I don't want to be taken away!'

'You shan't be,' Selene said very close to him. 'This is just you and me. Don't ask anyone else. Don't speak to your tutor.'

'Oh him!' said Philo. 'He's only bought.' Then he said, 'I think I remember my father. With his big bright...' His hands sketched the gesture of a breastplate and helmet.

'We've been allowed to remember Father.'

'Because he was really a noble Roman. Only he forgot to be.'

'We ought to visit his tomb some day. You and I.'

'But she's buried there too.' Selene said nothing.

Ptolemy Philadelphos whispered to Selene: 'When they took Alexander away—Mamma wouldn't say—Selene, where is he?'

'He is a ghost,' said Selene tonelessly. 'Only a ghost.'

'He's—dead? Killed? She wouldn't say.'

'She's very fond of you, Philo. Me too, I suppose. Only we're not free. Do you remember the Triumph? Do you remember the chains? Gilt chains, gold chains perhaps. I do.'

'Not really. Mamma doesn't want me to remember that either. She said it was wrong that we had to go through it. Wrong because of our father. I only remember a noise, a horrid noise and people, people. Only they weren't allowed to hurt us.'

'I suppose we were lucky. Juba was in the Triumph too, in chains like us. But he was older. He was old enough to be beaten. Beaten with canes by the lictors in front of everybody.'

'Poor Juba! But Mamma was kind to him after the Triumph. He told me so himself. You like him, don't you, Selene?'

She began to walk up and down the terrace, her brother following. The grapes were almost ripe on the long, leafy vine branches that stretched from one pillar to the next. Would they be going to the farm this year? Or—or what? If she said she wanted to go to Alexandria to visit her parents' tomb what would the answer be? She thought it would be no, but she couldn't be sure. And if she asked to take Philo with her? Could it be dangerous for him? And what was the answer to his question about Prince Juba? She wanted to give a true answer, as true as though Alexander her twin, to whom she had never lied, had asked her. At last she said: 'Yes. Yes, I think I like him.'

'That's a good thing, isn't it, if you're going to marry him,' the boy said and stopped to watch a procession of large ants crossing the path with some overwhelming purpose in view. He stood on a few of them, interestedly watching the swirling about of the others.

It was pleasant enough on the garden terrace; any breeze there was came there. But below in Rome it was hot. The Alexandrian quarter was better than some, but it was low-lying. There was quite a pleasant public bath there; the women went in the morning, the men in the afternoon; there was a small gymnasium, a garden where one could walk and a portico with second-rate frescoes. Eumenes had been ill from a mild fever but refused to see a doctor though Callimedon had urged him to do so. Nor would he see his daughter while he was ill. 'She makes me feel worse,' he said.

Elpis came, however, and brought fruit. If her father refused it Aristonoë wouldn't! 'How are things going?' Elpis asked.

'She says she is going to ask if she can visit her father's tomb.'

'Is that wise? Won't it put them on their guard?'

'She says not. And of course she would be looked after. In fact she would be an important guest and I suppose she'd stay with the horrible Roman Prefect! But of course if once she comes your father says it wouldn't be too difficult to snatch her away.'

'If she wanted to be snatched,' Elpis said and stooped down to her sandal which, fashionably, was mounted on a high sole. 'There, it's snapped!'

Aristonoë called Tahatre. 'Do see what you can do with this! Elpis, I'm sure she'd want to be snatched. She really wants to be with her own people. I've told her about the Queen: the true story. Yes, Tahatre, go and ask for some waxed thread, I'm sure they have it.'

Elpis looked at her. 'You speak openly in front of your maid—is it safe?'

'Of course. She's Egyptian.'

'No slave is safe.'

'She isn't a slave. She's from the estate of course. But—she's been my friend. Before I met you she was my only friend here.'

'You think I'm your friend now, Aristonoë?' Elpis looked away and felt a little choking in her throat. This nice kid taking on so much! Or thinking she was. Because perhaps it was all a nonsense. Perhaps what the Romans said and logically proceeded to do would turn out to have more force than anyone's dream of Cleopatra and the people. Perhaps even if Cleopatra Selene went to Alexandria nobody would care.

But Aristonoë reached over and grabbed her hand. 'I know you must be my friend. You're my cousin. But not like Hellanike. You're Aunt Charmian's daughter. I wonder what you'll think of her statue. You know, Father always took me to the tomb for the anniversary. It's always very quiet; that's partly because the Roman soldiers are on guard; but most people are praying or making little offerings. We always left flowers; anything else seemed like, well—

116

superstition. But he always said the statue of Aunt Charmian wasn't like her. It was just some hired Greek sculptor's idea.'

'Your father must be a nice man.'

'Oh he is, he is! I miss him so much. Will you miss anyone very much when you come back with us?'

'I don't know if I'm coming back. I can't tell yet. I don't think I would be happy living in Alexandria with my father glowering at me. There's a lot I would miss—here.' And she must decide, she must. Both poets kept pressing her, but differently. Horace who, in spite of being a Roman and seeming to believe in all the Roman ideas, was a good man underneath, tender and full of sympathy, even for her, a woman and an alien. But there was also Propertius who made her tremble and grow warm and soft inside like a ripe fig, who touched her so that she rang like a rubbed glass. But she must keep sane, must not give in to either, not entirely, and must not let them have those precious minutes alone at the end of the party which they both wanted. And she wanted herself. Or did she? If she was going back?

What would she really miss in Rome? Not the theatre. It was better in Alexandria. Or at least it used to be, though no doubt Roman money had lured away the best of the Greek actors. Certainly not the Games. She had been taken there two or three times, but found that she disliked seeing people killed even if they were criminals or had sold themselves voluntarily into the gladiator schools. Some people didn't seem to notice the smell; she did. There were some fine spectacles certainly and the machinery was most ingenious. Perhaps it would look better from the very expensive aristocratic seats. The wild animals? Yes. But none of them were so beautiful as the tame hunting leopards which there used to be in the palace, the Queen's special beasts. The racing? Yes, that was probably the best in the world, certainly a better stadium and longer course than the Alexandrian one. But everything had become so commercialised. Most people were more interested in the betting than in the horses, those superb, marvellously trained teams.

Yes, Rome could afford the best from everywhere, sucking it all in. Was this something to be so proud of? Perhaps, if you felt about Rome as some of the poets did—at any rate when they happened to be writing that way! But she could never forget that she was a foreigner. The kind of foreigner who was dragged along in chains for a Triumph: which was the kind of show they liked best. Things to please their senses from everywhere. Food, drink, marble and precious woods, incense and furs. And the streets and houses of Rome crammed with all those slaves from all over the world—poor devils. They'd never see anything else. Lalage now, she thought, she's got a chance of buying herself out. Hope she makes it.

But her nice cousin was going on talking in a sensible, matter-of-fact way. 'I think it will be much better if Selene is allowed to make the voyage,' Aristonoë said. 'You see, it would have been exciting to rescue her and arrange it all secretly, the way we thought of it first, and ride at night and perhaps let Tahatre stab someone. But it might easily go wrong. Uncle Eumenes mightn't manage it. He isn't very well and he can't do things quickly. As a matter of fact, Elpis, I talked to Callimedon and he says that it might need more money than we have brought. So if she's allowed to go officially, all that won't be a bother and we shall save the money. You know, Elpis, I'd hate all that family money to go to a lot of nasty dishonest Romans!'

'Yes,' said Elpis. 'It sounds as if Selene is a sensible girl. Perhaps even Octavia will help her.'

Actually, Selene had thought it all out and decided to go to Octavia and ask. She had not mentioned Aristonoë except to say that her Alexandrian visitor had spoken of the sea bathing and how one could go out on the fishing boats. 'And then, Mamma,' she said, 'it came to me that I ought to visit my father's tomb and pay my respects. After all I am old enough to do so.'

'My dear girl,' said Octavia and suddenly kissed her. 'Your eyes just now reminded me of his. I must think this over. I must consult my brother. If he were to say you could go you would have to be suitably escorted. You would stay with the Prefect, yes, that would be correct.'

'Of course, Mamma,' said Selene.

'You see, the natives might think—but no, it's all quiet there. But you would have to behave as—as I am sure his daughter would know how to behave. I don't think I could have you going out on a fishing boat.'

'No, Mamma, I understand. But perhaps if Philo came out with me, he could go on a fishing boat. Don't you think he stays in too much, puzzling his head over his mathematics?'

'You may be right, Selene, but I never found he wanted to join in outdoor games. Or even watch them. Perhaps I got the wrong tutor for him. But anyhow I shall speak to my brother and we will see what he says.'

Augustus came often to his sister's house; it was another home to him and there was so much to see to, with the wedding between Marcellus and his own daughter to arrange. It was to be hoped that the two young cousins would get to like each other and produce an heir. Marcellus was not too robust and Julia's tastes were somewhat different. But none of this could be allowed to matter. All would be done according to the old and time-honoured forms. Poor old Lepidus would have to be fetched back from retirement, one should not call it exile. After all, as Pontifex Maximus he was the religious Head of State. Then there were the ten witnesses to be considered: Agrippa, Maecenas, Statilius Taurus, of course. But it must not be too political. Perhaps one of the critics. Pollio? But he might disagreeably refuse and that would be awkward. The list of guests. And of course the dress for Julia, the sheepskin stools and all that. But Octavia would see to the woman's side of it most efficiently, and naturally she would arrange the feast for the men. Something very traditional. And solemn music. One of the poets would certainly write an ode.

So they talked it over at length, but when at last Octavia broached the matter of Selene her brother was firm: 'No, it would not be safe. Egypt is the centre of the corn supply for the whole Empire; we can't take risks.'

'I was so touched,' said Octavia; 'and she is a dear girl. She reminds me sometimes of—of her father in the old days—'

Marcellus, listening, said, 'Suppose we betroth her formally to young Juba and then let her go? It will be his responsibility. Poor girl, she has had a sad time.'

'That might be a possibility,' his uncle said. 'And it would certainly stop any Egyptian plot to kidnap her and marry her to someone there. They wouldn't want to antagonise Numidia.'

'Once they were betrothed, Juba might be allowed to see more of her and it might distract her from the idea of Egypt. Does she fancy him at all?'

'She is a quiet girl,' said Octavia. 'Obedient. Since she got over her first tantrums. Of course they saw one another as children. If you remember, Octavian, you asked me to take charge of him after your Triumph. He was rather shaken and had no relations in Rome.'

'Yes, my dear,' her brother said; 'you always do my dirty work for me.'

'No,' said Octavia suddenly reddening, 'not your dirtiest work!'

'Come, come, my dear. I didn't mean that. I was merely thanking you. Yes, a good solution and clever of my dear Marcellus to have thought of it. Tell her.'

CHAPTER NINETEEN

'That was lovely,' Elpis said. She had genuine tears in her eyes. Horace had come early with the new poem and had sat beside her reading it. 'I think you write marvellously about your friends.'

'Do you like it best when I'm serious like this, or when I'm gay? Be honest, my dearest sweet.'

'I think I like you best when you are serious and tender. I don't much like it when you go in for lectures. It doesn't really suit you telling people what they ought to do. Especially when it's something you don't do yourself!'

'And the fun poems? You know, darling Elpis, till you recited *"Natis in usum"*, I had no idea how good it was. I laughed and laughed. So did everyone.'

'Yes, I saw you! And I suppose you all want me to make you cheerful.'

'Don't we all? Don't you want to be cheerful yourself? Or— Elpis, lovely Elpis, what do you like best about me?'

'Tenderness,' she said low, 'and that's not very Roman is it? Ah, my dear, that's the way to catch me. But I'm not going to be caught. No. No!' She took his hand away or almost away. 'And the others will be coming in a minute. Please, please!'

'I know I'm not so young and attractive as the others. Time has left his footprints on me. Ah, Elpis, we are all mortally sick and there is only one kind of immortality. Can we not share it, you and I?'

'Oh, but you're not old, not when you write as you do! And you know I can't stand silly young men like Ovid pretending they know everything.'

'Propertius is younger than I am. I've seen you letting him kiss you. I've seen those wet lips of his slipping and sliding down, down, past your neck. One day, Elpis, one day you won't be able to stop him. Unless you are mine first. Which of us is it to be?'

She took his head in her hands and began to kiss his eyes. 'What is it that's getting at you tonight, my poor sweet? It's not just me, I know that. Tell me.' She tasted a tear: this was something a lot worse than unrequited love. 'Is it—politics?'

He gave a kind of wriggle of assent, then sat up. 'You understand me, Elpis. Better than anyone else. You could help me. We could get married and go and live on my Sabine farm. Looking down from under the trees, watching the slow white oxen. Making nosegays of flowers in their season. Forgetting about Rome and the idiocies of the rich and the cruelties of the powerful. When things like this happen you would be there waiting for me.'

'Things like what, my dear?'

He said nothing for a moment, then spoke stiffly, mastering himself. 'Varro Murena has been accused of conspiracy; he has been sentenced to death.'

'Has the sentence been carried out?'

'I think not, but—I have been with his sister, Lady Terentia. It is that much worse for her, not knowing. She can do nothing. I think she will never be beautiful again. For true beauty needs confidence. It means having the world on your side. Now that's for her no longer. Her husband does not choose to make any gesture towards helping. I find it difficult to understand, but he says there are higher values. He talks about the security of the State. But I have been with her most of the day. If this is what the good of the State means, it seems to me it may be no place for a poet.'

'No,' said Elpis, 'no, I see that. Alexandria was lighter-hearted. On the whole. Perhaps that's why it was conquered so easily.'

'The Alexandrians killed the great Pompey.'

'Yes, it was a mistake. Or so my father said. The King was badly advised.'

'You still think of him as the King. Yes, yes, of course. And how is the little Princess?'

'She is to be betrothed to Prince Juba of Numidia. After that she may be allowed to visit her father's tomb.'

'She will be betrothed from Octavia's house?'

'So my cousin says. She also says that she is taking me to the betrothal. That will be very strange because I have not seen her since—since they took me away. A party at Octavia's. Yes. Will that make me respectable, dear poet?'

'I respect you already, my Alexandrian muse. Have I not asked you to marry me? I don't think I have ever done that for anyone before—not seriously.'

'What would your patron think of that? I am an Egyptian snake.'

'If it is the only way to have you naked in bed with me—for always, Elpis—then there is no patron who will stop me. For always. Mine only. At home. In the shade of our own vine.'

'It might be—a happy dream.' He was leaning over her now, a little too close. She did not want to see the thinning hair, the fat on his neck, the wrinkles at the corners of eyes and mouth. Though they were kind wrinkles. For a moment she shut her eyes and softened. His knee was beginning to find its way between hers.

'Not a dream. A lifetime,' he said.

She pulled herself away a little. 'And all the other girls? How many feelings you will leave in ruins! And the boys as well!'

'Boys grow up. Girls slip into other arms. You would be mine. You would not be an Egyptian snake. You would be a lovely Roman nightingale singing all night to me in my arms.'

'A Roman nightingale? A dull little brown republican bird? No, Horace, you must think of something better than that or I shall turn into a laurel tree or a fountain!' Now he had got at her shoulder pins, oh dear, should she call Lalage? But then came a welcome noise of voices! 'No, hush, I hear the others—give me time.' She readjusted herself, stood up, smiled, shook out her dress, gave a quick comb to her hair, then laid her cheek for a moment by his in a half promise. But how did she really feel? Would it have been complete bliss to surrender, to open her legs to him? No, no, she certainly didn't want it desperately. It would be nice, it would be rest and forgetting, but not bliss, not being taken completely away and melted into fire. Could it ever be with him? To be married for always, his?

It was a small party, herself and a couple of friends doing all the entertaining, with Lalage accompanying them with flute, lyre or cymbals. If the men enjoyed it they'd tip Lalage properly and she'd put it all away against the time she could buy herself out. Madame had provided some amusing cookery. Not expensive, either. One of her friends could do some very pretty juggling tricks, the other knew all the Greek modes of singing. Garlands were handed round. Horace remembered that very incompetent garland that the young Antonia had made. But she was in a sense a great lady, utterly beyond him. Take instead the well-made garland from a foreign girl one happens to be in love with.

But Propertius? Interesting, thought Elpis, he touches my arm and I begin to heat like a pan of water. I can feel my leg muscles beginning to give. If only I could feel that way about dear Horace!

At the other side of Rome, Aristonoë and Tahatre were looking through the chests, deciding what should be worn at the betrothal party. When she got the news from Selene Aristonoë had been thrilled and wondered why Selene had looked at her a little sadly. But when she got home and told her uncle, he said that now it was all finished, Selene would never come to Alexandria, she would be under the authority of her husband from now on and he would never let her go. Aristonoë asked why not? Prince Juba was no Roman. But Eumenes said: 'He would do nothing to offend them. You will see. No, your Aunt Hipparchia's dream is ended.'

'But it wasn't only her!' said Aristonoë, very upset, 'it was—surely it was—'

'Her sister's dream also. My wife who is a statue.'

'But it was everyone's dream—the people! And Prince Juba might come with her or he might let her come—if he loved her—if she wanted it!'

'No, that kind of thing does not happen in real life. It was before the betrothal or never.'

'Then I suppose I've failed.'

'Yes,' he said heavily, 'you have failed. But I never thought you could do otherwise.' There was no more to say. It was sore like a bruise. It was the ending of something. But there was a party. Oh, she did long to go to a party! She had asked if she could bring her uncle and her cousin and was told yes by kind Marcella; nobody asked her who or what her cousin was. Yes, the best embroidered muslin it must be, and the underskirt not too transparent, no, Tahatre, not *that* one! But she did wish she had nicer earrings.

Octavia saw to it that Selene looked really well for her betrothal. She was Antony's daughter. Octavia had been more hurt than she ever said or let her brother know, when Antony's statues were thrown down and his name scratched off the official honours lists, above all when his house on the Palatine was taken over, although in some ways this house which her brother had given her was better and more convenient. But Antony must have loved his little girl in spite of—well, there it was. So Selene's long simple dress had been bleached to snow whiteness and her hair was specially done; it curled naturally as his had done in the old days. And then suddenly Octavia felt a great wave of generosity and asked Selene if she would like to wear the jewels which had come with her from the palace of Alexandria, which she had worn at the Triumph and never again. Selene had said yes, and then she had cried and cried and first Octavia and then Marcella had cried with her. It was a cruel world for women.

But the party was a good party; there had been no skimping over the eats. Or drinks. But ladies were not encouraged to join too openly over this. Elpis had lent Aristonoë a pair of earrings of her own, with chunky gold-set emeralds, completely in fashion. So long as Eumenes didn't notice! But as a matter of fact Eumenes had somehow got in touch with an old campaigner; they had met in Tarsus of all places. Now they were having more than one drink on the strength of it. He had not enjoyed himself so much since he had come to Rome.

People moved between the halls and courtyards admiring and criticising. Elpis kept out of Octavia's way, though she did not think she would be recognised; she could not trust herself to go too near Selene. If Selene suddenly knew her—and spoke—and Octavia was to hear— Did she, after all, hate Octavia? And Selene looked so different, in this long white Roman dress, from Cleopatra's Moonchild dressed in the brilliant gauzes her mother had loved to see her wearing. She tried to say some of this to Horace; he took her hand sympathetically, a good kind hand. But not the hand she would rather have held between hers—or anywhere else. Marriage, marriage?

The girls were in the crowd watching how Prince Juba put a gold betrothal ring on to Princess Selene's finger. He was a very grave young man, dark-skinned with close black hair. He wore a formal Roman toga but it did not somehow look quite right on him. He had the reputation already of a scholar with a distinct style of his own. Even Horace admitted it. But Juba was no poet. What interested him were strangenesses and anomalies, the oddest animals and plants, physical phenomena for which no explanation existed so far, comets and shooting stars, the furthest countries.

The furthest countries? What did that mean? Aristonoë thought. Were these the countries beyond Egypt, the countries which the Queen had visited or intended to visit, Arabia and India, the land of Punt? Perhaps Prince Juba will take Selene there!

But there was no sign of this. All was formal, orderly, Roman. When he became King of Numidia, Juba would be a client of Rome, keeping the bonds of the Empire secure. This he must most certainly be constantly aware of. Augustus in whose Triumph he had walked had spoken to him seriously and at length. He looked down at Selene's hand and she did not raise her eyes to his face.

CHAPTER TWENTY

Eumenes said, 'The last convoy before winter will be starting in a month's time. I suppose you are no further on?'

'Not really, my uncle,' Aristonoë said. 'She told me she would ask her Prince but I am afraid that whatever he says the Romans will still decide. But did you see the jewels she was wearing?'

'I knew them,' Eumenes answered, 'though it is many years since I saw them. Yes, they were her mother's gift. If she comes back others would know them. If.'

'It is still if,' Aristonoë said. 'But you must tell Aunt Hipparchia that I did all I could.'

'And—the other?' said Eumenes, low.

'She has, to my mind, made her own life.'

'Although I am her father. Other men's daughters owe some kind of obedience—respect—' He half choked on it.

'It is not her fault, my uncle. It was—the way Rome treated her. And nobody else was near.'

He did not answer, only turned slowly and went out; his crippled hand seemed to clutch at nothing. Tahatre, kneeling in the corner repolishing an already polished buckle, looked up as though to speak, then shook her head. 'If once he could think of her as his dear daughter. Only that,' Aristonoë said. 'If he could be a little kind. It is so easy to be kind.'

'She will not come back with us?' Tahatre asked.

'I do not think so. I think she will marry this poet who seems to love her and who offers security.'

'But then she would have to stop being an Egyptian. You wrote about her to my master, your father?'

'Yes, indeed, and he wrote back welcoming her. I know, too, that he will not blame me if things do not go the way we had planned.

Though I have a little hope still.'

'The Princess—she truly wants to come?'

'Truly. She told me so. She longs to see Alexandria again. Do you know, I have taught her a few words of Egyptian? I think—well, it wasn't quite strange to her. Oh, Tahatre, that splendid house where she lives is like—like the Augean stables now since the party! Of course we left before it was over. They must have behaved dreadfully after that. They are just not civilised!'

'Your father, my master, would never allow such things. Never!'

'But the Princess may long to come home and perhaps her be-trothed would let her come. Only what will be said by Octavia and —and Octavia's brother? It is very difficult. But my father also writes—Tahatre, do you remember a neighbour of ours, a son of the Queen's old councillor Pythokles who died before all the troubles? They had a beautiful house in Alexandria but it was confiscated. Some Roman army commander lives in it now. How-ever, they have the estate.'

'I know who that is,' Tahatre said. 'My mother's sister is married in his village. In the year when the beans all became spotted and mouldy he helped them with food. Also he gave an offering to the temple and so the next year the beans were healthy. Yes, we know them.'

'Well, Tahatre, he has a son who is a law student in Athens. In fact I remember him when he was a little boy, only little boys are all alike. This son is coming back from his studies, they say.'

'And then, my mistress? Then?'

'Well, the families will certainly meet. And it will be strange if this student and I do not at least see one another. He is said to be—'

'Handsome, my mistress?'

'And sensible. But we must make no plans yet. Only I would like not to have to have any more adventures or to take any more on my shoulders. For a little anyhow.'

'I hope this law student has strong shoulders, my mistress!'

They both laughed. Polemo had written with such love to his daughter that she felt comforted. How good it would be seeing him again! And if he had this present for her—yes, there had been times when she had looked swiftly at young men or, her eyes cast down, felt their nearness. And she had wondered with a little

128

shame how it would be when the time came.

On the other side of Rome, Horace would have said he knew well how it would be in any encounter of love, and yet somehow he felt that he did not know, not this time. He mentioned it to Pollio as casually as he could. Pollio was having a struggle with his last chapter. If it was to be the last. But if he actually finished his history how was he going to go on living? He was no longer much interested in the things which he had planned and done, even in that small public library which he had founded and had been so keen about. Now it was just a lot of old books. Was he then so determined to go on? Why? Was there not a time for sleep, for long, long sleep, unbroken, unbreakable? No waking to worries and discomforts, sleep like one had as a young soldier after a hard march. He used to enjoy reading his book aloud to a select audience. Dear Antistia used to listen too in a discreet corner. He would ask her if she had noticed this or that passage and she always had. But he could not be bothered now. Yet he would quite enjoy an audience if he did not have to put on his toga and read to it. He was always pleased to see Gallus. But today he was just as glad when Butas had come in and said that the other poet had arrived and was asking if he could pay his respects.

Now they were sitting in the courtyard next to the small pool where a few fish swam in an unpurposeful way. There was a leaf or two on the surface. They were beginning to turn colour here and there. On his own Sabine farm which was so much in Horace's mind and imagination, the barley had been threshed out, such as it was. There would be enough for barley bread for the farm servants, and plenty left for his own riding horse. He had been up there several times before the grape harvest, to make sure that everything was in order, and had duly made the sacrifices which his people would expect. He had seen that the vat and the presses were properly cleaned out and fumigated, that the grape hooks were sharpened and the basket cords renewed. He had seen to the pitching of the hogsheads; how had one managed before the days of imported tar? Resin? Charcoal tar? But it must have left a dreadful taste in the wine. He had a good pile of wood ready for boiling down the must. Then the smaller vessels, lead or copper, had to be scoured, and he had chased up the bailiff's wife and daughters into giving the wine cellar a thorough clean-out. On top of that he had investigated a brawl between some of the slaves, in which one had his arm broken—just before the picking began, too —and had a couple of them put into chains to cool down in the slaves' prison for a few days. One must be strict, though doubtless fatherly; he would not have them beaten this time, but they must not damage his property, in the shape of other slaves. There was just time for a pleasant canter in the evening, though not for hunting. That must wait until winter. Altogether it had been a pleasant, bustling time and his head had been full of gay tunes and cheerful phrases. But always at the back, the thought of how it would be to share it—next vintage perhaps.

Once he had persuaded Elpis to come with him. Together they had supervised the storing of the grapes which, with luck, might last over the next six months at least. The stalks of the bundles were dipped in hot pitch, and then the bunches were laid in dry chaff, not touching one another. Apples, pears and figs were all being dried; the smell seemed to reach to the back of one's throat, singing of warmth. Elpis had admired it all, indeed been enthusiastic, but at the end of the day pleaded a headache which appeared to continue all night; he had been allowed to comfort her a little but not enough for his own comfort. And though one of his favourite little farm girls had been more than willing, it was not like it used to be.

This year's wine might be tolerable, one could scarcely tell yet. The hives seemed to be full and honey must soon be taken out. He had the finely woven willow baskets ready for straining the combs. And now the chestnuts were beginning to tumble and the little pigs and children to rush after them. Beech mast would fall too from the great reddening trees. Then the time would come when the forests would bare themselves, showing their splendid boles and branches. To be there in winter with the wide log fire and the home-grown sheepskin rugs thrown down in front of it and Elpis in the flickering, leaping flamelight, married, willing!

Pollio said, 'You really intend marriage, Horace?'

'Not a grand marriage, of course,' Horace answered.

'Naturally, naturally. She is after all not a citizen, your Elpis. But free.'

'Unlike my own father!'

Pollio patted him on the shoulder. 'Who did so well by his son. But what will Maecenas say?'

'I wish I knew,' Horace said. This was something which worried him now and then. But Antistia had joined them; she looked affectionately at the poet.

'Our poor dear Terentia has not forgotten that you tried to help her,' Antistia said. 'It was good of you, Horace, for we knew you were, well, a little scared of the great man.'

'But it did no good,' said Pollio.

'Except to Terentia. She felt she wasn't alone. That was a big thing for her, Horace, just then. It may be hard for a man to understand, but she had never been alone and helpless before. And she had been such a beautiful young woman.'

'Until her husband preferred duty. *Pietas* towards the Princeps, not towards his wife. I shall stick to you, my dear.' Pollio crooked an arm into hers; yes, she had been a good wife to him, never tried to persuade him to act in his own interests rather than for his principles. He hoped their children were not being corrupted, but there were too many temptations for ambitious young men. He saw rather little of his son these days. His daughter at least had married into a decent family, one of the few left of the old *nobiles* after the proscriptions. A very respectable young man without political ambition. At least he hoped so; he and his wife had both been pleased about the marriage and he thought the young couple were quite content. Though not on fire as a poet might be.

'I hope you will be very happy, Horace,' said Antistia, smiling at him, almost as though he had been another son. But Pollio was thinking of something else. He had seen Quintus Dellius, who had made a respectful, formal call; after all Caius Asinius Pollio was still somebody. But he had got nothing, only the official line. Had the man genuinely forgotten? Or had fear—respect?—love of country?—no, fear, dirty old fear, actually rubbed out remembrance? If so it makes the historian's job more difficult but vastly more interesting.

He himself could not remember much about Queen Cleopatra, though they had met in Rome: an arrogant, intelligent woman, overdressed, asking too many questions. But not motivated, like most people, by fear or greed.

CHAPTER TWENTY-ONE

Octavia decided she must go down to the country for a week at least. There had been so much to see to and arrange, and after the betrothal party, what a mess! You would think people would behave better, especially in the best rooms, but men after they had been drinking—well, it couldn't be helped. But the smell must be got rid of, the ponds cleaned out after the fish had been rescued and the broken garden plants replaced. She gave her mind to it. Orders were to be carried out—or else! She would be back in ten days at the latest. All must be ready by then, everything exactly as before. Then she sent off a couple of riders to warn them in the country house and ordered the litters round for herself and the girls, as well as little Philo and his tutor.

Selene ,upset and feeling it must be her fault because it was her party, began to apologise, but Octavia cut her short: 'Some of my brother's new friends have intolerable manners. I wish he would speak to them. But of course he won't! I suppose it will be just as bad when dear Marcellus marries Julia. Worse, because there will be more wine. A great deal more, I'm afraid. Hop into your litter, dear, and stop crying. Prince Juba will come and visit us and you may walk through the garden with him. In you get, Antonia! No, take your parrot along with you. If you must have pets you must look after them yourself.'

It was cooler in the country and beautiful to look down on the lake past terrace after terrace of different vines, suitable for different purposes, all well laid out and weeded, though all but the latest grapes had been picked. There were still the last of the figs and a few mulberries, but the ground below the big trees was stained with juice. It was not so long since mulberries had been brought to Italy. Some of the sweetest grapes were drying in the sun, spread out on cloths; the sharp raisiny smell almost choked one. Prince Juba and Princess Selene walked past them quickly, then slowed down to see the blue of the lake dotted with a few little sails. They were out of sight of the house and Octavia. Here and there a slave, weeding or preparing a new seed bed, bent over his work, never looking up at them. The Antonias had run after them a little way, then decided it was boring; they did not even look softly at one another as a betrothed couple might do and be teased. Now they stood a little apart. What can we say, Selene thought, how can we begin? Then Juba's hand left his side and crept over to her hand and held it. What did she think of it? Was it right? Her wrists were as thick as his, her hands as wide and square. Nobody had held her hand like this before, not Antony her father, not even Alexander, her twin. For a moment she thought of him, then swung back. How slowly the little sails seemed to move. She wished now that she was more elegant, that she had put on a different dress; she wished she was beautiful, an ordinary, happy, pretty girl; she wondered if she ought to draw her hand away. Or not? His fingers were thin and strong; they fidgeted with the betrothal ring, pushing it against the base of her finger. Should he do that?

He looked away from her and said, 'Do you remember the Triumph?'

She jumped. Why had he said that? It was not anything she wanted to remember. At last she said, 'I cannot suppose I shall ever forget it.' And then, 'I remember you being brought to the house afterwards. You seemed to be covered with blood.'

'I was,' he said. 'They wanted me to scream. In the end I did.'

She turned to him quickly, looking straight into his face, it seemed for the first time. The centres of his eyes were utterly dark but the whites were clear and his eyelashes curled back. There was a smooth slope on his face like some Egyptian faces. His nose was straight and a little spread at the nostrils for the better sensing of all airborne scents. His mouth—it looked soft—no, no, she must keep her eyes away from it. But how dreadful it would have been, she thought, if they had made me marry a Roman. 'Forget it,' she said. 'Oh, please, forget it!' Perhaps she could help him. But would that be—too forward?

He said, 'They scarred me on purpose so that I would never forget. Just two or three places. On the back of my shoulders. The rest healed.' He was wearing a country-style tunic open down one side but belted in and falling neatly over his slim hips. 'Put your hand on the scars,' he said. She hesitated. 'Selene, you will be my wife. Learn to touch me.'

She bit her lip and put her fingers through the open side of the tunic, under his arm, feeling up, and suddenly felt a line of ridged skin and equally suddenly threw her other arm round his neck and buried her face in the breast folds of his tunic. 'Oh, it must have hurt!' she said. 'Oh, how could they be so cruel, my poor little boy!' For there he had been, so young, carried in after that treatment from the lictors and the watching crowd, his eyes half shut and tears of pain coming out of the corners and falling on to the marble floor. And Octavia had hurried her away. But gone back herself with sponges and towels.

He said, 'They did it to show the power of Rome. It has been on me all these years. But now you have broken it, Selene, Selene.'

'Have I?' she said, and raised her face, only to be kissed gently and often till her young skin burned with the blood behind it. Was this then the beginning of being married?

They sat together on the edge of a bank close and yet not quite touching, not yet. They could smell the dried herbs whose leaves they had crushed. And they talked about the Triumph of Octavian, each of them saying what had hurt them most and each of them aware that at last it could be shared so that the dumb shame and anger could be over. 'I hated them,' he said, 'hated them for my ancestors as well as myself. Did you hate them as much, Selene?'

'They had a cart with this horrible image of my mother—lying down and—oh, it was filthy! And we had to walk behind it. That was as bad as being beaten.'

'You had your brothers with you, at least.'

'But they had sent away Elpis, my lady-in-waiting. I don't know what happened to her. Nobody would tell me. Not even now. If Elpis is dead, I don't know where or when, and I can't even pray at her tomb! And then—you know about Alexander, don't you, Juba?'

'Of course. It was well known. I only hope Philo is not in danger.'

'I think he is more careful. He is a scholar like you, Juba.' And then she looked at him again and something seemed to become uncertain. 'You *are* a scholar?'

He began to draw things on the path with a stick he had picked up. At last he said, 'In a way. But it is my house I go into to escape them. My burrow. My dog kennel. But you must never, never say it is anything but real.'

'How can you think I would betray you to them, my—my husband?'

'If we can be sure that we shall never betray one another, that would be a strong roof overhead. A sword. But if they tried to make us—' His head had sunk, away from her.

'No. No!' she cried out, 'they do not have that kind of strength.'

'They have the strength of rocks,' Juba said sombrely; 'they know deep inside that they are the masters. The whip comes easy. They can always crush us. We rush at them and they close the spears on us. They take away our human thoughts and needs, our human love; even the dignity that all free men must have. If they choose, we are slaves.'

'They never took away your dignity,' she said, looking away from him, because if she had looked straight she could have melted into tears where now she must, for his sake, be firm.

'Carthage was their trade rival,' Juba said, and his voice dropped, even though there was nobody to overhear, 'so they had to win. They broke every promise. Yes, just as their image, Aeneas, broke his promise to Queen Dido, and for the same reason: the power and glory of Rome. Just as the divine Julius broke promises to Gauls and Germans.' He was speaking now almost into her hair; she stayed very still. 'They lied and lied about Carthage; they twisted history. Thucydides never lied for the sake of Athens; he set everything down for free minds to judge. Melos. The Romans could not have done that; Rome means more to them than truth. When it came to the siege and the destroying of Carthage, again they broke every promise.'

'How do you know all this?' she whispered.

'Because there were Carthaginians who fled into my country and settled. My father protected them; it was counted against him. Because when I was a young boy I listened.' Suddenly he hit his hand against a rock and the dust flew up. 'That was what they had to beat out of me! This thing of theirs: the rods and axes. Whenever I see it— Oh Selene, Selene, I have so much to tell you!'

'I will learn from you,' she said, 'I promise I will learn. All you want to teach me. I shall be as close and secret as—as the bud petals over the heart of the rose.' She laid her arm beside his arm, just touching; hers was pinky brown, not deep brown like his. Even when she turned his arm over so that she could see how light it was inside the elbow and on the palms, it was still a different kind of colour. He turned a little and the misery in his face began to break up. She wondered if she could kiss this arm of his, the palms of these hands pale with a darker line. But no, her cheeks were only now beginning to burn less. Softly she said, 'It's a lovely colour.'

'Oh no,' he said, 'yours is the nicest.' And then he laughed a little, the first time he had not been utterly serious. 'If you like it,' he said, 'you will love Numidia. We are like that. It will be good if the Queen is happy in her country. But you—I was afraid they would make me marry an Italian girl or a Spaniard, someone with Roman blood. Not an African like you.'

'But I'm not really even Egyptian—'

'Your mother died for Egypt. I think that buys you in. Selene, this is very strange. When we were betrothed I never thought we could be like this with one another. Speaking truth. Did you?'

'Not possibly. I only wanted you to say I could go back to Alexandria. Now that I am in your power instead of theirs.'

'You want to go back so much? Selene, Cleopatra's daughter, we will go back together after we are married.'

'You will come too?' She looked at him through blurred eyes. 'To see her tomb? To pray there?'

'She was your mother,' he said, 'the grandmother of our child when we have one.' He took her hand in his and moved it to the pit of his body; she understood what it was she felt. 'You are not afraid?' he asked, wanting to be sure.

'No,' she said, 'why should I be? When shall we be married?'

'They will settle that,' he said gloomily.

'But they cannot stop us,' she said and her cheeks were flaming again. 'Now.'

'Princess,' said Prince Juba of Numidia, 'have it your own way.'

CHAPTER TWENTY-TWO

'No, Tahatre, that's not worth taking back. Give it to one of the slaves.' They were packing now and the chests seemed as if they wouldn't hold everything even though she had bought so little while they were in Rome; she really didn't care for the taste here.

'Perhaps I could use it, my mistress?'

'No, Tahatre, you know I hate seeing you in my old clothes! I'll give you something new when we get back—if there's anything to celebrate.' Aristonoë shoved in a square box with some half-used jars of eye shadow and nail polish; there hadn't been many times when she'd wanted to put any on. It wasn't as if she'd even seen the sights of Rome properly; there was nothing in their quarter and it had always been the same way to and from Octavia's house. Once they had gone through the Forum, but she had barely seen it —the noise, the crowds! She had peeped out of the litter or covered chair from the great house, at the shops and the buyers and sellers on the street corners, the barbers and sweet-sellers and letter-writers. But Alexandria had been much the same. Eumenes and Callimedon had gone together to watch a day's chariot racing but there had been no thought of taking her and they'd lost money betting. They had not gone to the Games; these, said Eumenes, were disgusting and from what she had overheard this was clearly the truth. Elpis had offered to take her to a theatre once when there was a reputable programme, but Eumenes had said no. She spoke over her shoulder to Tahatre: 'You've got the mirror in, well down, haven't you?'

'There will not be a scratch on it. Oh my mistress, when we get home I shall give the mirror it's own sand, the sand of the desert. Useless, the sand here, coarse. The mirror will be glad to be home.'

'You know, Tahatre, that mirror came from Greece once upon a time! Or anyway it was made by Greeks.'

'The mirror has forgotten all that. It has become altogether Egyptian.' Tahatre had kissed it before snuggling it away. It was sad to see bright things going into darkness. 'Will you wear your bracelets, my mistress?'

'I'm not sure. No, they'd be safer in the chest. Oh Tahatre, there's one thing. I'm sure Aunt Hipparchia would like me to—this is a gold brooch she gave me. Could you get it to the Temple where we were? I expect—well, I don't think they get very many offerings, do you?'

'Not gold, my mistress. And it is told that—in *her* name—the Isis priests try to help the poor people. The women. They will offer prayers for your safe journey.'

'Oh, I don't want to bother them. I mean, Tahatre, I'm not doing it for that—'

'I know you are not, my mistress, but they would want to.'

'You've been there again, haven't you, Tahatre?'

'I have been there. They are my people. She is my Goddess.' But Tahatre came over and knelt formally in front of Aristonoë. 'Has Tahatre done wrong? But surely my mistress knew?'

'Well I suppose I did,' Aristonoë said, 'but you were taking risks, you know, going alone.'

'There are one or two going from the top flats, the cheap attics under the roof. We went and came together. All was well. There will be a feast for all on *her* day.'

'And you won't be there. Sorry, Tahatre! But we'll be on our way back home. You'll manage to slip over with the brooch later today? Oh yes, and pick up the shoes that were being re-soled.'

'Of course, my mistress. Perhaps they will give the brooch to *her* or perhaps to one of the ladies, to your aunt Charmian. Oh she is so badly dressed!'

'You mean you want to take one of my best scarves? No, stop kissing my foot, Tahatre, you tickle! Let's see. You can have the green linen with the papyrus head embroidery. There's a place in the middle a tiny bit scorched, but Aunt Charmian can wear it so that it doesn't show, and I'm sure she won't mind. All right, take that. But I'd much rather they'd sell the gold brooch for feeding poor people. Oh, dear, I do wish Elpis would come to say goodbye. I can't bear to think of not seeing her again.'

But there was no sign of Elpis that day or the next, and she could not go there alone, still less ask her uncle to take her. They were sailing at dawn from Ostia and must be on board that night. Tahatre had done her errands and the strong shoes were soled ready to wear if she needed them on the voyage. Had she seen the last of Selene? The Princess knew they were leaving, but no letter had come for her from Octavia's house. It was sad, but perhaps there was no more to say. And then the silent elderly woman who had met her the first time and whom she had sometimes seen since, came with a pair of sealed wax tablets. She broke the seal eagerly. Yes, it was Princess Selene telling her that after they were married Prince Juba would for certain bring her to Alexandria. It ended 'all will be well'. What did she mean? For herself? For Egypt? For what?

The day went on. No Elpis. The first wagon to take the heavy chests was at the door; she could hear the ox team jingling their harness and stamping. Two of the ship's officers were going down with it to see it safely stowed. Oh it was cruel of Elpis not to come! Unless the parting was going to be too much for her. Was it? But she was going to marry the most distinguished poet in Rome, even if his father had been a freed-man. No need for her to want to go back to Alexandria.

Then suddenly Elpis was there, heavily veiled and carrying a covered basket. Aristonoë ran at her: 'Oh you've come, you've come, I was afraid I'd never see you again!'

'You will,' said Elpis, 'I am coming with you.'

Aristonoë gasped, she couldn't say a thing. Elpis sat down quite calmly. 'But,' Aristonoë said, 'what's happened? Aren't you going to be married?'

Elpis shook her head. 'If I got married to Horace I know I would cuckold him with Propertius within a month and I couldn't do that. I couldn't. So I'm cancelling out. I'm going back to Alexandria.'

'Really, Elpis!' Aristonoë said, shocked. 'You're being stupid. How can you know you'll behave so badly?'

'Would it be bad? To be unfaithful to a Roman?'

'Of course it would. The poor man trusts you. Besides you are one of our family! If you feel like this about Propertius why don't you get married to him?'

'And live in one poky little room on the fourth floor of a

tenement? Oh God, I'd love it. For a week. But he hasn't asked me, little cousin.'

'But—wouldn't he?'

'That's not his line. Oh poor Horace, poor sweet Horace. I've spent most of today writing him a poem trying to explain. So that he shan't feel everything is against him. He mustn't do that, you see. But I'm afraid he'll hate me for a bit; well, I shan't know. And he'll find a nice girl, an easy girl, and he'll forget. It would be so much worse for him the other way. Aristonoë, will my father take me? Will you speak to him?'

'Are you sure, Elpis, quite, quite sure? Aren't you imagining things? Perhaps you'd love your husband after you were married and not—not want to do anything wrong.'

Elpis smiled and shook her head at her cousin. 'No, I'm sure. But I shall have to borrow clothes and things from you. Nobody knows I am going. Not even poor little Lalage. I've got my jewels in the basket; they'll pay my way.'

'Oh you mustn't bother about that. Elpis, how marvellous that I'll have you to talk to! I was so anxious—but here you are. Wait, I'll see your father.'

She rushed out full of excitement. Elpis! So she hadn't failed altogether! But stopped in mid-run. What was she going to say, what? Eumenes was coming out of his room with Callimedon. Well, he wouldn't answer anything bad in front of Callimedon. 'I have wonderful news, Uncle,' she said: 'Elpis is here and coming back with us!'

Both the men stopped and stared. 'My daughter—coming home?' said Eumenes. 'Is she tired of her life—in Rome?'

He nearly said something much worse, Aristonoë thought, then answered rather slowly: 'Whatever Octavia and the rest of the Romans did to her, she is one of us.'

Had that made him think about Elpis's mother, his wife Charmian, the Queen's mate? 'One of us? We are all our own making.' His face seemed to go far and dark. 'Even if all had gone as she had wanted, if Antony had truly wanted the Queen's golden age and helped it to happen, yes, even if we had won at Actium, even if the gods had not left us, it would have been all the same in five years or ten.'

'Oh Uncle, you can't say that!' Aristonoë cried out. 'If we had won, everything would have been different!'

'Would Elpis have been? Was it only Rome?'

'Of course, Uncle Eumenes. Aren't you being a little—sad? Elpis is coming because she felt that she could not honourably stay.'

'You use the word honour?'

'Certainly I do, Uncle Eumenes.' She stood very straight.

'She may use it strangely. As her mother did. But you say—very well, tell her she can come.'

Aristonoë threw her arms round her uncle, gave him a big kiss and ran back to Elpis. 'Uncle says you can come!' she cried and Tahatre behind gave a little jump and a light clap of her hands.

'I shall never see either of them again. Never,' said Elpis and pulled her veil across her face.

'But you don't want to, Elpis, oh surely you don't want to,' said Aristonoë. She felt utterly bewildered, near crying, and she'd been thinking she'd done so well! 'Elpis,' she said timidly to the still-veiled figure, 'aren't you happy to be coming back?'

Elpis looked out from her veil and her eyes seemed to be dreadfully tired. 'I am glad to be coming with you, dear Aristonoë,' she said. 'But happiness is in some altogether other world.'

PART THREE

Alexandria

THE NEW PEOPLE IN PART III

Egyptians

Pakap
Nesa
and others

Macedonians

Conon
and others

Roman

The Prefect
The Prefect's Lady
and others

From Beyond the Roman Empire

Queen Aba of Olba
The young Queen of Punt and her husbands

CHAPTER TWENTY-THREE: B.C. 25

'I've come to snatch you away, rabbit,' said Polemo, walking down between the rows. 'Back to town for a little rest. Your aunt Hipparchia thinks you should be looked after.'

'But Conon looks after me as if—as if I were a pearl necklace!' Aristonoë stood up, stretching, a little flushed, the curved knife in her hand, the basket of prunings at her feet.

'Does he indeed! Letting you prune his vines!'

'But I like to, Father!'

'Not as much as I would like a healthy grandson. Besides, I think I must pull myself together and be polite to you know who. And I want your help. Just a little smart talk about your grand friends in Rome.'

'You mean they won't confiscate any more of our land if I'm heard telling Hellanike about the parties at Octavia's house? Just that? Well, I'll come. I mean if my husband gives his permission.' She giggled. 'I suppose you've asked him! Well, I hope I shan't find myself spitting in anyone's face.'

'Of course you won't. We all have to pretend. And you are protecting Conon—as you know.'

'If you say that's what he married me for—'

'I don't, rabbit, I don't! But it may have been in the minds of the family. As a matter of fact, he thought he was protecting you. Come along.' He beckoned to one of the Egyptian vine dressers, who came, smiling. Aristonoë handed over her pruning knife and gave the man a few directions; he took a whetstone out of his belt. 'You're fluent,' her father said; 'quite right too. Is Conon?'

She shook her head. 'Not yet. Father, it seems so funny now, but he doesn't think of Egyptians like I do.'

'You usedn't to, my daughter.'

'I suppose not. But—for Conon they're just not Greek. Not—real people. Perhaps if he'd stayed in the country getting to know them it would have been different. It was all that going to Athens, away from our own land. But he'll learn!' They started to walk back slowly through the bright spring light, the sparkle of green coming everywhere.

'You mustn't despise Athens,' Polemo said. 'Even now. It manages to—exist. And make the Romans feel uneasy. Which is more than we do. What kind of grapes are these?'

'Amineans. Conon thinks we absolutely must have them for the wine and the soil seems to suit them. But I want some more fruit trees. Quinces. Lovely spicy quinces! One needs them for such a lot of cookery.'

'You've taken to cooking, have you, rabbit?'

'Well, one has to know or one can't tell one's people. Besides, Conon—' she blushed a little. 'Look, Father, we've moved the beehives.'

'Yes, it's different in one's own house, isn't it?' said Polemo, half teasing, half loving. He had been so afraid for her in Rome; he was only just beginning to admit it to himself. There were times he had been desperately angry with Hipparchia and with dead Charmian too, her sister who had chosen his rabbit to do her dangerous work and then gone where there was no arguing. 'I asked Tahatre to start putting your things together. You'll take her, won't you?'

Aristonoë hesitated. 'You know she's just got married.'

'No! I thought she was so devoted.' He frowned.

'Oh, but he's most suitable, a man called Pakap from the next village; he has teams of mules and takes pilgrims and sightseers. His elder brother is a priest of Sarapis, not high up of course, but I mean he isn't like an ordinary stupid villager.'

'You mean, Sarapis-Antony?' After a moment she nodded. 'And I suppose you went to the wedding?'

'Yes, of course! But Father, I did ask Conon for permission! And we had a simply gorgeous feast, beans done I don't know how many different ways and pigeons and kids, and they were all so nice to me and complimented me on my language and of course it's very, very good for my language practice. And Father, we asked the Queen's blessing on the marriage.'

'My dear, I'm glad. A time might come when it would help.

You've heard no more from the Princess?'

'No, but she only got married this winter. Oh, I know I'll get a letter! We were such friends, I know she'll tell me what's happening. And I'm sure Tahatre won't mind coming with me. I must just tell her which dresses—if you want me to impress the Romans. They don't always appreciate the real best, at any rate not these provincials.' She tossed her head a little; Polemo managed not to laugh.

But it was certainly useful to be able to talk about Octavia at the little gathering of the ladies of the Prefect's staff and to mention in passing that the young Marcellus had spoken graciously; and then there was the little joke about the latest toupée of the Princeps. 'And our cousin Elpis? 'said Hellanike. 'She was lady-in-waiting to Princess Selene—or wasn't she?'

Without exactly answering, Aristonoë said: 'You know she came back with us? The Princess was getting married so there was a change all round.'

'And she herself is to be married soon, we hear?'

'Yes, indeed,' said Aristonoë. 'To a friend of the family, a very nice widower with one child; he has written an interesting treatise on astrology. So we shall all be together.'

'A pity she didn't marry in Rome while she had the chance,' one of the other officers' ladies said. She was not an Alexandrian but perhaps from Sicily or somewhere of that kind. Aristonoë responded by quoting a line from the poet Horace, which was not difficult considering how often she'd found herself being Elpis's audience.

'She is very well educated, isn't she?' Hellanike asked.

'Oh, yes! Her poetry readings were famous.'

'The Classics?'

'And the moderns as well—including the Romans, you know. The poets used to bring her their latest poems long before they were copied.'

The wife of the Prefect had joined them, a kindly woman but always going in for rather stupid hairdo's and jewels which really did nothing for her. Her Greek was sometimes a little odd but the younger wives were fully aware that she must be kept sweet. 'Would your cousin give us a Virgil recitation?' she asked.

'I believe that could be arranged, madam,' Aristonoë answered. She thought she could persuade Elpis. It could well be a considerable help to the family. Of course Elpis would despise this audience, but that was all right so long as she didn't show it and surely she could manage that. In Alexandria it was a condition of success—whatever one's intentions.

Another of the younger group turned to the Prefect's lady: 'Is it true, madam, that we are to expect a visit from the Queen of Olba?'

'So the Prefect informs me,' his wife said proudly. 'I shall have to make the domestic arrangements. Duty, duty!'

'But where is Olba?' another of them asked. This was difficult. However, the Prefect's lady created a diversion by clapping her hands for the slaves who brought in sweet wine and cakes. Two of them were her latest purchases, a little Nubian and a little German from the two ends of the imperial frontier. Both by now were quite tame and used to being handled, especially by pretty ladies with cakes. Both wore little striped cloaks and nothing else so that real or supposed differences in their genitalia could be commented on and appreciated. Now they were sitting on the knees of two of the older ladies, only struggling and wriggling enough to make it amusing. 'Look, mine goes higher than yours!' 'Wait till I've got mine going! And just look at his sweet little nuts, I could eat them, the little cupid!'

Aristonoë had a feeling that Octavia would not have cared for this. And when the wretched little things grew up a bit and became stringy they would be thrown out and get no more cakes. Oh, well, better than being speared by a legionary, she supposed. 'Isn't Olba somewhere in Cilicia?' she asked her cousin.

'I think so,' Hellanike said, taking a sesame-seed and honey cake from the silver salver. 'I heard this queen has been doing a round of the oracles. She went to Delphi last year and didn't get quite the answer she wanted.'

'But who does?' said Aristonoë, remembering some of the uncomplimentary things her tutor had said about oracles. 'They keep people hanging on. The gods speak but it's the priests who make it plain. Or not plain. And a lot of money changes hands during the waiting time. Will this queen go to Siwa?'

'I suppose so,' Hellanike said, 'but there's some story about her. Oh, I don't know! Ask Aunt Hipparchia.'

And so the next day she did. Salampsio had wanted to know about the party and the dresses, including the Prefect's lady's new emeralds which really weren't the thing with her complexion. 'The

Queen of Olba,' said Hipparchia, thinking back. 'Yes, Aba. She is a priest queen, was initiated and so on. But her father took the throne by force. He was not the line and naturally the people of Olba wanted the queen and the right line; they wanted to be sure of the seasons.'

'But isn't that all nonsense, Mother?' asked Salampsio, who had inherited Zenon as her own tutor.

'Nothing that her people think can be nonsense to a Queen,' said Hipparchia. 'So Aba escaped and came here. There was a bad harvest in Olba that year and naturally it was said that this was because she had not been there to go through the rituals. No, Salampsio, I am not saying that this was actually so, but when people believe a thing passionately it arrives at some kind of reality. What I do believe is that all nature is one, and that how people live may affect the plants and animals around them. At any rate, Aba came here and got an audience at the palace. Yes, I remember her, quite young, in a very strange dress and mask or headgear. The Queen saw her and gave her help to turn her father off the throne of Olba. How? With money and soldiers no doubt. These were the means, added of course to her people's wishes. The father was killed and she was reinstalled, a friend to Egypt, if only a small friend.'

'I wonder if we shall meet this queen?' Aristonoë said. 'I'd like to!'

'If the Romans think that there is any reason why she should want to meet any who were—the Queen's friends—they will keep us apart. It would be easy enough. She is bound to be an official guest. Yes, she might leave Alexandria without meeting any Alexandrian—except the tame ones. They may want to impress on her that if great Egypt is now only a corn bin for Rome then little Olba only exists because they allow it.'

'Olba is not a big country?' Aristonoë asked.

'No, but it keeps its own frontiers and its own ways. There are so many small countries in that part around the Black Sea. Corn-growing mostly and with priest kings or queens. Places like Colchis or Paphlagonia or Marob. This Queen of Olba will no doubt wish to visit the tomb as well as to arrange her pilgrimage to Siwa. It would be only right. I wonder if the Romans will try to stop her. Yes, I too would much like to meet her. For many reasons.'

'Mother,' said Salampsio, 'do you believe in oracles?'

'If we have troubles and tell them truthfully to the gods some way out may be shown.'

'That's not answering me, Mother! What I want to know is whether the oracles can really answer questions about the future. Zenon says that isn't possible.'

'Put like that, of course it isn't possible. Stupid people get stupid answers. You would not expect the gods or their servants to use plain kitchen and bathroom words. Or would you?'

'No. I see. But Mother, did the Queen and Marc Antony ever go to Siwa? And did the oracle speak to them?'

'Yes, yes. When they came back together from Tarsus. The Queen told my sister Charmian a little but not all. It is said that the god who once spoke to Alexander had promised to be with Antony for a certain time, coming with voices and music in the air and leaving in the same way. There were some who said that at the end this had happened; nor were they all the uneducated and credulous. For myself, Salampsio, I heard and saw nothing.'

'It doesn't sound—rational.'

'No. But one would not expect that. Rationality is only one way of expressing what happens. It is a way of measurement. But some things are difficult to measure. Perhaps there are no standards. If Queen Aba goes to Siwa she will not expect rationality. But naturally one needs to work with both.'

'Yes,' said Aristonoë, accepting it. But her cousin Salampsio frowned, wanting rationality and the gods, whether Greek or Egyptian, kept in their places.

'By the way,' said Hipparchia with nothing in her voice to show what she was after. 'How is my niece Elpis settling down?'

'Oh,' said Aristonoë. 'I saw her just after the party. They wanted her to give a recitation from Virgil. And I thought it would be sensible; she'd impress them. She said she'd try the seventh *Eclogue* or perhaps the third; she would enjoy doing the different voices and I said, "What about the eighth, with all that lovely witch-craft?" But she wouldn't do it, she said it needed an accompanist and then she got sad thinking about the girl who used to accompany it for her, wondering what had happened to her. And then she said anyhow she didn't think that one was suitable for her in her position and it was only a Roman imitation anyhow, like their dreadful copies of statues. An imitation of our own Theocritus, you know?'

Hipparchia smiled a very little. 'I'm glad at least she takes it that way and does consider her position.'

'She—she's holding herself tight.'

'Very right,' said Hipparchia. 'She will do us credit yet.'

CHAPTER TWENTY-FOUR

Pakap was decorating the forelocks and collars of his mules slowly and carefully as he only did when he was taking pilgrims to the oracle of Siwa. Tahatre came over to the village with a broad basket on her head full of dirty washing. She and her sisters would do it in the canal a little above the mud houses. How proud they had been of the virginity stain on Aristonoë's bed linen after the first night! All the women of the village came to look and admire.

A skein of duck flew overhead. Tahatre stood behind Pakap. He knew she was there but did not turn round. She was his wife; her duty was to wait and be humble. She smiled secretly to herself but wiped it off when he turned a little and allowed himself to notice her.

'You are taking pilgrims to Siwa, my lord husband,' said Tahatre.

'Well perhaps I am,' he said.

'The Queen of Olba,' said Tahatre into the air.

Her husband turned round completely and came over. 'You have a message for them?'

'Send a quick rider back when you are near your last camp. They will come back with him and meet you.'

Pakap put his head down by hers. 'Is it—Queen's business?'

'That I would think,' Tahatre said and quivered as his cheek came brushing down past her ear. Would he turn and nibble it? Yes! It would go as was wanted.

The messenger duly came. They were ready. Polemo was mounted on the chestnut mare which he had managed to keep out of sight when the Roman army was around. Hipparchia and Aristonoë rode white donkeys with comfortable fleece-lined saddles. Salampsio, who had badgered them into letting her come too, had a less elegant grey one. Polemo had insisted on two servants, one of them to hold the bridle of Aristonoë's donkey all the time. Salampsio would be allowed to make her donkey canter—if she could! The guide went with them to the camp. Polemo knew more or less where it was but tracks between and over sand dunes look very much alike.

They started after the heat of the day and Polemo began to worry when night fell suddenly and the sand that had been gold in the late sloping light was quickly greying to black. But over the next ridge there was the twinkle of a fire and then the pale shapes of tents, lamplit within. They rode into the camp under the stars, presented themselves to Queen Aba of Olba. Aristonoë and Salampsio had been making up pictures about her and now had to revise them. Aba did not look very like a queen, but then, thought Aristonoë, harking back, neither had Cleopatra as she remembered her. On the other hand this woman had a most peculiar headdress in which her own hair apparently was taken up into a basket-like structure, a cone of serpents and lions, and over her body a kind of gold-wire cage on which the breasts were clusters of little knives. In the same way, little knives guarded her waist. Her skirt was deeply flounced, and apparently between the flounces—but no, the girls felt they simply mustn't look! This far-off queen lay on heaped cushions in the gently luminous tent, but there was something odd about the scalloped edges of the cushions, clearly her own.

Her face however was calm and her Greek only faintly accented. Her eyes were dark, but made darker and deeper by make-up of lapis. Her eyebrows arched like the entrance of caves. Her hands and wrists looked singularly strong and there was a curved scar on the back of her right hand which must have been made on purpose. She knew that they were coming and who they were, at any rate that they were not on the Roman side. For she was well aware that as an official guest she was only meeting those considered suitable. Even when she went to make her libation at the tomb she was attended by a guard of honour, for her safety it was asserted, legionaries without doubt; they had not cared for the ceremony, had fidgeted with their spear butts when it went on too long. At Alexander's tomb, where she also went, there was less fuss.

Hipparchia presented the simple gifts; a fine linen scarf, a pair of elegant slippers, a perfect honeycomb and a small basket of apples stored all winter, and even now scarcely wrinkled. Olba was in fact an apple-growing country, but as Hipparchia did not know this the apples, difficult to grow in Egypt, were a mark of great respect, and the Queen, quickly realising this, accepted them as such. All was laid carefully on a low table. In return Queen Aba had other gifts ready for her visitors. There was river gold in Olba and she put chains of fine links over the heads of Hipparchia and Polemo.

'So you are the Lady Charmian's sibs,' she said, and looked at them deeply. 'But Iras? Had she none? No, wait, let me think.' She stayed silent for a moment, her eyes shut. Then speaking rather differently: 'There was a brother. I saw him. Now there are black and red fishes all round.' She opened her eyes and stared at Polemo.

He answered: 'The brother was in command of one of the Queen's ships; it was wrecked on the coast of India. Every man on board was lost.'

'So,' said Queen Aba and motioned to the girls: there were brooches of worked gold for them. 'Come beside me, you two,' she said. 'I too have a daughter who one day will do my work. Are you afraid? Surely not?'

Firmly though not very gracefully Salampsio sat down on one of the cushions. Aristonoë more slowly took the other side, aware that the Queen was looking at her swelling belly and faintly uneasy. But Queen Aba responded by unfastening the clusters of knives. An oldish woman behind her reached over and took them into darkness. 'There should be a third,' she said wrinkling her face, puzzled. But had she been told or did she—somehow—know?

'Elpis, the daughter of Charmian,' said Aristonoë. 'But it is sometimes difficult for her to come. We will tell her everything.'

'Look now at the lamp,' said Queen Aba, pointing to a double-wick'd lamp of worked bronze hanging from a hook on the tent pole which reminded them of—what did it remind them of? There seemed to be dust or fluff flying round the slightly quivering wick flames or perhaps even flies, brightly coloured flies, or were they actually butterflies or dragonflies? But right in the desert? No, no, there was no desert, no tent, there was a river, a garden, singing birds in the branches which were coming in to fly around the lamp and beyond the birds were faces, some good, some evil, some with mouthfuls of roses, some biting bones. There was one face above all, seen through or behind the others, with hair drawn back and crowned with the high double crown of upper and lower Egypt.

154

It was Salampsio who stirred uneasily and rubbed her eyes. And there were no faces. Queen Aba turned to her and laughed. 'I—I am sorry . . .' Salampsio said. She was suddenly rather scared.

But the queen who was also a priest—but of what god or goddess?—merely turned to Hipparchia. 'She did a great thing for me, that one,' she said, 'when she was the Great Queen and I was suppliant. I had nothing. I had escaped in a small boat with little but my life. Who would have thought that I was the one the gods had chosen? But she knew. She helped me at first because I was a young woman attacked by a man, my father. She understood that it is not always those of a family who love one another. Yet she saw beyond that; she thought me worthy. Yes, even before she became a god she saw. So with her help I went back and became what I must be for my people of Olba. And so also Olba owes me to her and Egypt. What thanks do we give?'

Cautiously Hipparchia asked: 'You will be here for long, Ma'am?'

Aba said: 'That will depend on what there is for me to do or be. I cannot see it yet and your oracle spoke even less clearly than Apollo at Delphi. My daughter can take my place at the sowing. It comes later with us, barley mostly. Tell me, do they remember Queen Cleopatra in Egypt?'

'Yes, very well,' Hipparchia said. 'But Rome is strong.'

'As men are strong against women. As my father thought he was strong. Could Egypt throw them off? Would the people of Egypt want to?'

'Not without leadership.'

'Perhaps not even with leadership,' Polemo said shaking his head. 'Too many have become involved with Rome. Some who are not rich have seen their chance. Others have become richer. Many do not care either way.'

'But some do care. They pray to the Queen, who is also Isis.' Hipparchia spoke with deep passion, almost glaring at her brother. 'Myself, I do not think she is Isis, but when I remember her I get strength!'

'Praying and fighting, they're two different things,' Polemo said.

'I think so too,' said Aristonoë, suddenly remembering the little temple in Rome; 'the people who pray are mostly the weak ones.'

'But if a leader came?' Queen Aba asked, leaning forward, and the gold beasts on her headdress glistened and bobbed in the lamp-light.

'Why—why?' whispered Hipparchia. 'What do you know?'

'I know that her children are coming to Egypt,' the Queen answered.

Hipparchia and Polemo looked at one another. Salampsio was the one who asked: 'How do you know? By magic?'

But the Queen shook her head: 'Not by magic. No. There was no need. The Romans have been told.'

'But—but Selene would have written!' Aristonoë said. 'Written to me! She promised!' Suddenly she felt hurt in her heart; was this all it had meant? After all, Selene had not cared.

'And if she had written would you have got the letter? It would come in one of their ships,' the Queen said.

'Oh I see! If only she was careful what she said!' Aristonoë felt at once relieved and anxious.

'She will have been careful. She has been in a hard school. He too. They will bring the little brother.'

So it had come. Hipparchia said: 'This may be the time, Ma'am, when we may ask Olba to repay the debt.'

'But you do not know yet.' The Queen looked back at her steadily. 'You will get word to me. I shall be there. At least there are ways open for one who can hide. Like a serpent in a basket of figs.' Hipparchia's shoulders jerked, her head pulled back. Polemo gripped his daughter's hand. This woman knew.

It was Salampsio, always wanting to make sure, who said flatly: 'I don't understand. Are you talking about the Queen?'

'Yes,' said the Queen of Olba, 'but you must try to get under-standing.'

'How?'

CHAPTER TWENTY-FIVE : B.C. 30

They were in the upper chamber of the royal tomb. There was
still some treasure in the lower part though most had been seized
and taken away. But Octavian's legions guarded it. There was no
likelihood—no chance—of any rescue attempt now. The Queen
said: 'I think it will soon be time to die. I have done all I could,
even to speaking with Octavian. Even to making a pretence with
him. For the children's sake. For Egypt's sake. I can do no more.
You know that.'

'We know that,' said Charmian. 'We know also that we are not
going to be dragged in any Roman Triumph. Turn your face this
way, darling.' She dabbed the lotion she had made up on to the
deep scratches on the Queen's face, which her own nails had
made, digging in after she had looked up, knowing at last that the
heavy head on her breast was finally dead, that Antony had gone
to his gods, having died in her arms as he would have wanted. Marc
Antony who had given her complete loyalty and love, who had
tried to follow the flights of her imagination, who had lived as
long as he thought he might help her and finally knew she was
beyond his help.

'So long as we go together,' Iras said, a little shakily.

'That is arranged,' the Queen said. 'You two shall have worship.
Through you will come help and healing. You will never die so
long as women suffer.'

'And that will be always,' Iras answered, going over to the
window, the small window through which they had hauled the
wounded Antony, heavy, oh so heavy, unable to help himself,
staring up from eyes already strange.

'Not always,' the Queen said. 'We shall intercede. That is only
one step away now. One little step.' She moved her head im-

patiently as the lotion stung a little. 'It does not matter, Charmian,' she said; 'let me come to him with the scars. They are battle scars; he will understand, seeing them, that I was faithful to him once we married, as Macedonian queens have been before me. Yes, he will understand without words for I do not think there will be words where we are going. I whispered this as he died but perhaps already he could not hear my earthly voice. It will be otherwise soon. He was always afraid that I did not love him. Till the end. But how could we know till then? I thought for Egypt.'

'And the world,' said Charmian, softly, 'the world of hope which now we shall not see.'

'The Golden Age that never came. That was to come for our children. But I think, yes, I think this way I shall have saved my children. And yours, Charmian.'

'My poor little Elpis. My poor wounded man.'

'You cannot help Eumenes now, my darling.'

'No, no. He knows that my honour tells me to be with you now. And his own honour. Hipparchia will take care of him. I saw Hipparchia. Before—before we knew for certain. She will tell Polemo's daughter.'

'Aristonoë. Why?'

'She is, I think, braver than Elpis. And Elpis may be with the Princess. Wherever they are. And Salampsio is too young. Yes, Hipparchia will tell Aristonoë when the time is ripe and we shall be there, in her, in the future.'

Hearing the names she knew so well, Charmian looked for the people they stood for, but the people were already shadowy and far.

'The future,' said the Queen, 'the dark future. And we are so near to it, rushing out of the present into the state and knowledge of being Isis. Of pure godhead. You with me. Oh Charmian, oh my dear kind Iras, I can hardly wait!'

Iras was at the window again. She noticed a stain of blood on the sill, but it was too late to do anything about it. Much, much too late. The sound of the sea, the lapping, continuous long ripple came faintly. She said, 'The Roman soldiers are still marching up and down.' She drew back sharply. 'One of them looked up,' she said, spitting in disgust.

'And beyond?' the Queen asked.

'There are people standing. Some of them I think are praying.'

'Already!' said the Queen. 'That is good. They will pray more later. We three women. Men and women will pray to us. We three Macedonians. We children of Philip and Alexander. Egypt will pray to us.'

'But how shall we hear when our ears are stopped with dust? How can it be?' For a moment Charmian felt herself near despair, near a darkness she could not, dared not look into.

'Have I ever lied to you, Charmian, my mate? To others, yes, and often and gladly. I do not lie to you over this but I cannot tell you how, although I think I know the messenger. The priests have spoken to me but they have tangled their own words till they mean nothing. If I knew for certain how, I would find death less interesting. One does not want to go a known way. Ah Charmian, I feel like a young girl again, a virgin, afraid and not afraid! Look out again, Iras. What can you see?'

Iras went to the window again; more faintly even than the sea sound, she heard the low singing from the small temple of Isis, one phrase repeated over and over, calling them. The Queen had spoken of the knowledge of Isis, the pure godhead. For them all. Was this what the calling was? Half turning she said: 'There are more people beyond the soldiers. Some of them look like country people. There are a few of them giving presents to the soldiers. Yes, and they have let one of them through.'

'Iras! Tell me, what is he carrying?'

'Why? I can't see yet. Oh yes, he has a basket. One of those rush baskets that country boys carry fruit in. I believe he is coming to us. Yes, it looks like figs, beautiful ripe figs.'

'Beautiful ripe figs splitting woman-fashion to the desiring tongue, the oozing sweet drops. Beautiful figs!' The Queen was breathing fast, watching the door.

Charmian looked at her deeply. 'What is it, my Queen, my Queen? Are you showing us some way? Are you taking our hands in yours?'

'Unbar the door, let him in,' said Cleopatra, 'and dress me in my royal robes.'

CHAPTER TWENTY-SIX : B.C. 25

The endless waves that had been blue through green or green through blue had now darkened to purple, but the occasional tossed crest still glittered gold. 'Wine dark,' said Prince Juba, savouring it, taking a quotation from Homer on to his tongue. Selene was thinking of something that the elder Antonia had said to her before they left Rome: 'Aren't you bored with all those silly quotations of his?' She had not answered then. What was the use with the Antonias? It just bounced off them. But how could one be bored, hearing it in his voice? It was as though he had dug an old quotation up from the dark mine of the classics and thrown a golden light on to it. As the evening closed in she moved nearer to him, feeling him all down her side. His hand running gently up her arm from waist to shoulder sent her deliciously spinning. Her nearer breast seemed to be turning tautly towards the hand.

The Romans had spoken of her mother as a witch who stole men and whose inner heat melted them into her playthings. Even Octavia had spoken like that. Could it be so? Could one want to change a man, to take him out of his own perfection? Surely it would be better to change oneself, to become wiser, nobler, more worthy, to let him, her Juba, be the one to melt her with the heat and fire of his hammer blows on her core. Juba, who opened her into a shedding rose. No, not to think of it too much till it was happening, till it was on her again, and the night boat rocking through the water, no longer wine dark but lucent black like his eyes drowning her.

Ptolemy Philadelphos was watching the water at the other side; sometimes you could see the fishes dart away, a streak of underwater fire. Selene had said that perhaps he could go out with the fishermen of Alexandria, watch them throw the clever weighted nets. She had watched this sometimes from the palace balconies, she and Alexander. But he himself would be close, observing and noting, he would be able to see and touch all the slimy brilliant fish and the half fishes, the creatures of the depths and crannies. And he would go to the marshes and shoot fat ducks. He was not very good yet with a bow and arrow, but here it might be different. And there would be all the animals Juba had told him about, elephants and river horses and great running birds. But would he find these beasts near Alexandria? Wild? He wasn't sure. Alexandria. And of course there would be the library, so much bigger than anything in Rome. The actual manuscripts of Euclid. There would be the Pharos, the dream of the mathematicians come real in marble and bronze. And the mirror at the top. Some people said it was magic, but he himself thought it must be science. Alexander his brother had thought that.

He turned and saw his sister and her husband fused into one stillness, his cloak round her. Well, that seemed to be what they liked. But it worried him a little that they seemed to trust each other so much. One should have secrets surely? Did she speak to this dark husband about—Alexandria and all that? There were things he would always keep to himself. He shook his head. No, it was getting cold; he was going down to his own cabin.

One of the greyhounds came up to the still figure in the wrapped cloak and sniffed at it. Juba burst out and cursed the dog till it cowered away. Selene giggled. 'So you still keep your Latin!'

'For dogs,' he said fiercely, then laughed. 'When I was a dog they spoke to me in Latin, before you made me a man.'

'Octavia was kind to me in Latin—mostly.'

Juba ran his hand along the dank gunwale. 'All over the world,' he said, 'people are hating Latin. They have had to learn to answer, to run, perhaps to speak. But—it grates on the tongue. These are ugly heavy sounds.' But was that right, Selene thought, going back to the songs and dances she had learned with Marcella and the two Antonias. Well, if he said so. He went on: 'In the Triumph were men from all over who hated Latin and were killed in Latin. At the end. Hearing it in their ears while they were being strangled. Kings of the Gauls who had rebelled. Germans. Parthians. Spaniards.' He was breathing hard now. Selene turned towards him, pulled his head down, the tight crisp curls, the soft nose snuggling into her neck. Let him not remember! There was the water all round. The

161

light slap of the waves on the counter of the boat and the lightness in the sky to the East ahead of them, the rising of her own goddess. 'Selene, my moon baby,' said Juba, his mind shifting again. 'What will they say to us in your Alexandria? Have you thought about it? No, attend, stop kissing; if you don't, I ... I ... I don't know what I shall do!'

'Do it, do it!' said Selene, 'afterwards—I will think about Alexandria.'

So afterwards, lying on the spread cloak, the risen moon creeping over them, bars of black shadow from the rigging moving a little with the boat, they spoke of Alexandria, and what might happen. If the people knew they were coming, the daughter and son of the Queen—'Then what?' said Juba. 'We shall all three be in the hands of the Roman garrison. Guests. Prisoners.'

'They will see us at the tomb.' She thought briefly of her dead mother. Would it matter being dead if once one had been happy all through? Fulfilled. Had Antony done this for her mother? Oh she hoped so. 'It would be possible to find some way—'

'Wait,' said Juba. 'I have been thinking about this. Almost ever since you spoke of it first. That day. I know that you have seen yourself as Queen, not of my Numidia but of your Egypt. Am I right?'

Tears prickled. 'Yes, perhaps,' she said; 'but with you, always with you!'

'I am Numidia. Listen. If they suspect that you and your brother have any thoughts of—of Egypt rising, two things will happen. They will kill Philo. And they will take away my kingdom.'

'Oh no!'

'But they will. We must face it. They must never suspect that I am not wholly with them. If they suspect, all is over for Numidia and also for me. No, be quiet, love, and listen. If they do not suspect, you shall build another Alexandria for my people, who will be yours.' She was silent for a while; accepting this as already she had accepted all from him, taking him as the father and guide she could barely remember, Antony who had loved her mother: and also loved Octavia. What was he giving her? Another Alexandria? Would it be possible? He seemed to sense this, for he said: 'We have marble. We have gold and ivory.' He pulled the cloak away to look at her bare young breast in the moonlight. 'Ivory. Like that. But I am afraid we too will have a Roman garrison.'

'It will be the only place where you will have to hear Latin. Juba my husband, I shall be speaking to our people in our own language.' She murmured something and he laughed.

'You must learn the plurals!' he said. 'And the formal greetings. You must learn to dream in it.'

'I will,' she said, 'oh I will!'

CHAPTER TWENTY-SEVEN

In practice Hellanike's mother did most of the running of the estate. Her son-in-law had of course installed a Roman bailiff to give orders to the natives, but this had not been altogether a success. The man didn't seem to be able to understand that certain crops which everyone grew on their estates or in their gardens in Italy just wouldn't grow in the Nile Delta, whatever threats or inducements he used. And he had taken against the alternatives; one must have decent olive oil, not this sesame-seed muck. But the olives obstinately died, even when thoroughly mulched with human manure from the slave stables. Still, the estate was at least in one sense safe. It did not suffer from the special levies and encroachments which went on elsewhere. And Hellanike herself was safe—as safe as a woman can ever be. Several of her set had married into the occupying staff. No doubt the time might come when their husbands would be shifted, possibly to another province, or perhaps back to Rome. But you cannot shift an estate. Nor was sale a straightforward matter, as the Alexandrian lawyers were seeing to it that this should not be so. Probably Hellanike and her friends were doing rather better for their families than, say, Polemo's daughter.

Hellanike meanwhile was picking up whatever information her husband let fall. Lucius Mindius was pleased that she was pregnant. 'See you make it a boy,' he said. 'I want a little soldier!' And he insisted that she should go to certain temples and not to others and fussed about what she ate and drank. Secretly she thought this was all rather silly, but if he liked ordering her about over this he would do it less over other things. And he had given her a pair of handsome bracelets. Besides, he was good in bed, no question of it. She had let drop a few discreet statistics to some of her friends and they were agreeably envious. But all these queens and princesses? It looked like being quite a summer.

The Prefect was pleased in a way. It all went to show the importance of Alexandria. Well, he knew that already, and at least they had taken over most of the old palace, so that there need be no question of the various parties meeting unofficially. Arrangements for surveillance were not too difficult. Fortunately the original building had been designed partly with that in mind. Also, they had conveniently been able to take over some of the earlier staff, who had been well trained in this particular skill. The Queen of Olba and her suite had one of the smaller palace buildings; she had come for the oracle and of course this was most respectable and he did not think any very special precautions were needed, though it was always usual to have a guard for anyone wishing to visit the royal tomb. With all this Alexandrian mob that had nothing better to do than hang about looking for trouble, it was better to be safe than sorry.

But the message which had come North by way of Meroë and upper Egypt about a visit from the Queen of Punt? Doubtless the main motive was trade. It was understood that this queen would not take the lengthy river route, but would travel from her own land to the coast and then up. The Prefect was somewhat uncertain as to where exactly Punt was. He ordered a memorandum to be made and submitted about the coastal trade. Doubtless she would bring rather special gifts. He had a menagerie and would like to add to it and to send something suitable to Rome. The Queen would have rather a large entourage, he gathered. What was she like anyhow? Un-Roman, no doubt. So long as there were some decent interpreters. And where had they better go? Perhaps a wing of the main palace? Those extraordinary Moesians who had turned up alleging they were chiefs could be moved, in fact must be moved, however much they protested Moesia's loyalty to Rome.

But of course the Prince of Numidia would be the main guest and the main worry, considering who his wife was. There would be those who would try and make capital out of the visit. The girl had of course been brought up by Octavia; she should have the right principles. The boy too; he was said to be a scholar, not interested in sport or natural pleasures, but then many of the Ptolemies had been a little queer. All the same, one never knew with foreigners. A crafty lot without the benefit of Roman virtue. He would have to watch.

Meanwhile the ladies of the establishment were looking over a new consignment of interesting goods from Rome. Hellanike did not think there was anything so very attractive. The woollens were good, but winter was over. If she was to have imported muslin she would rather have some of those fascinating Indian ones with gold thread woven through them. Or of course, if she could talk him into buying her a piece of silk ... but that cost the earth, coming from even further than India. Well, if he did make a success of his career—! The jewellery was dreadfully inelegant. But they did have a lead in wigs—no doubt they cropped those German slave girls—and also in certain kinds of cosmetics; and as for the packaging! Well, you wouldn't have the face to buy some of them. It might be different in Rome, but here one was expected to have some sense of delicacy.

Finally she decided to buy some woollen material to make up for her husband; he had this extraordinary idea that one should always wear wool next to the skin because it brought out a healthy sweat. The main thing of course was to help Madam Prefect to choose her new necklace, holding the amethysts up against her scraggy old neck, exclaiming about them. Oh well, if she wasn't entitled to all the flattery she could get, who was? It was said that both her brothers had disappeared during the proscriptions. Her father, perhaps fortunately, was already dead and respectably interred.

Hellanike described it all to her cousin Aristonoë. Somehow she got on better with Aristonoë than she used to do. Could it be because Aristonoë had been to Rome? Or that she herself wasn't quite so sure that she'd done the right thing. Oh but she had! There was no future in marrying another Alexandrian. Conon was never going to get to the top or anywhere near it, whereas her own Lucius Mindius—well, these days you didn't have to belong to one of those stupid old Roman families. The Princeps had put an end to that. So he might rise, with the help of a clever wife, to almost any height. Of course they'd be going to Rome, but not to the dull Alexandrian quarter where Aristonoë had stayed. No, they would be in high society. So long as she was sure to get her figure back after the baby. But she would. Lucius would insist on a wet nurse so as not to spoil his very special delights. Anyhow, for the moment she and Aristonoë could laugh about Madam Prefect and her neck-lace.

'Tell me,' said Aristonoë, 'will there be a reception for Numidia?'

'I suppose so,' said Hellanike; 'but we shall have to be specially careful. Not so much him as—well, you know.'

'We both know, don't we?' said Aristonoë, looking at her in rather too cousinly a way.

Hellanike fidgeted, feeling her Roman baby, her little legionary, kicking at her masterfully. She was three months ahead of Aristonoë. 'They can't possibly think there's anything—for them—here,' she said. And then, 'After all, Numidia itself is equally—'

'Awkward,' said Aristonoë.

'Part of the Empire,' Hellanike amended. 'Have some nuts. They're delicious, from Gaul, they say. They have some clever way of doing them up.'

'Advantages of an Empire,' said Aristonoë. But had she meant it nastily! Well, anyway she was eating the nuts! After a little she said, 'No doubt poor Selene will want to visit the tomb.'

'Of course. That will be arranged immediately. Nobody—nobody wants to hurt her—it's only that it's to be hoped that nobody else will be stupid enough to think that—well, that Egypt could possibly rebel.'

Aristonoë didn't answer. It was possible even that Lucius Mindius had told his wife to keep an eye on her cousin. And quite possibly it was correct to suppose that such thoughts were stupid, without foundation. Wasn't that what she had herself said to Aunt Hipparchia? It was only that it was—unacceptable—from Hellanike.

CHAPTER TWENTY-EIGHT

'Mother,' said Selene very quietly. 'Mother?' This had been the room. Yes. But the bed was—where? She ran her hand along the walls. It was dusty between the lotus petals of the deep plaster-work. Not very dusty. Someone must come in and clean, no doubt. But there was no smell of roses or incense. The big mirror had been there—or there? And that was the door that used to clang back when he came in, with his scarlet cloak and helmet under his arm. But now Selene had a father again. Only, not a mother.

She had held herself back at landing; she had only murmured and bowed gentle acknowledgement to the Roman greeting; she had kept her eyes away from the trumpets and legionaries. Were there people behind them in some places, crowded, peering be-tween the spears, whispering? Perhaps, but she must not look. Not yet. But Philo looked and tugged at her once or twice; she had turned and frowned. Later the questions came pouring out: he wanted to make sure. Is this really the palace? *Our* palace? 'Theirs,' Juba had said; 'remember.' It was *they* who had the main rooms of course, the Hall of Justice, the Council Chamber, the broad steps and the lotus-pillared outer hall. They had the rooms with bal-conies towards the harbour or the street, as well as the dining apartments and kitchens. But the palace was huge, a little town within a great one. Guests could be fitted in and kept apart. The royal Numidian party, as they were called, had the rooms which looked into a pleasant little garden court, but Selene did not remember it at all from the old days. In these rooms one was not even aware of the night glow from the Pharos which she now remembered from her childhood. The first day there had been a reception. 'Was there anybody you might have seen before?' Juba asked afterwards.

She shook her head, 'Not yet. They were almost all Romans—or at least provincials. And with you?'

'It was Latin all the time. The humble Latin of the conquered.' His nostrils flared and his teeth showed a little. They had worn Roman dress; it was expected of them. Selene had worn her Roman emeralds, although she had brought her mother's jewels with her; Octavia had wept a little, nervously giving them to her before she left, but this once Octavia had not consulted her brother. Dear kind Octavia who had herself been so pushed and harried and who hoped Selene would be happy and virtuous, always within the divine power and glory of Rome. But these Egyptian jewels stayed in a locked chest for now. Selene put her arms round her husband's neck; whichever of them felt most angry must always be comforted by the other. In a while, half comforted, he set her astride his knees like a father with a little girl, but also ... also ...

The next day they explored cautiously, turning back before they were turned back. On the main paved roads through the palace grounds there were Roman soldiers only too delighted to lay hands on any female, but deterred by the knowledge that these happened to be distinguished guests. It was possible to observe that there were other guests in other suites of rooms with their own bit of garden. Selene half remembered it all. There, for instance was a small palace where her big brother Caesarion had lived and met his friends; there had been rather a lot of boys and girls from the town, music and laughter and sometimes screams. And then there had been a cage of monkeys down there by the fountain and two tame gazelles. But not now. At one or two points they found the guards were Egyptian auxiliaries. The captain of one of these, saluting, asked Juba to wait, but said that he would take it upon himself to allow the Princess through if there was anything she wished to see. This part of the palace was empty; the doors were barred between it and the main reception rooms.

It was so quiet. What was she then, the Queen who had died in her royal robes, taking with her the two ladies, all to become immortal? Was she here? If so, why did she not speak to her lost daughter? Selene leaned hard against a wall as if she could force out an answer; she knocked on the plaster with her open palm, but the sound came empty and frightening. Was there nothing left? Nothing?

Then there was a movement. Someone coming towards her, wear-

ing a strange striped dress, cut close to the body, edged and belted
with peculiar gold, and a tall headdress. 'I am Queen Aba of Olba,'
the woman said in Greek; 'your mother helped me. Perhaps I can
help you.'

'But how did you get through?' Selene asked, taking hesitating
steps towards her. The woman only smiled. 'Who are you—truly?'

'The Romans think my country Olba is too small to be worth
breaking. We pay taxes. But our own gods remain. I am the priestess. I came to visit the gods of Egypt.'

'My mother...' said Selene, and could not go on.

'The serpent destroyed her mortal body. But we are more than
our bodies. She died for others and to defeat her conquerors.'

'But did she defeat them?' Selene asked. 'In Rome they say—
about her—and I was taught ...' Again she could not speak, only
her eyes implored this strange queen.

'Do not be anxious. Conquerors try to do that; they try to stamp
on men's souls, destroying their honour. It does not hurt the gods.
Cleopatra-Isis is not stamped upon, she remains and will remain
under other names. Some day perhaps the conquerors will feel
shame.'

'A Roman never feels shame. Except for something he might do
against Rome. Never for something against others; they don't count.
Even Athens. Even Alexandria.' Selene turned her head away, half
crying in the sad, empty room and suddenly wondered if this
queen was a spy sent against her.

But the Queen was besider her, holding her hand. Would a spy
do that? Perhaps not. 'It will not always be Rome,' she said. 'And
your Mother is at peace in the place of the Gods. But take care,
you are watched. Be yourself a serpent, protector of Egypt. We
shall meet.' And then, as Selene blinked away her tears, the Queen
of Olba was gone—through one of these heavy doors that she had
thought locked and barred? Or how? Yet somehow she felt stronger. A thing had been said. A designation had been made. A faint
scent had been left in the air of bruised leaves from rocky slopes
perhaps, masking the smell of emptiness; she turned and went
back almost gaily to Juba who was waiting for her.

She had asked to visit the ancient tomb of Alexander and the
tomb of her parents and had been told it would be arranged. In
fact, the visit to the tomb of Alexander had been organised almost
immediately. It moved Juba greatly, this battle-carved marble, but

not the other two. Meanwhile, Madame Prefect had prepared an entertainment for Princess Selene, a poetry recital by a gifted performer. 'Latin,' said Juba with a half grin. He himself had behaved with due deference to the Prefect and the military establishment and had mentioned—even with something that seemed like real affection—the young Marcellus who was climbing so rapidly up the careers ladder. Almost too rapidly for old-fashioned people, who did not care for hot young consuls. But Marcellus was to be the heir, the precious vessel to which would be entrusted the power of Rome. 'But we hear rumours of sickness,' the Prefect had said with a little anxiety.

'Only a mild fever, and naturally he has the best doctors in the world.'

'The Princeps will hope for a grandson,' Lucius Mindius had said. But Juba was non-committal, thinking that it might take more than Marcellus to bring life into the harsh womb of Octavian's daughter.

After a little hesitation, Selene had decided to wear a somewhat Greek-style tunic for the recital and, with it, some of her mother's shoulder and hair jewels. Not the very best, not the royal ones. She would keep those for Numidia. But the dress was right for an artistic occasion and went with the white-flowered wreath she was given. She was placed on a cushioned seat among Madam Prefect's ladies. The Queen of Olba, she noticed, was on the far side of Madam Prefect. For a moment they caught each other's glance, then both quickly looked away. Sweets were passed round : honey-soaked almond paste had been made up into little coloured shapes, some of which Selene found a tiny bit shocking.

There was a slight introduction : competent harp music by two slave girls, probably Egyptian, kneeling beside their instruments. Then the curtains parted and a girl classically dressed and wearing a wreath of green leaves stepped in and made a gracious reverence to the audience, then tapped her foot to the harpists to break off. What was she going to recite?

A poem by Horace, the nice friendly poet who used to come sometimes to Octavia's house. In those days, Selene thought, I had stopped hating Rome and had not learned to hate again. We danced and played games and our daily task of spinning and weaving was not too hard. Marcella—would she ever see Marcella again? But perhaps it was wrong even to think kindly of any Roman. Juba

171

thought so, deep inside himself, deep where only she had been allowed to look. Friendship with Romans was only in the outside skin.

The girl now gave them something rather uninteresting by Gallus, a poet she had heard of but never seen, one of Pollio's clients. Pollio? Yes, hadn't she heard he was dead? But it was just before they started and she was so busy and happy she hadn't really noticed. The girl went on to one of the *Eclogues*. Yes, Selene remembered, she'd had to learn some of this by heart herself. But who—who was the girl? It was beginning to worry her, she should know. And now it seemed as though this same girl was looking at her as if— Suddenly she knew it was Elpis and took a quick breath and held to the edge of her chair, not listening any longer to the Latin, but thinking, thinking, with painful, disturbing stabs of memory.

'Perhaps,' she said to the lady next to her when the *Eclogue* was finished, 'I might meet the performer?'

The lady crunched up her mouthful of nuts, then leant across and tapped the knee of another, who was sitting back under the weight of her pregnancy. 'Hellanike, the Princess wants to meet that girl. Cousin of yours, isn't she? Fetch her in.'

'Perhaps it would disturb everyone less if I left you for a moment?' Selene said.

'Just as you like, Princess,' said the other, carelessly. There was going to be a juggler now. One of the slave girls was coming round with fresh garlands; threaded rose petals don't last long and have no value. Selene lifted the curtain and slipped out into the next room with Hellanike.

'Elpis,' said Selene. 'It *is* Elpis? You're different somehow. Where have you been?'

'In Rome,' said Elpis, 'like you, Princess Selene.'

'But how? Why did I not know?'

Elpis shrugged her shoulders a little, looked at Hellanike. 'It was not allowed,' she said.

'But now? It *is* allowed? You can visit me? Oh please!'

Hellanike said, hurriedly and worried: 'We must ask! But I'm sure— You are enjoying your stay, Princess?'

'Of course, of course! But would you ask also if I could see Aristonoë, the daughter of Polemo?'

Yes, said Hellanike, to be sure she would ask, but they should go

172

back to the other room now. People might wonder. No, of course you are perfectly free, Princess, but you are a valuable person, you must be guarded. No, not against anything one could name, but there were undesirable influences. From the bad old days. It would be dreadful if they were to try and use our guests in their own interests which were not those of Rome. Selene stood very quietly, in her young dignity, her eyes wide, and all the time she was speaking Hellanike kept between her and Elpis, as though she were afraid that some touch—some message—what? But nobody suspected Elpis, Hellanike said to herself, she must not exaggerate. It was only that her husband had told her to watch, given her a good pinch to remind her. Because if there was anything and it came into the open through him, well, that might be the making of his career.

But Selene and Elpis stood looking at one another across her. At first there was nothing and then Selene began to cry a little and tremble a little. 'After the Triumph,' she said, 'Octavia took me away and *he* was lying on the floor and you—you were gone— and since then—nothing. Why did you never—never tell me? You could have been dead.'

'Yes,' said Elpis, 'I could have been dead.' But she stayed dry-eyed.

CHAPTER TWENTY-NINE

The library of Alexandria had remained much as it was. Even during the fighting and other troubles, those who were continuing their researches firmly did continue them, which would have been the more laudable had the researches been something other than, for example, counting the Ands and Buts in a pseudo-Homeric fragment. From the alcoves of the library came a bee-like murmur of people reading aloud to themselves. Now and then one or two conferred. Voices might rise, perhaps to an epigram nicely sharpened. Juba found himself in the centre of an admiring concourse. They had copies of some of his historical and literary observations; well, if that was what they liked he could play their game. They were pleased, patronising—for he was neither Roman nor Greek— but envious, because he was a prince. It did not seem to be leading anywhere. He wondered when he and Selene would visit the tomb and whether, when they did, anything would happen. Why should it? What kind of thing? But it might.

It had been arranged that they should visit the Pharos next day. Philo was deeply excited. He had read all he could about it. But also he wanted to go out with the fishing boats. He had watched them in the harbour at Ostia while they were waiting to sail, and again when they were making for Alexandria. Whenever they came within sight of land the coastal sea was being flogged for food with the clever nets. Meanwhile, he had come to the library with Juba but had found his way towards the rolls of mathematics and optics, so many ingenious ideas, but who was making use of them? Perhaps it was right that ideas were important but use something slavish? The Roman army engineers didn't think so, nor yet the builders of the Pharos. Anyhow, what fun!

But out of a corner of his eye he had seen someone speaking to

Juba, cutting him out of a gossiping crowd as a hound cuts out the one deer from a running herd, or the one ox from a field of grazers. This man spoke quickly to Juba, who looked uneasy, and then someone else had come across deliberately, or so it looked to Philo, breaking the conversation up. 'Who was he?' he asked, when they were alone, walking back.

'He said his name was Polemo and he was brother to Charmian, the Queen's lady,' Juba said quietly. 'He said the people were sad not to have seen us yet. He said that we mattered to them.'

'You and Selene?'

'And you. But I do not think we should listen. I believe the people of Alexandria are still hoping, in fact I'm sure of it. That is useless. And could destroy us. Very easily.'

'Us? I suppose you mean Numidia. We Ptolemies are destroyed already. Aren't we?'

'You are growing up, Philo, but no need to grow up into destruction. If our souls are untouched, nothing else counts. We have the victory over any oppressor.'

'I've heard that before,' said Philo; 'the Greeks have had to say it, haven't they? They've got to be able to think that there's still something. Even now. Me, I think it's a slave's idea. Did this Polemo say anything else?'

'I think he would have, but somebody came up to us. On purpose I suppose. When that happened and the chatter began he took leave. I couldn't help asking myself if—there was anything planned.' His voice had dropped to a whisper.

'Well,' said Philo, 'I hope we get to the Pharos first, anyway.'

Horses and mules were brought round for the palace party. There were guides, one of whom was a mathematician from the library, but also a guard of armed, stocky legionaries. Selene tried not to notice them. They did not take the great middle road between the Sun and Moon gates of Alexandria, the wide, paved and colonnaded way always crowded with people. Instead, their guides took them by the narrow road along the edge of the harbour under the palace wall and so on to the causeway. Riders with whips went ahead to clear the way; again, Selene did not want to look. Down in the harbour, there were the Roman corn ships eating away Egypt's prosperity. Warships too, big and shining and dangerous. But Philo reined in his mule twice to watch the almost naked fishermen twirling their nets out in a circle, then tightening the cord at the bottom and hauling in. And then the exciting glitter of the tumbling fish!

The lighthouse road across the island was full of donkeys, going slowly with loads of wood weighting them down, wood which had already travelled by boat or pack-beast before it got to Alexandria. Then the same donkeys trotted easily back, unloaded. All that wood was for the great bonfire on the top storey of the Pharos. Wherever there were people standing, the guides hurried them on, but here and there they were recognised. In one of the fishing villages a small crowd of ragged-looking people, men and women, had got together on a rocky outcrop above the road and were shouting. It was not in Greek, still less in Latin, but Selene recognised some of it and drew herself together to show nothing. For they were shouting: 'The Queen! The Queen!' 'Queen's daughter!' 'To us!' and, more dangerously: 'Foreigners, get out!' Then, at a sharp order, the guards went for them at the double. Juba laid a hand tight over Selene's on the bridle rein. She turned to the chief guide and said, 'What was it? I do not understand.'

He said, 'They were shouting rude things. We cannot have our guests insulted.'

'It does not matter, not at all!' said Selene, but watched to see what the soldiers were doing. The men had all got away, except for one old one who was dragged along screeching and a couple of women. 'Oh no!' Selene cried. 'Let them go! It was only a rudeness, I forgive them. No, let them go or I shall scream, I cannot bear to see people beaten!' Reluctantly, they were let go and hurried off with nothing but a few kicks. Selene hoped she had established that she knew no Egyptian and hoped that this would be reported. If only she could have given them some sign! She looked back. The guards would take it for curiosity; she hoped the village would take it for something else.

And yet—it was all so useless. As Juba had told her. Now she was half wishing she had not come to her mother's Egypt. It was being pain. But the lighthouse was close ahead, the walls of the courtyard and then the square tower of the main building, so much higher than any temple. Yet Poseidon crowned it in immense bronze, the god with power over all seas, worshipped by all sailors under many names.

The square block in the middle of the courtyard had stores and offices and, in the middle, a gateway into which the laden donkeys were driven. Here there were pulleys and clanking chains and devices with counter-weights. The chief engineer came out to welcome them and explain and answer dozens of questions, mostly from Philo. Then they set off up the stairs and so out on to the first of the balconies, with an octagonal further storey and a great bronze-lettered inscription. More steps, more questions, another balcony and a gradually increasing view, far out over Alexandria, over Lake Mareotis, a pale glitter, and the long, snake-winding arms of the Nile. The green, green fields made a chequerboard between the small writing of the canals, wheat, barley, flax, luscious fodder crops, sesame, plantations of date palms or vineyards, sometimes brown fields waiting for the rotation, but mostly just now in strong growth. Philo, standing close to his sister, whispered: 'That ought to be ours. And I'd be your husband!' Selene blushed and pushed him away. 'I'd let you have him as your lover,' her brother said, and giggled.

But she couldn't any longer just think of it as play. Her brother was no child any longer; he was beginning to be a man. And because of that in danger. She thought back so strongly to Sun, her twin, that her throat seemed to narrow and tears came into her eyes. It was not to happen again! But what could she do? Guides and guards all round; Juba and the mathematician arguing amiably.

And above them, one more climb, and at last the chamber of the mirrors. Here the ashes had been swept out and the hollow for the fire prepared. While the head engineer explained everything, two of the lighthouse slaves were laying the sticks in an exact pattern. They were speaking in Greek. The engineer, who knew he was indispensable, couldn't be bothered with Latin, and when he got a question from the officer in charge of the guard who had come up with them he firmly refused to understand. He demonstrated the mirrors, showing how they were continually shifted during the dark hours to reflect the light from the blazing fire in as wide an arc as possible.

Here was the oil for the fire. Here was a special polish for the silver sheets. And here—the head engineer carefully brought a bronze tube set on to a tripod so that it could be moved—is a lens which gathers in the light rays and spreads them again, and its nature is that it can show a thing far off as though it were near. He pointed it at a boat some way out and all in turn peered and exclaimed. In the middle there was a picture of the boat as though

177

it were close in. But the edges of the picture blurred and twisted. Juba and the mathematician began to argue with the head engineer; Philo joined in. Selene stood looking out, wondering if her mother used to come here, or if perhaps Queen Cleopatra had thought about it as something secure and scientifically certain, which she need not be anxious about. And so the lighthouse went on, warning and guiding ships, even if these ships' cargoes went to the profit and glory of Rome instead of Egypt.

They went back and the fishing villages were silent. Only as they turned down towards the causeway a hard flung stone took off the helmet of one of the guards. Just one stone and in the bustle and drawing of swords impossible to tell where it had come from. A boy chucking stones about? Probably not. The officer shouted threats at nothing. A few women with baskets or pots on their heads stared and moved on. But perhaps they knew.

The next day Elpis came to see Selene, her Princess, her charge. She remembered the palace well but as if from an altogether other life. It was better to divide one's life sharply. When she had agreed to the marriage which the family arranged for her she separated this clearly from any thought of the poets far back in Rome. Certainly there would be aspects that she would not care about, but equally there would be benefits, both for herself and for her father, towards whom she felt a kind of debt, owed not by herself but by her dead mother. She did not love him but she would like to repay something of what he had lost. She liked Polemo, her mother's brother, and she liked her cousins Aristonoë and Salampsio, yes, they made up for a lot; she could laugh with them. Hipparchia? But Hipparchia was always pressing her towards an action of which she was doubtful. Hipparchia and her memories.

As to her future husband, he was an honourable man, not rich enough to provoke envy nor poor enough to be constantly anxious; he was related to the family, was something of a scholar. The child by the first wife seemed healthy and friendly. There would also, Gods willing, be her own. That perhaps would be yet another life. She wished she could have brought Aristonoë with her to the palace as Selene had asked; but it had been hinted that this at the moment would not be suitable. After the visit to the tombs. Perhaps.

Selene had been a child. Her mother had hoped she would be a queen. And a queen she was, though not of any of the lands she had been awarded that far off day when she and her three brothers were dressed in gold and silver and given all the kingdoms of the world before the people of Alexandria. 'Your mother,' said Elpis, 'would be glad that things have gone well with you.'

'Elpis,' said Selene, looking round quickly, 'do you think—she knows?'

'She is a God,' said Elpis. 'The gods know everything.'

'It is so difficult,' said Selene. 'I used to love playing with her scent bottles and make-up sticks.' She looked from side to side in a despairing kind of way. 'But after that I began to believe what Octavia told us.'

'Yes,' said Elpis, 'I suppose you loved Octavia.' They were walking slowly round a little courtyard. There was a tiny central pond, marble-bottomed with a mosaic of fishes; a few real fish rippled the pictured ones. There was a scent of jasmine and roses. A gardener was watering and trimming, his brown slender back appearing and disappearing between the foliage; he did not understand Greek. But the awkwardness about the palace of Alexandria was that there were persons whom one must constantly encounter, male or female, or perhaps not quite either, who were certainly listening and watching, acting as extra eyes and ears for Rome; one had to watch for them. They had ways of their own, curtains and passages, so that one must always, always, be half on guard. Had her mother the Queen in her time had this army of spies? And had the Romans simply bought them up? Perhaps. She would never know.

Selene wondered now whether what she had felt for Octavia, whom she had called Mamma, was love. Could one have that for a Roman? 'My husband tells me,' she said, 'that it was not possible. I could not have loved—one of them. And yet...'

'And yet...' said Elpis. 'Quite so. And now that you are back in Alexandria, Princess Selene, you will understand that there are those who see your mother in you.'

'What do they expect?' said Selene in a flat whisper.

'They expect that if a lead is given, the people, remembering Cleopatra, will rise.'

Hearing it said flatly, Selene gasped. 'Could that happen?'

'I have been away from Alexandria too long to know. The people, I think, love the memory of the Queen and the story of the Queen. But it is another thing to risk one's life.'

179

To risk one's life, Selene thought, for me? No, for *her*. But if they did that I would risk—him. He told me we must be so careful, or else—we might lose Numidia. To remind herself she said a few words in Numidian, half aloud.

'What was that, Princess?' Elpis asked quickly. 'Was it— Egyptian?' And suddenly she was frightened in case after all her princess, whom she had been told to guard and cherish, had made her contacts, her secret bond to the people of Egypt. And then what?

But Selene shook her head. 'No. That was—Numidian. I shall be Queen there. We shall build a city.'

Elpis felt herself breathing easily again. But yet—her aunt Hipparchia had told her to find out how the princess felt—and when Elpis answered that the whole thing seemed impossible and senseless, Hipparchia had said bitterly that she had learnt slavish ways in Rome. Had she? Or had she seen a hard truth that her aunt refused to see? 'Queens,' she said, 'all you queens! You have spoken with the lady of Olba, I think?'

Selene nodded. She had indeed. Only that day Queen Aba had suddenly been beside her and said, 'Do not let the boy go to his mother! Keep him back, keep him here!' But when she wanted to ask more one of the persons she did not care for was coming towards them with a respectful smile that could hide—what? But the warning must have been about the tomb and how could she stop Philo? Should she speak to Elpis? No.

Elpis went on. 'But the new one, the Queen of Punt, she will be here in a day or two. People are talking about her already. They say she is very peculiar indeed. Fat and black. She is carried on the shoulders of thin, tall men. Oh, there are a great many kinds of queen!'

CHAPTER THIRTY

'No!' Hellanike shrieked. 'Please no!' She was on the floor, the rug skidded from under her, she was protecting her belly with the baby—his baby—and he was tugging at her hair, hitting her head against the chair legs—oh, no, no! She shrieked with pain and felt blood getting into her eyes; suddenly it stopped, she lay quite still feeling the blood trickle, looking blurredly at tumbled furniture and cushions, a flower pot broken and the earth spilling slowly out. The lily petals bruised and dirty. Then his arms were round her and he was lifting her up, shouting for her maid Nesa, who had rushed in, but was now cowering in a corner. Water was being dabbed on the cut, he snatched the cup from Nesa to dab the water on himself, spilling it all down her dress. 'You are not hurt!' he said. 'My own darling, you are not hurt!'

So if she said she was? No, it might set him off again. 'Not—not too much,' she said shakily.

'That's a brave girl,' he said. 'But now you must tell me every-thing.' He pulled her on to his knee and began to fumble for her breasts. 'You know you love me, you belong to me. Right?' She nodded dumbly and turned close against him so as to keep his hands away. 'Then you must tell me. Everything. No secrets from me! This woman who was killed, she was your aunt. Right?'

'My step-aunt,' Hellanike said, defensively. 'My mother was married to one of *them* first, he died, then she married my father.'

'I bet she had a nice estate! Maybe nice between the legs too. It could run in the family!' Now he was at her buttocks, slipping his hand in, always the same after these scenes! But this last one was worse than most. After a small scene she didn't mind, not at all. It was the nicest way to end up. Well, of course, everyone likes scenes, every woman who *is* a woman! A hot scene about a bit of jewellery or something like that. Good strong jealousy that made you feel you were someone! But now, with Aunt Hipparchia lying dead with a great spear gash in her throat! 'Then I was born, darling, from this second marriage. I wasn't brought up with my cousins, so we were never close. I didn't have any idea that this could happen! No idea at all!'

'What about this cousin of yours, this Aristonoë? I've seen you two with your heads together. What was she saying, what? What? No, you've got to tell me, my little pigeon. Didn't she mention something? Now, no lies! She did, she did!'

His hands were away now, looking for a nastier grip on her, her hair, her throat, oh, please not again! 'Only that she wanted to see the Princess—'

'Ah, we'll stop their little game! Now that's two estates—'

'But—but you can't—I know Aristonoë so well and she never said a word about rebellion, not a word! She was in Rome, she met the Princess at Octavia's house, Octavia used to send her own litter to bring her over. Oh, she loved Rome! She'd have liked to stay!' No, thought Hellanike, no, they shan't get the family! I don't care if they hang some of the mob but not my cousins and I won't give in to him! I'll make him believe me! 'You might as well accuse me!' she said and made big eyes at him. He began to soften up, so if she went on now, if she could keep it up—'and you know how much Madam Prefect likes Elpis and Aristonoë too! We mustn't think of anything which would upset Octavia, she's powerful still! And it isn't as if the Princeps hadn't put up these statues to Charmian and Iras himself, so if he thought they were honourable we ought to, and it would look very bad—I can't have you doing something which could look bad in Rome!'

'Are you really thinking about me?' he said. 'Are you, you little bitch?' Big eyes again and slightly tearful. 'You think Madam Prefect might bite? Or even Octavia? Look, come off it, would Octavia care?'

'Yes, and Marcellus too. Aristonoë was in the highest society. There—in Rome. That doesn't happen for nothing.'

'And then she comes back and marries a little Greek!'

'I know. We aren't all lucky.'

'Just some of us,' another squeeze. 'So the Prefect would say she was all right, would he? And that father of hers—they say he was in the crowd.'

182

'But he was stopping them—didn't you hear?' If only he'd fall for that!

'How do you know?' He looked at her close. 'Lying again?'

'But you see, darling, he was a soldier. He knows that one can't stand against Rome. He knows how strong and wonderful the legions are. Any soldier knows that. It's only sense. Why, that was what happened, if he hadn't been there it might have been worse. much worse! It's only stupid ignorant people and poor silly women like Hipparchia who think anything else about Rome. I know, darling, I'm keeping watch. Better than you sometimes believe. But it's my life too. You and I. Together—in Rome.'

He thought about this for a moment, fiddling with the handle of his dagger. 'What about that husband of Hipparchia's? Was he there?'

'Oh, I don't think so. He's a Rhodian you know. They're different, and of course the boy has been away for months in Athens. He wouldn't know a thing.'

'Subversive place. All that philosophy. And nothing but a lot of Greeks, after all.'

'I know, darling.' Big eyes again. 'As if one wanted a Greek!'

'Feeling fine now? How about a little...?'

'Well, be careful, darling, because of—him.'

'Ah, he's a soldier. He's my little legionary. He'll be fine, he'll like it.'

There was however quite a consultation between the Prefect and his staff, including Lucius Mindius. What had been the behaviour of the Prince and Princess at the time of the incident? It seemed fairly certain that after a formal sacrifice the Princess was weeping in a perfectly proper and womanly way. This was after all the tomb of her father, Marc Antony, the noble Roman, even if the foreign bitch was buried there too. A whole crowd looking on, some of the women howling too, but that seemed suitable. Then it all burst, a real old Alexandrian mob in full cry. She had lifted her head—yes—but the prince had seized her and held her close. They did not think she had actually seen what happened when that foolish shouting woman ran straight on to the spears. Nobody wants to kill a woman of good family, but it couldn't be helped this time. She was shouting forbidden words. She must have known. And there had been an ugly mob rush held. There had been a few

183

respectable people but apparently they got away, no doubt with the connivance of the mob. The prisoners, who would be hanged or possibly crucified, were all the lowest of the low. It was not certain whether Hipparchia's husband had been there. He would be placed under arrest and suitably fined.

'What do you think the estate is worth?' the Prefect asked. It would be useful to the Treasury. There would probably also be some works of art, jewellery and so on. The body would be given back to the family only on condition that there was a completely secret burial and a general willingness to meet conditions. 'And then,' said the Prefect, 'the incident will be closed.'

'I'm not sure,' said Lucius Mindius. 'Listen!' Outside they could hear another wave of the mob, more yelling, 'The Queen lives!' 'Cleopatra-Isis!' All that. But they weren't armed, or only with sticks and stones. No need to bother. Yes, now they could hear the order to the guard, the stamp and rattle and then the screams, dying out as the mob turned and ran. 'I wonder if our guests can hear it—in there?' said one of the other officers.

'Shouldn't think so. No windows that way. Even if they do— young Juba has sense. He knows his masters. They made a good job of him in Rome.'

'But what about the boy?'

'Ah, there now, that's not so easy,' the Prefect said. 'The boy was on his toes during the incident. Juba tried to keep him quiet as well but it wasn't too easy. That's the report. Seems he shouted back. Funny, but it looks like he was treated too well by Octavia. Some time or another you've got to show these provincials. Got to break that nasty subversive spirit. You agree, gentlemen?'

They did indeed agree. But it was not an entirely simple matter. The boy was a guest and after all very young. No danger really. They dispersed. But the Prefect called Lucius Mindius back. 'That wife of yours—you're sure of her?'

'She's my best source of information. Knows what's what. As a matter of fact she did say that she thought this woman, this step-aunt of hers, should be kept from the Princess. That was done, but maybe I should have taken it further.'

'What about this boy? If he's like this now he might grow up dangerous.'

'Well,' said Lucius Mindius, 'if you think so there are always ways and means.'

'These poisons are all very well,' said the Prefect. 'But it might look bad, especially if it got back to Rome.'

Octavia again, thought Lucius Mindius. He said: 'An accident would be better. We could devise one. The boy has been out with the fishing boats; we could arrange something there. I have one or two agents. The fishermen are quite poor and a little money would look big. They need only turn their backs.'

'We might,' said the Prefect, 'proceed along those lines. Meanwhile I have to look after this Queen of Punt. You know, my poor wife is quite overburdened. This—this lady—has certainly brought an unrivalled collection of curios. The feathers and furs alone! A little hairy man, or so it seems, stuffed. Not to speak of ivory and packets of incense. My wife is having some of the feathers made up into a very elegant fan. Unique in fact. Do you think your Hellanike would like some?'

'I'm sure she would, sir!' Yes, that would put it right, cure those weeping eyes, poor little pet.

'One or two specimens for my menagerie as well. Or possibly for—you know who, though I never think they look after them properly in Rome. But the Queen of Punt insists that she must be surrounded by her—ah, courtiers.'

'I hear, sir, that they're actually—'

'Yes, her husbands.'

'I'd need a good bit of ivory myself before I acted husband to that bag of fat!' Both laughed and made several jokes.

'Yet she appears to be able to converse in passable Greek. My wife and she have managed some conversations. One asks oneself why and how.'

'One does indeed!'

CHAPTER THIRTY-ONE

The first time he had been out in a fishing boat Prince Philadelphos had been quite unable to throw the net so that it spread into a circle when it reached the water. He could see the mathematics of it in his mind, the twisting of the rapidly flattening cone; but his hands appeared to be unable to follow the brain's instruction. Irritating! However, the fishermen, chosen from the most respectable families on the waterfront, were patient and admiring. His tutor, who did not really think this a suitable occupation but had been nagged into it, and the two guards, who were bored stiff, waited on the steps of the causeway. Prince Philadelphos practised with the fishermen in the boat and learnt a few Egyptian words as well as fishermen's Greek, which was almost as difficult. They applauded, saying he was the Queen's true son. One of them indeed went further than that, asking him if he was not here to bring back the Queen's time. He had been tempted to answer yes, for were not these all friends? He was all the more tempted because it seemed to him that his sister Selene was pushing all this away from her, was refusing to answer to their mother's Alexandria because of the new Alexandria which she and Juba were planning. But he did not let himself be tempted; he remembered that he was no longer a child. Instead he had said shortly that the Queen's time was long ago. 'But we remember it,' said one of the fishermen.

'We got good prices then,' said another. 'Now they beat us down or the soldiers take our best catch, the dirty Romans.'

And the man who had seemed most enthusiastic said: 'But there are many who remember. If there was someone to lead. Do you not think, Prince, the garrison could be swept away? The people of Alexandria—determined! If they had a leader—yes, it would

186

happen! The stones would fly. No more Romans—instead, you!'

Again he was tempted and yet there was something about the others, some kind of strain. He looked at them one by one carefully to see if they could meet his eye. He said with a snap which he had not known himself to be capable of: 'You don't know the power of Rome—none of you know! Stop being stupid. Now I want to go on casting. I shall master it, you'll see!'

All the same he had not managed that day to master the net. It refused to go out in the even circle, the thing it did so easily for any of the crew. He began to get angry, his hands shook. The oldest fisherman said: 'It takes time, Prince. Egypt was not made in a day. Let us show you the merchant ships before we go back.' And he hauled up the sail into the breeze and they went lightly across the harbour. By the time they had looked at the big ships and then rowed back Philo was laughing again. Next time it would be all right!

And then a few days on, came that hot afternoon when they had gone to the tomb and the crowds had so suddenly and disastrously burst on them, and Selene had turned away with Juba holding her, but the crowds were calling for him—yes, him!—and he could not tell what to do and even if he had managed to burst through with the guards packed between him and them, could he have led them to overwhelming victory or would he have been dead, gashed, bleeding crazily into the gutter like that woman and her hands had flapped once like a landed fish and then there was nothing? Selene had begun to cry, even while she was making the sacrifice with him beside her; but of course she could remember their mother. He hardly could. Nor indeed their father, for whom also they sacrificed, no, nothing was left, nothing to remember, in spite of all Mamma had said, in spite of the marble head in her room that she said was him. He remembered his nurse much better and how she had been pulled off him at the last, screaming like he had screamed. Oh, so long ago. And the Romans had laughed. If she had been in this crowd? What was the use of wondering that?

He wasn't going to think about it. For now the fishing boat was pushing off again. His tutor, still disapproving, waved from the causeway and pulled out his writing tablets; this was his opportunity for a memoir. The guards went to sleep. Now Philo was gathering the net as they had shown him. He stood balanced on the thwart. There were seven in the crew, seven. What was one of them whispering? It didn't matter. What mattered was to see the signs of fish as they pointed down, a rough excited head against his bare leg and then the spin, the jerk of the elbow, the ripple-edged cone flying out and look, look—this time the circle patter-ing evenly down over the rich oily water! The voices were all round him: Well done, Prince! You'll be a fisherman yet! The words of Egyptian or rough Greek, the friendly hands, then the pull on the tightening cord that brought the net together and, all together boys, haul in! Yes, yes, fish in the net, a dozen fish and one beauty, what a face, what whiskers, what a ripple of colour! And now the cord was loose and they were pouring out into the boat flapping and splashing and he looked round in delight and noticed that there were now six in the crew; he looked from one face to another. Nobody spoke. The missing one was the man who had—yes, who had wanted to make him talk. 'What—what hap-pened?' he said, and then: 'Was he ...' but couldn't think what. The oldest fisherman filled in for him: 'A spy.' And then, 'If you could have an accident so could he.'

With a weak feeling Philo knew how near death he had been himself in the middle of his pleasure. 'The Romans,' he said, 'will they know?'

'A story can be made,' said a fisherman. 'We shall miss part of the money. But you are *her* son.'

Philo looked from the dripping net to the dark sea, secret as a shut box. 'He is—there? I heard nothing, nothing.'

'He made a small splash,' said a fisherman. 'But—it was so.' He grinned and hit the big fish on the head with a heavy stick. It stopped flapping. 'Prince, we will row a little and then you shall cast again.'

Neither the tutor nor the guards noticed anything. They had not bothered to count a few fishermen. Whatever plot they were in it was not this plot. Philo swung the big fish and demanded that the tutor, who kept his princely purse, and at least the Romans weren't mean over this, should produce gold. He gave a handful to the crew. Would the spy have done better? Or perhaps not so well. Some of the fishermen kissed his feet. He would come again, now he was one of them! They went back to the palace. Someone called the tutor aside. He came back to say, 'The Queen of Punt has asked Prince Philadelphos to honour her with his presence.'

'What,' asked Philo, 'the fat one?'

'Yes. She is anxious to see both the Princess and yourself.' The tutor shook his head. 'It is most extraordinary that she should speak Greek. One would suppose that such people come from beyond the ends of civilisation; even Herodotus did not describe their country.'

The Queen of Punt received Cleopatra's children in the apartment which had been set aside for her and which she had decorated in a queenly manner with leopard and lion skins and others which neither Selene nor her brother knew. Two elephant tusks engraved with a network of meaningful lines reared themselves above her cushions; a gold plate hung between them. Two tall and feathered men beat softly on drums, another occasionally reached up to strike a golden bell. There seemed to be some kind of altar of carved wood behind the Queen. Her large and deeply pendulous breasts dropped like curious fruit from an all-brown tree. Her kilt of orange fur showed luscious folds of flesh; her knees were dimpled, gartered with gold, her smile of welcome was genuine. 'So you are her children!' she said. 'Come near, my darlings. I will tell you. Long ago your mother, who is now a God, came to visit my mother. I was only a little child but I remember that lively lady. Yes, I remember.'

Her cup bearers brought wine that had certainly been acquired in Alexandria, but also curious dried food, sweet and crisp, and a darkish thing which Philo mistrusted. It could have been something crawling once. She pulled Selene a little unwillingly down beside her and patted her with sorrowful exclamations at her boniness. Philo and Juba stood admiring the leopard skins and the spears and knives of the men. Juba was memorising the detail to write down later; at some point he must manage to ask a number of questions, though perhaps not at this first interview.

'Yes, my darlings,' the Queen said. 'So when I was made the chosen daughter my mother bought me a Greek to teach me the language of trade with your mother's land. I learnt. I learnt. Oh, how I made him teach me!'

'And you travelled, Madam Queen, yourself?'

'Oh, yes, I traded, darlings. I spoke with many, many, peoples up to the time of my milk feeding and also after. Between the little sea and the great sea. Then I had daughters with these'—she swept her hand round the room and the feathered, silently moving men—

'my kin-brothers. They can speak with drums but not one can speak Greek, my darlings. When my own Greek whom my mother had bought for me died we made a sacrifice for him, so that he had wives to care for him in the other world. And I speak to him in the night.' Suddenly, disconcertingly, she recited a stanza from the *Oresteia* in a high, half singing voice. She ended, but her eyes were on Philo and he took it up, coming a half step nearer, no longer either afraid or mocking.

The Queen dabbed at her eyes, 'Beautiful, my darlings, so beautiful. I am glad.' Then she looked from one to another. 'You are in danger here. Much danger. Do you know?'

Selene said nothing, only looked at Juba, who smiled a little, reassuringly. But Philo suddenly said, 'Yes, they tried to drown me, only the fishermen were on my side!' He gave a little jump and laughed. Was it real?

'You never told me!' Selene said in a half scream, and her spread fingers went up to her face. 'You too!'

'Already,' said Juba. He had almost expected it after the affair at the tomb. But that it should have come so soon! The poor boy, so young still. He hated the Romans in silence as so often.

'We will stop that, my darlings,' said the Queen of Punt. 'You were her children. But for a little be quiet. The leopard will take time before his next strike; he will look for another tree. In that time we will have made a trap for him. You will see.' She made a hand sign and the drumming rose in pace and volume. 'You will come back soon, darlings,' she said. 'I will buy the best horses in Alexandria. Though I will not myself ride them!' And she threw herself back laughing while they bowed their way out.

CHAPTER THIRTY-TWO

The family were all in mourning; this at least they could do for
one another, though only in the home. Tahatre had mourned,
thrown ashes on her head and torn her cheeks to bleeding, calling
on the Queen's name. Others had come in from the village in tears,
but it was urged on them to keep their grief within their own
breasts, not so much as throw dust on their heads. Polemo was
carefully keeping Salampsio in, within walls. Zenon had brought
her over and very thoughtfully, as it turned out, had taken the best
of the book rolls and made Salampsio take all the jewels she could
lay hands on. A few hours after, the legionaries were in, all the
rooms sealed and the inventory being taken. Mikion who had in
fact not been at the tomb, was under arrest, protesting that he
knew nothing, but reasonably certain that he would be tortured
and would have to admit something. A letter had been sent to Kerkidas in Athens telling him how his mother had died, but also
telling him to stay there, to be very discreet and if necessary to go
into hiding. Probably if he let drop the correct sentiments in such a
way that they would be overheard he would not have to suffer. So
long as the letter got to him. It went by a friend, but you never
knew nowadays.

Polemo was grieving, grieving. He should have been able to stop
his sister. He thought now of words he ought to have used: too
late, too late. He had begun to realise that some of those they had
trusted were useless or worse than useless. Alexandria still remembered the Queen. Fine, but what did it come to in action? The
priests of Isis and Serapis would be with them, but not until the
issue was almost certain. The same went for others, old friends,
he thought bitterly. But when one remembered the penalties ...
Which he might have to suffer yet. So now Charmian's sister Hip-

parchia had joined Charmian, leaving him and Eumenes. Yet Eumenes had, it appeared, been unsurprised at what had happened. There had been enough surprise and shock in his life to last him for ever. It was as though now Charmian's sister had gone, finally, to some mystery, some expiation which must be suffered by some human so that all should survive. The pattern of suffering and death which came to women even more than to men. Eumenes kept on speaking about Elpis's marriage, trusting that this would not be delayed. If he could see just this small bit of security. If security it was going to be, although also, in part, as he knew and they knew, expiation and casting out of the gods of Rome.

It was a sad house and not unafraid. If it was decided up at the palace that the legionaries should come here? Polemo burned some papers, gave others and some of the money to his bailiff, with instructions to bury it in various places which had already been thought of; he knew which parts of the estate were likely to be taken, if it came to that. So long as they left him some. No use turning it over and over. He wished he had enough belief in the gods to pray. Conon had been with them, but was now getting some advice from a lawyer friend. As though that would make any difference to the palace! If one estate went, the greedy creature would wake up and reach out its claws for more.

Salampsio sat with her face turned to the wall, her shoulders hunched. Then there was a knock on the outer door, no, probably not what they were afraid of. That would have been louder. Polemo called to the doorkeeper to slip back the bolts; he took a deep breath and eased a smile on to his face. But it was one man only, the captain of a sailing ship, bearded and oiled, a Tyrian perhaps, his flung back cloak showing a handsome striped tunic for use in port. He had a letter, a pair of old-fashioned sealed tablets. 'For Aristonoë, the daughter of Polemo.' He looked round. Polemo sent Salampsio off to find her cousin and sent the servant for wine. The Captain drank, wiping his beard with the back of his hand. 'I hear you've had troubles,' he said non-committally.

'Enough to last my time,' said Polemo.

'The Gods avert more,' said the Captain, superstitious as all seafaring people were, and made the sign of Melkarth. 'May this letter help.'

Aristonoë came in. 'My daughter,' said Polemo.

'To whom the letter is addressed,' said the Captain. 'May it be good news, lady.'

Aristonoë stood straight and took the tablets, looked at the seal. 'But,' she said, with only a tiny tremble in her voice, 'this is from Octavia, this is her own seal!'

'That is so, lady,' said the Captain. 'The lady Octavia gave it to me. With her own hand.'

Aristonoë was murmuring the letter half aloud: 'She greets Selene too and dear young Philadelphos. She wishes us well. Oh Father!' For she knew as well as anybody that a letter from Octavia meant refuge. The rock would not fall and crush them.

Polemo took off one of his rings. He had put on several in case— well, in case. This had an amethyst engraved with a palm tree set in gold. He pressed it into the Captain's hand.

'The Lady Octavia paid me,' said the Captain. 'But of course if you insist! I shall treasure it. And I have another letter, not from the Lady Octavia, but from—well, a noted poet, not that I care for poetry myself, unless it's to help on the windlass. Addressed to Elpis, daughter of Eumenes. Can you help me?'

'Naturally. I'll send a messenger at once,' Polemo said, and clapped his hands. The slave went off at a brisk trot. 'I may see your letter, rabbit? Another glass of wine, sir?' He sat down beside Aristonoë with his arm round her. They read the letter to one another, half aloud; there was not much news, mostly greetings and remembrances. Marcellus had been having a fever, was now better. The Princeps had a fever too, sacrifices had been made—the Vestal Virgins—preparations for the marriage of Antonia, Marcella soon to be betrothed to Agrippa—Aristonoë suddenly turned to her father with a flush of anger: 'Oh poor dear Marcella, having to marry that cross old peasant! And she won't say a word. You'd never have made me do a thing like that, Father!'

The letter went on. Octavia writing from the country estate. The vines. The olives. She hears that her dear Aristonoë is married. She hopes— 'I should show this to Madam Prefect,' said Aristonoë, 'soon. I think—don't you father?—we need not be so anxious now!'

It was not too long before Elpis and her father came. The Captain, while the others were all reading Octavia's letter, managed to beckon Elpis away from them; he dived in under his tunic. The letter this time was a small parchment scroll, rolled and sealed. 'For the lady's eye alone,' he said.

Elpis bit her lip and looked away, feeling a blush spread uncomfortably all over her face and neck. 'That would be—wrong,' she said.

'He said—'

'Never mind. My cousin shall read this letter, my cousin whom the lady Octavia befriended. Aristonoë! She shall decide who is to read or not read.' She broke the seal and they sat down together. Women, thought the Captain, there you are. You never can tell. They were reading silently, not murmuring it over. Elpis began to cry.

'It's a cruel poem,' said Aristonoë. 'How can he be so cruel? How can he accuse you like this?'

'I hurt him,' Elpis said. 'Poor Horace, poor dear Horace. It's so much too easy to hurt a poet. And so he wrote. The other— he wouldn't even bother to write a poem. By that time there would be someone else. But look at what he says in small letters at the bottom. Look, Aristonoë!'

'He forgives you.' Aristonoë caught Elpis's hand. 'But of course he does. He will remember you always. He hopes you will remember him. Will you, Elpis?'

'I have never forgotten,' said Elpis and a tear rolled down her nose on to the parchment. 'Either of them. But it is past, past! Can you make my father understand, Aristonoë? I must not keep it secret, and yet...'

'They won't really notice because of the other letter.' And then she whispered, 'Have you got something to give the Captain? That pearl pin you don't like much...? Fine. Now we'll roll the letter up.'

'I suppose I could always recite it,' said Elpis, and she gave a dry kind of laugh. 'The very latest from Rome. They need never know it's about me!'

'Don't be silly. Don't hurt yourself as well as him! And stop crying, Elpis. No, you must stop. Look, I'll give him the pin. He won't expect so much from you. Anyhow, I'm sure he was properly paid in Rome.'

After suitable goodbyes the Captain left them. Zenon was invited to read the letter from Octavia as well. 'Strange,' he said, 'this may save the family. This letter from—am I right?—a rather

194

unhappy woman who has lost or is losing those she loves. But who thinks of others. Would you care for me, sir, to see that a message arrives in the ears of Madam Prefect? I could approach the lady Hellanike. One might say that fate acts strangely. None of us knows what the next hour will bring. Nor must we be too confident.' But none of them were that. Not yet.

'Will this help Father?' Salampsio asked abruptly.

'We hope so,' Aristonoë said.

'Are they hurting him?'

'We don't think so.'

'Can't you make sure?'

'No.'

CHAPTER THIRTY-THREE

'Listen to me,' said Queen Aba, 'carefully. I am repaying a debt. This also is between queens.' Philo nodded. He was rather scared. He had thrown a piece of meat from his own plate to one of the dogs and the dog had died. If he had been hungrier or the dog had died less quickly—well, that wasn't something he liked thinking about. 'The Queen of Punt is leaving today, having given suitable gifts to the Romans. Tomorrow six of her husbands will come back. Your rooms do not open to the street. One of mine does. You are to jump from it. It is small, but not too high. They will catch you and gallop away. They have the best horses in Alexandria. They will not be caught!'

'But—where to?'

'Out of here. Out of reach of Rome. Perhaps to the land of Punt.'

Horrified, Philo took a step back. 'No! I—I can't, not there.'

'Listen, Prince, your mother went there.'

'But she didn't stay there. How could she? No civilised person could. It was only a trade visit. I know that.'

'Nobody was trying to kill her as they are trying to kill you, and will succeed quite soon if you don't escape, Ptolemy Philadelphos, son of Cleopatra and Antony.'

He stood very still. Could this be true? Did he have to escape out of civilisation, leave everything, leave cities, libraries, books, science, never again see the Pharos, never quite understand the magnifying lens? Never again see his sister. But, then, if she went to Numidia where would he be? He had never thought. Had she meant to take him with her? Who else of his own had he? He had been fond of Mamma, Octavia, but he had half known when they left Rome that this parting was an end. He would never again call for Mamma when he had a summer fever.

Cautiously he said: 'But I cannot speak their language, even. How can I live there? Truly I do not even know where it is.'

'She speaks Greek. Their language can be learned. Once you want to learn it, Prince Philadelphos.'

'I couldn't ever want to learn it. No!'

'You will want to. It is, as they say, a blessed land full of fruit and flowers, birds and beasts. Winter does not come. There are no Romans. Also the Queen of Punt has daughters—'

'Oh, that would be horrible! Horrible. I couldn't bear to touch one!'

'You will see them before the time of the drinking of milk, when they are lively and beautiful. One day, two years, three years from now you will remember speaking with me and you will laugh at how foolish you were and how little you could foresee.' She was looking at him burningly and her headdress seemed to catch the light, almost as the mirrors of the Pharos. Was it after all possible? The dog had howled hideously and bent its back, kicking. Then it was dead. 'I do not think they will try poison again for a day or two. But be careful, Prince. Do not take a present from anyone. Trust nobody yet.'

So if it was to be like that, why stay? Even the library might have enemies in the alcoves. He stood thinking. Those ideas in the library that nobody had done anything with; he understood them. One could do nothing with them here, but perhaps some quite other place would be different. He might make the ideas do work. He had learned how to cast a net; there was nothing he could not learn. And master. Suddenly he said: 'Can I say goodbye to Selene?'

'No,' said Queen Aba, 'she might try to stop you. But you can write her a letter and leave it with me. I will see that she gets it. And also that she destroys it when it has been read.'

'Why?'

'For reasons. There is something which the Romans must believe. It will make it easier for all of us.'

'Us?' But Queen Aba did not answer that one.

Juba was looking at the dead dog. Yes, it must be poison. They must be badly frightened to do this. Philo had been lucky. So far. Would they try for Selene too, Selene his wife, the Queen of Numidia? If they do, he thought, I will not rest till I have killed them all, even if I have to lose my own country. Coldly he considered this, a matter of honour. At a certain point the masters go too far; when that happens they will first be inconvenienced, as by the slave revolts, and then destroyed. As by—what? One does not know the end of history, only that it is approaching.

There was to be a chariot race the next day; they had been invited, but one of the guides or guards had arrived in a state of politeness to explain that it would be better if they did not put in an appearance. The crowd was always disorderly at the chariot racing; they were apt to bet madly and then lose; policing was difficult. If in addition they were to be inflamed by stupid and reckless speech-makers, lives might be lost as in the unfortunate earlier incident. The Prefect regretted having to make this decision, especially as his own favourite team was running and he would have liked to have the Prince and Princess with him, but it was really for the best. Was there any alternative programme which they would care for?

Yes, Princess Selene would like to hear a recitation from Elpis, the daughter of Eumenes. The message was received. It was regretted that she was—well, indisposed. Perhaps another performer? Madam Prefect would see to it.

'Prince Philo and I will visit the library again,' said Juba. 'There are certain points in physics that I am anxious to discuss. It was a privilege to visit your Pharos and I would like to know the basis for certain of the phenomena.' When we found our new Alexandria, he thought, we shall have a Pharos, smaller no doubt, for Numidia has no corn-giving Nile, but certainly more advanced than that fire basket contraption at Ostia, and when we are there I shall be able to watch over Philo. They would hardly dare—not in the library.

'Certainly, Prince Juba,' the man said. 'There are some models which might be of interest and indeed the original drawings for the Pharos.'

One could hear from the library the row and din of the chariot racing. I suppose, thought Juba, I shall have to encourage this kind of thing in my new city, at least if I have to have a Roman garrison. No, that is incorrect; it is not only the Romans. My own people enjoy horse racing and even donkey racing. They like making a noise, drinking, getting out of ordinary life. Just as they like to have gods. Or a leader. He shook his head and went back to the drawings of the mirror complex. Expensive. But on a smaller scale it should be possible. Someone was showing Philo some of their most interesting manuscripts. Euclid, Archimedes. And then the poets. All the plays. Yes, Aeschylus knew what it was all about, oppression and reaction. Philo was looking very serious, touching the slightly faded, beautiful parchments gently and solemnly.

How was he going to protect Philo? He didn't know at all. So far he had not told Selene about the attempted poisoning. He was surprised that they hadn't managed it more competently, seeing for instance, that any dogs which were about were too well fed to take any more. Perhaps the local poisoners whom they probably employed, on the assumption, usually correct, that anyone would do anything for money, had not cared for the job. How long does oppression go on, if it has the means? For ever? Or is it possible that, after all, there are gods watching? It did not look like that to him.

The Queen of Punt had left Alexandria after much sightseeing, to which she was carried in her special gold-plated litter. She had also had some interesting trade discussions and had made purchases of cloth, both linen and woollen, dyes, scents, two Egyptian harps with spare strings, certain kinds of weapons and utensils, glass vessels, amber, glazed pottery, red, yellow and purple, as well as two plates of Chinese ware—expensive, those!—and of course a number of jars of wine and sacks of wheat; she had come with pack animals but had also bought some of the finest horses in Alexandria. Her husbands and their interpreters had been very insistent and had spent a day putting them through their paces.

However, she had sold some very handsome ivory, in fact, some of the largest tusks that anyone had seen; there had been keen competition for these. Her packets of gold dust had been of the highest quality and some of the furs were something which had not been seen even in Alexandria within living memory. There was much discussion about what kind of animals some had come from and the interpreter was not helpful. Apparently certain of the trimmings as well as many of the feathers came from even beyond the land of Punt. Imagine that!

But now she was gone. Soon no doubt there would be other visitors to Alexandria, just as interesting and extraordinary. One year or the next everyone came here. The Prefect's collection of gifts grew in a most satisfactory way.

Prince Juba had given himself some interesting sessions with her, asking questions and getting sometimes unsatisfactory answers. He felt she might be exaggerating about the curiosities of the land of Punt, still more those of its neighbours. It was annoying too to find absolutely no correspondence between the language of Punt and that of Numidia. He had theories about Africa which were not being upheld and as he was in the course of writing a rather dry poem about them this was a little annoying. Meanwhile the Queen spoke to him seriously about feeding Selene on cream and fat roast meat dipped in honey and described to him the extra pleasure this would give him. He doubted it.

Among the relics of the visit, Hellanike's new feather fan, exquisitely mounted on an ivory handle, was certainly one of the most beautiful; the only other one belonged to Madam Prefect, but who wanted to see her poor old eyes peeping over the scarlet and orange shimmer? There had been moments during that dreadful scene when Hellanike really thought her husband was out for blood. So when he brought her this unique gift it proved that it was only another scene, that her Lucius Mindius truly loved her. Nesa, patting ointment over that cut above her eye and bringing her soothing juices, insisted that this was so. But maids were sly things, much too well aware of what was going on. It was she who had told Hellanike all about Aunt Hipparchia at the head of the mob rushing at the legionaries. As though she wanted to be a sacrifice, Nesa had said.

Aunt Hipparchia. She had lived beyond her time. So that she began to imagine things. Like imagining that Roman rule of the province of Egypt, solidly part of the Empire, could be disturbed by a rising in Alexandria. Why, even if—well, even if the Roman garrison could be thrown out and that couldn't possibly happen, another garrison would be on its way from the nearest centre. The Queen herself, even with Antony's own legionaries to help her, had known it was useless to struggle.

And yet people like Aunt Hipparchia couldn't understand. And so they got themselves killed. And the dead are dead. Of course the Egyptians never quite thought that. She wouldn't have dreamt of speaking of such things to Nesa, but everyone knew that for Egyptians to die was to open a door and go for a long journey, but one for which you were prepared. Stupid! To die was to die. Danger was danger. Suddenly Hellanike wished her mother wasn't fussing so much about her confinement. It was going to be all right! Of course. She wished she could see Aristonoë and tell her how she had, well, probably saved the family estate. Aristonoë however was not leaving the house and perhaps that was wise. But I am bored and lonely, Hellanike thought, and summer is coming on, all this dreadful heat and I want—I want—what? Well, I shall go over to Madam Prefect, give me the mirror, Nesa! She peered into the polished silver and no, that bruise doesn't show. But she was pale. Nesa must put her on some colour. And a change of dress. And some scent—no, the other bottle, stupid!

There, that was better. She walked the short distance, too much bother getting out the litter and she didn't care for the jolting. Nesa accompanied her, as well as two armed slaves, though it was a quiet road and one didn't expect trouble. But once inside the gate oh, what a commotion! One of her friends, another young married from the staff group, rushed to tell her. Prince Philo had been carried off by six of the Queen of Punt's husbands, armed to the teeth, into the desert and they had murdered him and eaten him up! Yes, yes, several people had heard him screaming but they had galloped off on the fastest horses in Alexandria, black cannibals, to think of that poor innocent boy under the protection of Rome killed and cooked and eaten—we can hush it up of course but all the same—why, Hellanike, you are looking quite faint!

CHAPTER THIRTY-FOUR

Selene was doubled up on the floor, crying, crying. Juba knelt beside her, his brown narrow hands on her shoulders, trying to reach her, trying to comfort. Surely it couldn't be true! He had seen the Queen of Punt and her court; they weren't like this, they couldn't possibly have done it. Or had the Romans simply bribed them to carry off and kill the boy? If so—if so—but what? How terrible to feel oneself powerless. Even if one knew that in the long run evil would not go unpunished, yet it was in the short run that one lived and acted.

And then Queen Aba of Olba came in without guards or even the old attendant woman who mostly followed her. 'Selene, daughter of Cleopatra,' she said, 'I have a letter for you.' Slowly Selene unbent and stood up, her face blotched and wet with all this crying. It was a wax tablet, one that her brother used for making notes and mathematical drawings. 'Look,' said Queen Aba.

'But it's from him!' Selene said. 'Lady Aba, what have you done?'

'I have paid a debt,' she said. 'I did not think it would be this way. I hoped—yes, I hoped it would be otherwise, but that was not possible.'

'But—is he alive? Was it—? Oh, was it one of their lies?'

'He is alive,' said the tall Queen; 'read. And then wipe out the wax.'

He had written a rather long goodbye letter using formal words. Selene would have wished to keep it; she held it in her hand, looking imploringly at Juba. But he shook his head and brought over a lighted lamp. She ran the tablet across the heat, erasing all. 'Octavia will be sad again,' she said; 'poor Octavia, poor dear Mamma.' So often hurt through the fault of others but accepting it if it was for Rome and the family. The wax was smooth again.

'If he had stayed,' said Juba, 'something would have happened. One can be sure. This cannot be wished otherwise.'

'So far away,' Selene said, 'so very far.' She dropped the tablet; it cracked across the joint. She began to cry once more, but this time Juba slapped her on the cheek.

'Stop,' he said. 'Your brother will take with him everything he has learnt. He is himself: unhurt. He will never be dragged in a Triumph. He is going no further than your mother went.'

'But she came back,' murmured Selene, and began to wipe her eyes.

'It could have been better if she had not come back. If she had made a country that Rome could not reach.'

'She might have been destroyed as Alexander was destroyed when he too went beyond the limits.'

'And so? We are all destroyed in the end. But some part of us lives. Is that not so, Queen Aba?'

'The grain lives though the plant dies,' Queen Aba said. 'That is always true. I have paid my debt now.' She turned and swept out with no goodbyes.

Madam Prefect was extremely upset. These young people were the guests of Rome. Naturally nobody had mentioned in her presence that there was anything against the boy, still less that means had already been tried to rid Imperial Rome of a potential danger to the steady corn supply. She had not been there to see her husband exchange looks, a quizzical raised eyebrow, with Lucius Mindius. It had immediately occurred to the young officer that it might be allowed to be supposed that he had some hand in organising this. He would of course deny it completely to his wife, but that would be understood. She, after all, was, well—a native.

'What can we do for our poor little Princess?' Madam Prefect asked, distractedly. One of her ladies mentioned that she had asked to see Aristonoë, the daughter of Polemo, whom she had known in Rome. 'Of course, of course! Have her brought at once. And perhaps that nice young woman Elpis; we must ask for another recital soon.' By now it had been decided that Prince Juba knew his place and would see to it that his wife knew hers. So after a little consultation Madam Prefect's wishes were duly carried out.

When the loud knock came on the door Polemo thought, this is it. But one of the servants, watching from the roof, called down,

'Not many soldiers!' All the same he tried to prepare himself. If only one really believed in the Gods, not Dike, Ultimate Justice, but some closer saviour. Then there would be something beyond oneself to hold to. As it was—well, there was honour. Tahatre ran pattering and kissed his hand, whispered: 'May the Queen strengthen you, master!' Yes, if one could believe in Cleopatra-Isis as the common people believed!

Then there was Aristonoë, his daughter, beside him with a cloak wrapped round her and her hand at her breast over the letter from Octavia. 'It will be all right, Father,' she said with hardly a tremble. 'I'm coming too.'

But the officer ushered in saluted courteously and gave the message from Madam Prefect. 'We have a litter for you, Lady Aristonoë. Yes, naturally we can wait for you to change your dress. Yes, certainly you can bring your maid with you. We shall also be calling on Lady Elpis, but we have eight men on the litter poles, so not to worry. Thank you—' To Polemo: 'A little refreshment never comes amiss.'

When Aristonoë left to change her dress the officer leant over and asked Polemo if he had heard the news. But Polemo had stayed so much in the house that it had not reached him yet. He found it difficult to take. Was this a Roman trick? The last of the Queen's sons. As well perhaps that Hipparchia was not there to grieve and grieve. 'Perhaps you should warn Lady Aristonoë yourself, sir,' the young officer said kindly. He himself had liked the lad and been shocked by the news. One day he had commanded the guard of honour for the Queen of Punt—and her husbands. Could he truly have seen cannibals, eaters of men, with his own eyes? But once you got beyond the bounds of the Empire anything was possible.

Polemo left the room and told his daughter, adding in an undertone that it might be a lie, but that possibly the boy had been murdered. Not necessarily in the way that was said. He held her hand firmly. 'Show them nothing, rabbit,' he said. She nodded and gasped. When she came through it was high-headed, even with colour rubbed into her cheeks. Tahatre helped her into the litter; she ignored the young officer; she could at least give herself that pleasure!

Behind the curtains she and Elpis whispered. It did not matter that Tahatre overheard, though it appeared that she was lost in

204

prayer. The young boy had joined his older brothers; they would guide him. At the palace Tahatre waited in the anteroom; it still had old paintings whose significance the Romans did not know and would probably not have cared to admit. She looked at them and her lips moved; in a while two other Egyptian servants, older than she was, joined her.

Selene threw her arms round Aristonoë. 'At last!' she said. 'Oh, I've missed you. I wanted to write earlier but it was better not. I knew you would understand, that was why it had to be.'

'I did, I did!' Aristonoë said. 'But—this terrible, wicked thing that has happened. We are all grieving for you—and for Prince Juba—' Elpis joined with the murmurs of grief.

'Do not do that,' said Selene, gravely and low, 'it is not the way the Romans said. My brother has gone to a kingdom.'

Aristonoë thought she understood and spoke back as gravely as the princess. 'The kingdom of—Dis, where all must go. Yes, death is surely a kingdom.'

'But this is a kingdom of life. Such as our mother prepared for him. No, do not ask. Do not even look happy. I can say no more. Not yet. They must never know. Elpis, remember!' She looked from one to the other.

Juba came in. He was a little anxious, wishing that he and his wife could leave soon in case something else happened. What else? He didn't know. One never knew when one was in the power of the Romans. If one had not abased oneself sufficiently the unexpected fart of their thunder god, Father Jove, would blow one off one's feet into a gutter of retching misery. He had seen it happen to others, not only outsiders but those who were inside, thinking themselves safe, but pridefully allowing their actions to deviate. 'You have told them,' he said to his wife accusingly. 'Is it wise?'

'I am used to keeping secrets,' Elpis said; 'very used. Whatever comes of this there will be no story from me.'

'Let the Romans tell it their way,' Aristonoë said. 'As they tell their story about the Queen your mother. We know what is truth and what lies. But we do not speak. Remember there was a time, Princess, when you yourself believed what they said.'

Juba said: 'We can despise them for lying. And for being stupid. And for thinking so much all the time about money grabbing.'

'Money is useful,' said Elpis. 'You will need money when you are King of Numidia.'

'To build our new Alexandria,' Selene said; 'where you two will visit me.'

And all of a sudden his wife was looking at him joyfully. Oh, they would go in the first possible boat, leave Alexandria and sail West. He knew the Prefect would be glad to see the last of them and if he said they intended to go, the Romans would not be tempted to do anything to hurt Selene. He would not care if he never saw the library again. They too would build one!

'Yes,' he said, 'we shall need money. But there are things we shall not do in order to get it. Or so I hope. One thing is to give way totally to the Romans. As they want. As they think we have done. But it is only our bodies which give way. Is that not true?'

'Certainly not our minds,' said Aristonoë with a toss of her head. 'In Athens they understand that.'

'I suppose Conon says that,' Elpis said. Aristonoë blushed because of course she had taken it from him. 'They have not all managed very well, even in the shadow of the Propylaea. Though I expect Conon has!'

'We can all try,' said Aristonoë stubbornly. 'Also in Egypt it is said that the Romans cannot touch the soul.' She thought for a moment of what Tahatre had said and others in the village.

'We can use them against themselves,' said Juba. 'But this means cunning, perhaps of a slavish kind.' And suddenly he found himself longing to be a real king and his wife a real queen as her mother had been. Yet perhaps their own tongue, the language of Numidia, might be some kind of cloak around them. Perhaps it was so also for the Egyptians. Did they remember that they had been great in a world where Rome was only a struggling village?

Aristonoë went over to Selene and put an arm round her shoulders. We must not ask any more of what has happened to the boy, she said to herself. Under the breast fold of her dress she felt the corner of the tablet with the letter from Octavia. Yes, she would probably use it. Hellanike could be allowed to help, after all! But was it not possible that Octavia had meant her to do just that, knowing she might need protection? The mantle of Rome? She frowned.. No, that wasn't it. It was just a kind of friendliness between women who stand a little away from the cruelty and power of men. But what was Prince Juba saying now?

He was speaking low, tapping with his fingers against the edge of a table: 'However much the people had cared about the Queen

I do not think they could have altered the way things are. Not now. That piece of history is over.'

'If they had been properly armed, if better preparations had been made—if Aunt Hipparchia had not suddenly thought she could lead them—'

'No, Aristonoë,' said Juba, 'it could not have succeeded. Do not think that. We have to do it another way.'

'The poetic way,' said Elpis. They all looked at her. And then she wondered if that meant anything.

CHAPTER THIRTY-FIVE : B.C. 30

'What did the Queen say?' Who asked? Where? The slow dishevelled words formed themselves and came at her out of the air, with the smell of figs. With enormous difficulty Charmian straightened the diadem and the necklaces, touching flesh that was still warm. Her hands trembled. But were these her calm practised hands or were they birds fluttering now near, now far? One had a streak of blood on it, a thin streak, why? These unattached birds folded down the lids over the Queen's eyes since now her sight was inward, other-where.

The question, yes, and Charmian must be herself and must answer Iras her mate after all these years. 'She said: The children.'

The voice had become a low grating whisper. 'I heard. And then?'

'As she became God she said...' But what was it she had said? Egypt? Selene? Yes. '...said Selene. So that the word stays with the child.' The fluttering remote birds picked up the Queen's limp right hand, laid it across her breast over the blue wings of eternal life. The figs rolled on the floor. The basket, yes, the basket, it could lie there. But the little guests that had been in the basket, they were away, having done what was asked of them.

Beyond the square of the window appeared a great blue funnel of light, a dazzle of movement. Lines shot out and away crossing and vibrating and merging. The lines came from herself, from the tiny bleeding spot which was taking her mortality, saving her from the Roman Triumph. Within the dazzle a palace built itself and dissolved. She could watch forever entranced. But their mate was already within the palace or devising it. Charmian, Iras, she calls. Her dear voice. And they were coming, coming.

'Are you with her, then, Iras my darling?' Yes, yes, lying across the foot of the couch. Gone. Let me straighten, let me close. We shall not fear. We have oppressed no man. We have caused no hunger or hurt. The way is open. We are called.

Charmian! Iras! But the voice is now not hers. It rings harshly. Whose then? Feet on the stair, hammer at the door. But it is open, we left it open. How not, now? The men come in, the soldiers, the Romans with their hard dark faces under the bright hurting helmets. And they stop there and huddle, staring, and one puts his foot down on a fig that bursts, bursts. They are looking at the Queen and one of them points and speaks, angry, so angry, the stupid man from whom we have escaped. 'Was this well done, Charmian?'

Very well done. And now I too am escaping, am going. Am gone.

FICTION

Mitchison, Naomi (Haldane)
Cleopatra's people.

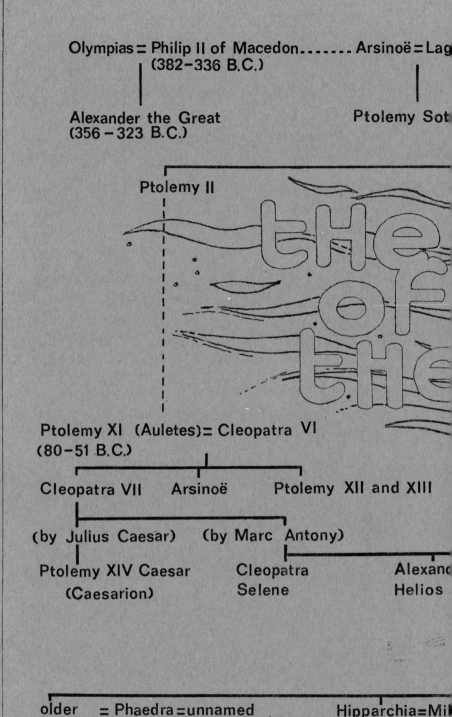

Olympias = Philip II of Macedon . . . . Arsinoë = Lag
     (382–336 B.C.)

Alexander the Great   Ptolemy Sot
(356 – 323 B.C.)

Ptolemy II

Ptolemy XI (Auletes)= Cleopatra VI
(80–51 B.C.)

Cleopatra VII Arsinoë Ptolemy XII and XIII

(by Julius Caesar) (by Marc Antony)

Ptolemy XIV Caesar   Cleopatra   Alexand
(Caesarion)   Selene   Helios

older = Phaedra =unnamed   Hipparchia=Mi
brother   second husband

Hellanike=Lucius Mindius   Kerkidas